The Sinclair's Mysteries

THE MIDNIGHT PEACOCK

The Sinclair's Mysteries

THE SINCLAIR'S MYSTERIES
THE MIDNIGHT PEACOCK

KATHERINE WOODFINE

EGMONT

EGMONT

We bring stories to life

First published in Great Britain 2017
by Egmont UK Limited
The Yellow Building, 1 Nicholas Road, London W11 4AN

Copyright © Katherine Woodfine, 2017
Illustrations copyright © Karl James Mountford, 2017

The moral rights of the author and illustrator have been asserted

978 1 4052 8290 1

www.egmont.co.uk

A CIP catalogue record for this title is available from the British Library
Printed and bound in Great Britain by the CPI Group

63962/1

Stay safe online. Any website addresses listed in this book are correct at the time
of going to print. However, Egmont is not responsible for content hosted by third
parties. Please be aware that online content can be subject to change and websites
can contain content that is unsuitable for children. We advise that all children
are supervised when using the internet.

For Anna and Sara –
Three Amigos forever!

SINCLAIR'S

Mr Edward SINCLAIR &
Monsieur César CHEVALIER
cordially invite you to attend
the first annual

SINCLAIR'S NEW YEAR'S EVE BALL

Welcome in 1910 and celebrate
the launch of Maison Chevalier's first fragrance
MIDNIGHT PEACOCK

At Sinclair's Department Store, Piccadilly, W1
From 9 o'clock p.m. on 31 December 1909
Fireworks at 12 o'clock midnight
Carriages at 2 o'clock a.m.

Dress accordingly

R.S.V.P.

PART I
The Mystery of the Haunted Mansion

'Who goes there? Show yourself!' declaimed Montgomery Baxter,
the courageous boy detective.

CHAPTER ONE

Tilly knew quite well that there were no such things as ghosts. She said so, very plainly – much to the annoyance of Lizzie Hughes, who had come rushing into the Servants' Hall, eager to pour out her tall tale.

Some people would do anything to get out of a spot of dusting, Tilly thought.

'The East Wing's not haunted,' she said, from where she was sitting at the table, finishing off a bit of mending. 'That's just a lot of old nonsense.'

Lizzie turned on her at once, hands on hips, nose in the air. 'That's all very well for you to say. *You* weren't there. I'll have you know I heard it myself – with my own ears!'

Sarah and Ella, the scullery maids, were both staring at Lizzie. 'What was it?' Ella asked.

Lizzie lowered her voice to an important whisper. '*The sound of the ghost's footsteps!*' she announced.

'Oooh!' they exclaimed together.

'What did they sound like?' gasped Sarah. Her eyes

were as big and round as the plates in Her Ladyship's best dinner service.

'Loud – and echoing – and coming closer and closer by the minute! Then the most terrible chill swept over me. It was as if my blood *froze*! I dropped my duster and ran away as fast as my legs could carry me!' Lizzie collapsed into a chair, as though the very memory of it would make her swoon. 'It didn't half make me feel peculiar!' she finished up.

Tilly rolled her eyes. 'You didn't actually see this "ghost" at all, then?' she demanded.

'I was hardly going to go looking for it, was I?' exclaimed Lizzie indignantly. 'Who knows what might have happened to me?'

'So how can you be so sure that what you heard *was* a ghost? There's bound to be a completely ordinary explanation,' said Tilly. 'Maybe it was mice.'

'It couldn't possibly have been mice! No *mouse* could have made a sound like that!'

'Well, then, it was probably one of the under-footmen playing a trick. I'll bet it was Charlie. He thought it was a great lark to put salt in William's tea last week – remember? Pretending to be a ghost to give you a fright is just the sort of stupid thing he'd do.'

But Lizzie shook her head. 'It couldn't have been a trick. That terrible chill – why, I've never felt anything like

4

it in my life!'

The other two looked awestruck, but Tilly just snorted. 'It's *December*, Lizzie. It's cold – and the East Wing is freezing. I think that probably explains your *terrible chill*.'

Lizzie turned her back on Tilly and addressed her next remarks to Ella and Sarah: 'I s'pose you've heard the old story about the ghost that walks at night in the East Wing?'

'No – do tell us,' Ella urged.

In a low voice, Lizzie began: 'Hundreds of years ago, the old Lord who lived here at Winter Hall had a daughter that he loved like no other. She was good and sweet and as beautiful as the day. But then, on her sixteenth birthday, she fell ill and died. The old Lord went mad with grief. He locked himself up in the East Wing and *never came out again*.' She paused and then went on: 'When they finally managed to break through the doors, they found that he was *dead* – as dead as a doornail. And ever since then his ghost has walked up and down the long passage of the East Wing. If ever a young girl is to go alone to the East Wing at night, the ghost will lure her to her death, as vengeance for his own lost daughter,' she finished up with a flourish.

'Oh heavens! I shall never dare set foot in the East Wing again!' exclaimed Sarah.

'There's no ghost in the East Wing,' interrupted Tilly. 'You ought to know better than to believe that sort of codswallop.'

Lizzie turned on her. 'Well, Tilly Black, if you're so clever, then why don't *you* go into the East Wing and see for yourself?' She stared at Tilly crossly for a moment, and then added: 'Right now – on your own. Go on – I dare you – or are you too *afraid?*'

Sarah and Ella exchanged wide-eyed glances.

'She doesn't really mean it,' said Ella after a moment. 'It's so late – and dark – no one would blame you if you didn't fancy it, not after what Lizzie just told us.'

'What Lizzie just told you is a pack of nonsense,' said Tilly, getting to her feet. She was going to nip this in the bud at once – otherwise Sarah would probably keep her awake half the night having nightmares. 'I'm not in the least bit afraid to go to the East Wing,' she declared. 'I can tell you for certain that I won't find any ghosts there – but perhaps, if you're lucky, Lizzie, I'll be able to finish that dusting you're in such a hurry to avoid.'

With that, Tilly walked swiftly out of the Servants' Hall, and into the passageway.

Sarah came running after her. She had only been at Winter Hall for two months, and she still looked very small and unsure in her starched white apron and cap.

'Tilly!' she burst out. 'You aren't really going to the East Wing are you?'

'I've said I will, and so I will,' said Tilly crisply.

'But – but – you *can't!*' exclaimed Sarah, hastening

to keep up with Tilly's longer strides. 'There really is something funny about the East Wing, honestly there is. Old Mary told me she'd heard noises there late at night. And Jamie, the gardener's boy, said that he'd seen lights floating around high up in the windows. Even Mrs Dawes thinks there's something queer about it. I heard her saying so to Mr Stokes.'

This was quite a long speech for Sarah. Tilly stopped and contemplated her for a moment. 'They're just rumours,' she said, more gently. 'The East Wing isn't *haunted*. There are no such things as ghosts, Sarah.' She added in a sharper tone: 'And don't start hanging about with the gardener's boy. Mrs Dawes won't like it.'

'But how can you be *sure* that there are no such things as ghosts?' Sarah persisted.

'Because it isn't *scientific*,' explained Tilly, striding off again. 'There isn't a single spot of proof that ghosts exist, you know. I read a book all about it. All the scientists agree. Ghosts are just . . . *made up*.'

'Well, you should at least let me come with you,' spoke up Sarah bravely, as she scuttled along beside her. 'You can't go there all alone!'

'Of course I can,' said Tilly. 'I've been in the East Wing at night alone dozens of times – and nothing terrible has happened to me before, has it?' She didn't wait for an answer, but went on: 'Anyway, you should get back to the

Servants' Hall, or Ma will be wondering where you've got to. I'll be back in no time – promise.'

At that, Sarah nodded reluctantly, and disappeared back towards the Servants' Hall. Tilly grinned to herself. She knew Sarah wouldn't want to risk trouble with Ma, who was Cook at Winter Hall, and ruled all the kitchen and scullery maids with a rod of iron.

Of course, Ma wasn't *really* Tilly's mother. She'd worked that out for herself before she was five years old. It was plain as day to anyone with half a brain that they couldn't possibly be related. Ma was small, round and rosy, with fairish hair that was always pinned back smoothly into a neat knot under her cap. Tilly, on the other hand, was tall and rather bony, with a lot of curly black hair that was a struggle to twist into anything even halfway resembling a neat knot. Her eyes were dark brown, her eyebrows were black and bushy, and her skin was brown too. It wasn't just that she didn't look like Ma, she stood out like a sore thumb amongst the other maids, with their blonde hair and pink and white complexions.

Tilly's real mother had been a lady's maid in this very house. She'd died here, giving birth to Tilly, fourteen years ago. No one seemed to have any idea who Tilly's father was; Ma said he was probably just some common good-for-nothing who had turned her poor mother's head, God rest her soul. 'And let that be a lesson to you,' she would say to

8

Tilly, although Tilly was never quite sure what the lesson was supposed to be.

But it didn't really matter to Tilly that she didn't have a father. After all, Ma and the other servants at Winter Hall had been all the family she had ever needed. She'd been helping Ma in the kitchens since before she could walk properly, and now that she was almost fifteen, she was a proper housemaid with a frilly white apron for when she served tea in the Drawing Room. She felt quite grown-up – certainly far too grown-up to pay any heed to Lizzie's nonsense about things that go bump in the night.

Now, she pushed open the green baize door that separated the servants' quarters from the main part of the house. From here, she could hear the familiar sounds of the family and their guests in the Dining Room: the clinking of glasses; the rumble of conversation; Her Ladyship's tinkling laughter. The big hallway looked exactly as it always did, with the enormous grandfather clock ticking, and the faces of generations of Fitzgeralds gazing down upon her from the oil paintings that hung on the walls.

Tilly couldn't recall a time when she didn't know every inch of Winter Hall – from the cobwebby wine cellars down below to the attic bedrooms up in the rooftops. She knew each creaking floorboard and each of the old leather-bound books in the Library. When she had been very small, she had even given names to every one of the stuffed foxes and birds in His Lordship's study. Now, she was different: taller, almost grown-up, but nothing at Winter Hall had changed a bit. In spite of the recently installed electric lights and the wonderful new motor car, everything always felt exactly the same.

Once, she had loved that sense of comforting familiarity. It had meant *home*. But lately, the sameness of Winter Hall had begun to get on her nerves. Tilly longed for something new and different, but her days just kept on going like clockwork: the gong sounding for luncheon; tea served promptly at half past four; Her Ladyship scolding her maid as she dressed for dinner; and below stairs, the maids ironing and the footmen polishing the silver and His Lordship's valet brushing his shoes. Even the story of the supposedly haunted East Wing was an old tale that she'd heard half a dozen times before.

Just the same, as she went down the corridor, Tilly suddenly wished she had let Sarah come with her after all. It wasn't that she was scared – of course she wasn't, she wasn't an *idiot*. But this part of the house did feel rather dark and lonely.

The East Wing was the oldest part of Winter Hall. Once in a blue moon, Her Ladyship would bring some visitors to look around; they would exclaim in delight over the antique furniture, the beautiful carved chimney-piece, the canopied bed upon which it was said Queen Elizabeth herself had slept. But most of the time, the family didn't come here, preferring to keep to the plush comfort of the more modern West Wing with its electric light and running hot and cold water. The only one who was really interested in the East Wing was the youngest Fitzgerald daughter, Miss Leo: Tilly knew she sometimes spent hours here, looking at the pictures or making drawings of the old curiosities she found.

Now, Tilly pushed open the door to the East Wing. It did not creak exactly: Mrs Dawes was far too particular for that. Instead, it made a strange little sighing sound – rather like someone letting out a breath. The dark passageway yawned ahead of her. As she stepped over the threshold the flame of her candle guttered in a breath of air, and for a moment, she thought it would go out.

She could hear all the little noises of the house settling, a window rattling, and the wind howling outside, whirling about the house like a wild creature trying to get in. It sounded ghostly enough, and in spite of herself, Tilly shivered.

But immediately she reminded herself that there was nothing to shiver about. It might be cold, but that was because fires were not usually lit in this part of the house. There might be an odd, sour smell in the air, but that was nothing that a good airing wouldn't soon fix. And it might feel a little strange and old – but that was no surprise, as this part of the house had been built well over three hundred years ago.

A small light glinting a little way along the passage made her stop short for a moment, her heart thumping. But no sooner had she halted than she realised it was just the reflection of her own candle in an old looking glass. She shook her head at herself: she was being jumpy and silly.

'There's no such thing as ghosts,' she muttered, as she went on, feeling colder than ever, as the wind howled louder outside.

Halfway along the corridor, she glimpsed something lying on the floor, and realised it was Lizzie's duster. She reached down to pick it up, and as she did so, she felt a sudden rush of air that made her skin bristle. It was ice cold.

Nothing more than a window left open somewhere, she thought – but then she heard something else. It was a sound – quite loud and unmistakable in this empty, dark, creaking part of the house. The hollow, echoing pad of footsteps. Footsteps that were moving slowly but purposefully towards her along the corridor, growing louder and louder all the time.

It was a trick – it had to be. 'Charlie, I know it's you!' she called. 'Come out and stop playing the fool!'

But there was no reply, no answering snigger. Instead, the footsteps just kept coming towards her along the passageway – slow and heavy. Too heavy to be the steps of a young under-footman. Her chest tightened.

'If this is your idea of a stupid joke . . .' she began, but the words seemed to choke her, and fell away.

As she stared, she saw to her horror that a dark shape was moving steadily towards her. A tall, billowing, unearthly shadow, stretched into the shape of a human figure, advancing closer and closer along the wall.

A bitter cold wind swept over her. Every instinct was screaming at her to run, but she seemed to be frozen to the ground.

The shadow stretched towards her – a long, thin, black shape like an arm, reaching, reaching, until it could almost touch her.

Then the candle suddenly snuffed out, and in the icy darkness, Tilly screamed.

CHAPTER TWO

'We shall be delighted to welcome our special guests to the first Sinclair's New Year's Eve Ball.' Mr Sinclair's voice - clear and strong, with a hint of American twang - rang out across the Press Club Room at Sinclair's, London's most famous department store. 'I intend this new event to become a regular fixture of London's social calendar.'

It was a few days before Christmas, and outside, the London streets were very cold, the first flakes of snow beginning to fall from a heavy grey sky. Inside, the wood-panelled room was warm and brightly lit, and crowded with journalists, all of them listening intently to Mr Sinclair. A thick cloud of cigar smoke hung above their heads, blending with the rich aroma of Sinclair's at Christmas. It was the warm smell of cinnamon and toffee and spiced oranges, the sharp metallic tang of tinsel and silver paper - and something else too, something more difficult to identify: the tingling scent of anticipation.

From where he stood at the very back of the room, Billy

Parker, the youngest Sinclair's office boy, could sense a buzz of excitement in the air. All around him people busily scribbled down Mr Sinclair's words in their notebooks, whilst at the front, several photographers with cameras and tripods were jostling for position, each hoping to get the perfect shot of the man himself.

Of course, this scene was not exactly an unusual one. Ever since the news had first broken that New York millionaire Edward Sinclair would be coming to London to open the city's finest department store, he had instantly become the darling of the press – and really, Billy thought, it was little wonder. After all, Mr Sinclair always seemed to be planning some extraordinary new scheme, from ballet performances in the roof garden, to a showing of one of the new 'moving pictures' in the Exhibition Hall. He was frequently to be seen at London's most exclusive social gatherings, attending the first night of a fashionable new West End show, or dining at the best table in one of the city's finest restaurants. What was more, his department store was a place where sensational and dramatic things seemed to happen. Already, Sinclair's had seen everything from the daring robbery of precious jewels and priceless paintings to (it was rumoured) a narrow escape from a bomb concealed in the store's famous golden clock. In less than a year, Mr Sinclair had given the press a great deal to write about.

But it wasn't only the journalists who were endlessly fascinated by the debonair department store owner, Billy reflected, as he craned his neck to try to catch a glimpse of the elegant figure – immaculate as always, right down to the perfect orchid in his button hole. They might have been working for him for many months, but Mr Sinclair's own staff still speculated about their employer just as much as ever. Although he could be seen at the store almost every day, although his photograph appeared most weeks in the society pages of the illustrated papers, Billy thought now that there was still an awful lot that they did not know about the man they called 'the Captain'.

'Of course, as you know, gentlemen – I do beg your pardon, ma'am, gentlemen and *ladies*,' Mr Sinclair was saying, with a courtly bow in the direction of the single female journalist in the room. 'As you know, we don't do things in any ordinary, commonplace way here at Sinclair's – so you may be sure that this will be no ordinary or commonplace entertainment. We shall be welcoming in 1910 in truly spectacular style – is that not so, Monsieur Chevalier?'

He turned to the man standing beside him: a smartly dressed gentleman with a pointed black beard. 'Indeed we will,' said the gentleman, speaking with a strong French accent. 'I am honoured – most honoured – to be launching my new scent, *Midnight Peacock*, at the wonderful Sinclair's. What finer setting for a *fête* unlike anything we have seen before – *incroyable et inoubliable!*'

There was a murmur of appreciation from the journalists, as Mr Sinclair went on:

'Decorations, costumes and entertainments for the ball have been specially designed for the occasion by Monsieur Chevalier himself, taking inspiration from *Midnight Peacock*. Helping him to create the spectacle are artist Mr Max Kamensky, and the West End's renowned duo Mr Lloyd and Mr Mountville, who are producing a special entertainment for the evening.'

'I say! They really are going to be putting on a show,' Billy heard one journalist whisper to another amongst a frenzy of excited scribbling.

'Our guests for the evening will enjoy refreshments from the Marble Court Restaurant courtesy of our celebrated chef, Monsieur Bernard, a showcase of *Maison Chevalier*'s latest styles featuring our famous mannequins, and of course, the opportunity to be amongst the first to sample this magnificent new perfume,' Mr Sinclair continued. 'What is more, although the ball itself will be for invited guests, the festivities will spread out on to Piccadilly – and I hereby extend a cordial invitation to members of the public to gather and share in the countdown to midnight. With the support of our neighbours, we have arranged a special firework display from the rooftops of Piccadilly Circus, which will be a fitting conclusion to our evening of celebration.'

'Good heavens,' the second journalist whispered back. 'Fireworks as well? Sinclair doesn't do things by halves, does he?'

'I'll wager he'll get such a crowd the authorities will have to close off the street!' said another.

'What else d'you suppose he's got up his sleeve?'

But at the front of the room, it was clear that Mr Sinclair was bringing his address to a conclusion. 'I believe we have time for one or two questions,' he said.

A forest of hands surged into the air. Mr Sinclair singled out a young man with a curled moustache, who Billy recognised as a journalist for one of the fashion papers.

'Can you tell us more about what we can expect to see at the ball?' he asked eagerly.

'Ah – we do not wish to give away too many of our secrets,' said Monsieur Chevalier, his small dark eyes twinkling. 'For that would spoil the surprise – would it not?'

A bluff older man with grey hair was selected next.

'What do you make of Mr Huntington's plans, announced just this afternoon, to hold a New Year's entertainment at his store?' he demanded. 'Do you see the Huntington's New Year's tea dance as a rival to your ball?'

'I am sure Mr Huntington's little party will be a most delightful affair,' answered Mr Sinclair, his voice as smooth as cream. 'Of course, our entertainment will be in a rather different league – a tea dance this certainly isn't.'

There was a warm bubble of knowing laughter, and then it was the young lady journalist's turn to speak: 'Is there truth to the rumour that His Majesty the King will be amongst your guests?' she asked.

Mr Sinclair gave her his most charming smile. 'Now, of course, I couldn't possibly comment upon His Majesty's engagements – but what I will say is that we think this will certainly be a celebration *worthy of royalty*.'

At these words, a murmur of excitement ran around the room, and more hands were thrust into the air, but Mr Sinclair was already shaking his head.

'No more questions, I'm afraid. If you require more details, please apply to my private secretary, Miss Atwood. But for now, I would like to cordially invite you to remain here in the Press Club Room for a festive drink, to thank you for your support for Sinclair's during our first year of business. And when you leave, do look out for our special *Midnight Peacock* window displays. Ladies and gentlemen, thank you – and may I take this opportunity to wish you a merry Christmas, on behalf of all at Sinclair's.'

As the members of the press accepted glasses of sherry from waiters with silver trays, two floors above them, Sophie Taylor was sitting in the window, watching the dizzy, dancing swirl of snowflakes fall on the street outside.

The clock on the mantelpiece had just chimed four o'clock, and the light was already fading, but down below her, all along the street, the shop windows were bright and twinkling, and the pavements were thronged with people, wrapped up in overcoats and mufflers. Groups were gathering before the windows of Sinclair's to admire the parade of Christmas trees, beautifully dressed with gleaming silver stars, candied apples and bonbons wrapped in shiny paper. Another cluster of people were exclaiming over the window dressed all in purple and gold which advertised *Maison Chevalier*'s forthcoming *Midnight Peacock* perfume. Beyond, uniformed porters hurried out to waiting motor cars and taxi cabs, their arms piled high with Sinclair's parcels, and all the while Sidney Parker, the Head Doorman, stood at the top of the steps ringing a bell to welcome people in.

Through the great doors and into the store, the Entrance Hall was crowded with shoppers. Even during the grand opening, earlier that year, Sophie did not think that Sinclair's had ever been as bright and busy as it was now. Of course, everyone in London wanted to buy their gifts at Sinclair's, and at that very moment, Sophie knew that gentlemen were purchasing pocket handkerchiefs for their young ladies, mamas and papas were selecting train sets and teddy bears, and ladies of fashion were choosing fans and gloves for their dearest companions. The Confectionery

Department would be busiest of all, crowded with people buying sugar-dusted Turkish Delight, silver cones of rose and violet creams, and box after box of glorious Sinclair's chocolates, nestled amongst feather-light layers of snow-white tissue, and tied with a blue satin bow.

Sophie had a box of the chocolates beside her on the desk at that very moment. The confectioners had been experimenting with a new festive recipe, and Billy had brought up some samples for them to try. Now, she popped one into her mouth, tasting the melting sweetness of caramel and chocolate as she gazed out at the falling snow, and the shoppers surging in and out of the store.

As she watched, she saw the figure of a tall gentleman with a military bearing. For one heart-stopping moment, she thought that she recognised him. Then that sense of familiarity vanished as quickly as it had come, and he was just a stranger again. A little girl was clinging to his hand, obviously nervous of the crowds – his daughter, she supposed. As she watched, he paused and bent down to comfort her.

She turned abruptly away from the window. She had done quite enough daydreaming for one day, she told herself sternly, trying to fix her attention on the document that lay before her on her desk. But even as she began to read, the typed heading *CASE NOTES* blurred before her eyes and she found herself reaching up to trace the thin,

21

curving line of the white scar that ran across one side of her forehead.

The scar was barely visible, but for Sophie, it was important. It was a sign – perhaps the only sign – of everything that had happened to her in the past year.

There was nothing else to show that she was different. She hadn't grown as much as an inch in the last twelve months – and as for her long, fair hair, however much time she spent arranging it, it still had exactly the same annoying habit of slipping down. Her clothes, perhaps, were nicer than they had been, and here she stroked the skirt of her well-cut frock with satisfaction. Mr Sinclair liked them to wear the very latest styles, and had given both her and Lil a generous dress allowance to spend in the Ladies' Fashions Department. They both enjoyed choosing new frocks, but whilst Lil liked ornamenting her outfits with all the most fashionable accessories – dramatic fringed scarves, beaded chokers and pendant necklaces – Sophie always found herself coming back to the same old string of green beads that had once belonged to her mama.

She was wearing them today, and now she let the cool shapes of the beads run through her fingers. Sophie had never known her mother, who had died when Sophie was very small, but she had thought about her a good deal in the past few months. She felt full of questions about her – but there was no one left to answer them now.

Could it really have been only a year ago that she had first heard the news that Papa had died? Since then, her life had been turned upside down. She had gone from having a father and a home at Orchard House, to being all alone in the world – and then she had found a new place for herself at Sinclair's. Somehow, she had found friends and a job that – unexpectedly – she had turned out to be rather good at. For a moment, she grinned to herself. Twelve months ago she could certainly never have imagined that she was about to begin a career as a detective.

But the smile was only a fleeting one. For thinking of that only made her recall all the other things that had happened in the past year – and especially her encounters with the villain called the Baron.

Last Christmas she had never even heard that name – but since then, she and her friends had crossed the path of London's most notorious crime lord on several occasions. Between them, they had managed to prevent his scheme to destroy Sinclair's with an infernal machine – even after being locked up in the summerhouse in the roof garden by one of his henchmen. They'd exposed his disguise as the aristocrat Lord Beaucastle and helped to liberate much of London's East End from the stranglehold of his vicious gang, the Baron's Boys. Most recently of all they had rescued two valuable paintings by the Italian artist Benedetto Casselli, which the Baron had stolen on behalf of a secret society known as the *Fraternitas Draconum*, or the Brotherhood of Dragons. Though the society itself remained a mystery, it was thanks to their efforts that several of the Baron's accomplices were now in gaol – and that the Baron himself was a wanted man, on the run from Scotland Yard. He hadn't been seen by anyone since she had come face to face with him in a darkened Chelsea alleyway some months ago.

Of all their encounters, it was that one that she thought of most. Perhaps that was because it had been the first time that she had faced the Baron alone – or perhaps because he had confessed to her that he had killed not only her beloved papa, but her mother too, many years earlier. She had escaped from the encounter with no more than the scar on her forehead. Now, in spite of the warm fire, she shivered, thinking how lucky she had been.

I could have killed you a dozen times, he had told her. The words still puzzled her. It was true: so why hadn't he? The Baron had a reputation for ruthlessness, for exacting the most horrible revenge on anyone who crossed him. Yet he had let her go, saying only: *Farewell. This time I know I'll see you again.*

She found she was tapping her pen irritably against the desk. When it came to the Baron there were always these questions: the same frustrating spiral of mysteries and riddles. She counted them off the ever-growing list. How had the Baron known her parents? He had told her that he had once been a friend of her papa's – but how could she possibly square the memory of her kind-hearted father with what she knew of the Baron's cruelty and greed? She knew her papa had travelled during his military career, so perhaps the Baron had crossed his path – but how could he have met her mama? She heard the whisper of the Baron's voice again. *When she was by my side, she was the toast of Cairo . . . she gave all that up for a home and a husband – and you.*

Cairo . . . What on earth had her mother been doing in Egypt? She knew nothing of either of her parents ever having travelled there. Ought she even to believe a single word that the Baron had said?

She got up from her chair and walked over to the fire. She'd promised herself that she would stop going round in circles like this. She'd spent weeks after her last encounter with the Baron, mulling over everything he had told her, trying to piece together each tiny piece of evidence. It had been their friend and adviser Mr McDermott – himself a private detective – who had put a stop to that. 'I'd advise you to leave it alone. The Baron is the only one who can answer those questions – and with Detective Worth and Scotland Yard's top men on his trail, he would be foolish to set so much as a foot in this country. Try to forget about him – and focus your attention on Taylor & Rose.'

Mr McDermott had been right, of course. He usually was. Reluctantly, she'd taken down the photograph of the

25

Baron and her parents from the wall and filed it away in the folder in their office that was neatly labelled '*The Baron*'. For that was what she was going to do with the Baron now, she told herself: file him away with the rest of their paperwork on the office shelves. Far better to put all that aside and keep her attention firmly fixed upon new mysteries.

They certainly had plenty of those to keep them busy. In their first two months of business, Taylor & Rose had dealt with half a dozen different cases – from missing jewels to strange anonymous letters. Thanks to Mr Sinclair's appetite for publicity, everyone knew about his latest innovation: London's first (and only) young ladies' detective agency. From where she stood beside the fire, Sophie could see its name, *Taylor & Rose*, printed in curving gold script across the glass panel of their office door.

Plenty of people had already come through that door, curious to see Mr Sinclair's 'young lady detectives' for themselves. At first, the stream of visitors had made Sophie nervous. She lay awake at night, wondering how they could show everyone that two young girls really were capable of being detectives.

But little by little, she found her confidence was growing. With Mr McDermott's guidance, Taylor & Rose was beginning to thrive – and Sophie had suddenly found herself a person of some consequence at Sinclair's. When she had been a shop girl, she had been all but invisible, passing unnoticed through the crowds of shoppers. Now, people turned to look at her: salesgirls stared curiously in her direction; customers nudged each other, recognising her photograph from the newspapers; and some of the older doormen shook their heads, muttering that they 'didn't know what the world was coming to'. It would seem that not everyone approved of the idea of a young lady becoming a private detective.

But Sophie paid that no attention. She loved being part of Taylor & Rose. She had never really felt like she fitted in with Edith and the other salesgirls in the Millinery Department. It was not that she had minded selling hats for a living – in fact, there had been times when she had rather liked it. But her new work fascinated her like nothing else. Of course, the cases they dealt with were not on the same scale as the Baron's schemes, but each was engrossing just the same. They put her brain to the test, forcing her to trust her instincts and hone her powers of observation – and they absorbed her completely.

But today for once she was struggling to keep her mind on work. It was almost Christmas; and the office of Taylor & Rose was unusually quiet. Mr McDermott was away on the Continent on business, Lil had gone out to visit one of their clients, and whilst the rest of Sinclair's hummed with people, on the first floor, Sophie had been alone all the afternoon. The office was a pleasant place, attractively decorated for them on Mr Sinclair's orders, with a pretty sitting area, furnished with elegant chairs and a table spread with the latest fashion papers. There were two desks, one for Sophie and one for Lil, and even the telephone which Mr Sinclair had insisted must be installed stood on its own dainty little table beside a vase of flowers.

Yet in spite of Mr Sinclair's ladylike vision, the office of Taylor & Rose had swiftly acquired its own particular atmosphere, which was not really smart or elegant at all. It was a place where friends came to call, where crumpets were toasted before the fire on wet afternoons, where tea was poured from their own teapot, books and newspapers were read, and the latest cases were discussed – Sophie usually pacing up and down on the rug, whilst Lil leaned back in her chair, resting her boots on her desk in a most unladylike manner. In fact, the office had begun to feel like *home*, Sophie thought – in a way that nowhere had since she had left Orchard House a year ago.

But thinking of Orchard House led her back to Papa, and thinking of Papa led her back to the Baron, and that was no good at all. Sophie went back over to the desk, curled herself in her chair, and pulled the sheaf of documents decisively towards her. She must stop thinking about all that, and actually do something useful.

CASE NOTES, she read – but before she had got any further, there came an unexpected knock on the office door.

CHAPTER THREE

'It's only me,' said a familiar voice, and Billy came into the room, bearing a stack of envelopes. 'We've just finished downstairs. Mr Sinclair had the journalists eating out of the palm of his hand, of course. They're ever so excited about the New Year's Eve Ball. Here, I've brought up your post.'

Before he handed it over, he paused for a moment to shake his head at Sophie. Billy was always very keen to ensure that Taylor & Rose operated as professionally as possible. Though he continued to work in Mr Sinclair's offices, reporting to Miss Atwood, he had been given permission to spend one day a week, helping Sophie and Lil with their new business. And *that* was a jolly good job, he was given to remark, since neither of them had the first idea of how an office ought to be run.

'If you want Mr Sinclair to take you seriously, then you have to do things *properly*,' he reprimanded Lil half a dozen times a day. Billy had been well trained by Miss Atwood, and in his book, doing things properly meant writing reports, filing documents, keeping careful accounts with neat red lines ruled in all the right places, and making sure their desks were always tidy. That was an easy enough matter for Sophie, who rather liked putting things in order, but an almost impossible task for Lil, who was forever surrounded by a jumble of crumpled papers and spilled ink. Most importantly of all, Billy said, they must always be ready to receive clients who might turn up without an appointment. Now he looked at Sophie disapprovingly. Sitting comfortably curled up in a chair was not what he considered properly businesslike.

But Sophie just grinned at him. 'I don't think we'll get any new clients this afternoon,' she said. 'They're all downstairs, choosing presents and buying delicious things to eat. Christmas just isn't the season for mysteries. Why don't you sit down? I'm sure Miss Atwood can spare you for a few minutes, and I was just going to make some tea.'

Appreciating the logic of this, Billy shrugged, and flopped down into a chair. 'Oh – are those the notes from the Albemarle case?' he asked with interest. 'Let's have a look.'

Sophie passed over the documents willingly, as she flicked quickly through the afternoon post. At first glance it all looked quite usual: two letters from clients that she put aside to read later; some bills and circulars; and the latest edition of *Theatrical News* for Lil, who combined working for Taylor & Rose with performing on the West End stage. But underneath them was a narrow envelope with a foreign stamp. She frowned. Surely that handwriting was familiar? She swiftly ripped the envelope open – but her gasp of surprise was stifled by the bang of the door opening again as Lil burst into the room, her cheeks rosy from the cold.

'Hello, all!' she announced breathlessly, casting off a stylish coat with a fur collar, and tossing a pair of new kid gloves carelessly down upon the chair. Whilst she might look very much the glamorous young actress these days, Sophie knew that underneath the fashionable clothes and hairstyles, Lil was just the same girl that she had been when they had met at Sinclair's for the very first time. There could certainly be no doubt that she still talked just as much as ever, Sophie thought with a smile.

'Gosh – I don't think I've ever seen the store so busy before, have you? Oh yes, it all went quite well. Miss Balfour said she was awfully pleased with everything we've done – and she's going to recommend Taylor & Rose to all her friends. I say, just look at how the snow is coming down! It makes it feel like it's really Christmas. Isn't it cosy in here? Joe's on his way up and look – Leo's come to tea with us. I've promised her cake, so I jolly well hope we've got some.'

Sophie saw that another girl, of about the same age, had

followed Lil into the room. In her plain, dark coat, now speckled with melting snowflakes, Leo Fitzgerald could easily have been mistaken for any ordinary schoolgirl. But the big portfolio she carried, and a certain dreamy gleam in her brown eyes were clues to the fact that Leo was a promising young artist, currently studying at London's prestigious Spencer Institute.

'Hullo, Leo!' exclaimed Billy.

'Come and sit by the fire and get warm – it's so cold outside,' Sophie urged her. 'I didn't realise you were still in London – I thought you'd have already gone home for the Christmas holidays.'

Leo carefully set down her portfolio, and the cane she always used – a rather beautiful one, made from a rich, dark wood, with a handle carved into the shape of a lion's head. 'I'm going tomorrow,' she explained, as she unwound her scarf. 'Some of us students have been helping Mr Kamensky with the scenery for the New Year's Eve Ball and there's been an awful lot to do. But it's been good fun – and truthfully I've been rather glad to have an excuse to stay in town a little longer. I'm in no rush to go home,' she confessed. 'In fact, that's what I wanted to talk to you all about. I wondered whether you had plans for Christmas?'

Sophie did not answer at once. She wasn't quite sure what to say. She knew that the others would be busy on Christmas Day: Billy would spend the day with his mum and Uncle Sid, and she expected that Lil and her older brother Jack would go home to see their parents. But she herself had no plans at all. 'Oh – I think I'll just have a quiet day,' she had murmured, when Lil had pressed her. The truth was that she didn't want to think about it. The idea of another Christmas without Papa was something that she couldn't quite bring herself to contemplate.

Luckily no one noticed her reluctance to answer the question, for just then Joe came in, with Daisy at his heels.

Officially Daisy was the Sinclair's guard dog, but Joe had looked after her ever since she had arrived at the store, and she considered him her owner. She slept on his bed in the rooms above the stables, and followed him wherever he went. When she was on guard duty, she could be fearsome, but the rest of the time she was gentle and playful, and loved nothing more than a frolic with Mr Sinclair's little pug, Lucky. Now, she sniffed around the office, greeting each of them with an enthusiastic lick, and then laid one big paw on Sophie's knee, tilting her head to the side, with a hopeful look at the chocolate box.

'You *know* you aren't allowed those, you daft dog. Come over here and sit down,' said Joe, grinning around at everyone and settling himself next to Billy. Joe still worked in the Sinclair's stables, but like Billy, he was very much part of Taylor & Rose. He was sometimes allowed to act as Sophie and Lil's driver, accompanying the two young detectives on their investigations – with Daisy coming along to help too, of course.

'Look, now we're all here, just listen to this,' Lil was saying excitedly, as she spooned tea leaves into the teapot. 'Leo's got a terrific idea! She wants to invite us – all of us – to spend Christmas with her at her home, Winter Hall! What do you think of that? Isn't it awfully kind?'

Leo's face flushed pink. 'Well, I have to be honest – it's not really very kind of me at all. The truth of it is, I'd have an awful time at home on my own. Mother and Father always have a big house party for Christmas, and they invite lots of society people. None of them have a single thing to say to me – except for my godmother Lady Tremayne, of course. You'd like her. She's the one who persuaded them to let me go to art school in the first place. Anyway, Mother said that I could invite some of my own friends this year. I thought that if you would all come for a few days, it would be much better – rather fun, in fact.'

'What about your brother? Won't he be there?' asked Lil, handing her a cup of tea.

Leo gave a little snort. 'Oh yes, Vincent will be there all right. But he's – well – you'll see what he's like for yourself, if you come.' She looked around at them all. 'Do say you will. I know I haven't made it sound very enticing, but Winter Hall is beautiful at Christmas – I'd love to show it to you. I've already asked Jack and he says he'll come if

34

you will.'

'Well, thanks for the invite – but I reckon I can't get away,' said Joe, as he accepted a slab of the iced plum cake that Billy had found in the cake tin. 'You see, even when the store's closed, we've still got the horses to look after. Most of the other fellers want to go home to their families, so I said I'd stay on and look after things.'

Sophie gave him a quick smile. Like her, Joe was all alone in the world, with no family that would expect him on Christmas Day. It was just like him to volunteer to shoulder the work, so that the other stable boys and grooms would be free to go home to their loved ones.

'Me neither,' Billy was saying. 'I've got Christmas Day off, of course, but apart from that, I'll be here. There's an awful lot still to be organised for the ball, you know – and Miss Atwood says I'm to expect to be rather busy. Besides,' he added candidly, 'Mum wouldn't half be mad if I wasn't at home for Christmas dinner. She's already ordered the goose. You ought to come and have dinner with us, Joe, if you can. Mum's a grand cook.'

'Well *I* definitely want to come, Leo,' said Lil, taking a second piece of cake. 'I think it sounds perfectly marvellous. I'm starting rehearsals for a new play in January you know, which is set in a country house. It's a mystery and my character – Daphne De Vere – is to be horribly murdered in the first act. Rather thrilling, don't you think? This will be absolutely perfect for research!' she exclaimed happily.

'But won't your parents mind, if you aren't at home for Christmas?' asked Billy.

Lil shrugged. 'Neither Jack nor I are exactly in the good books with the Aged Parents at the moment,' she explained. 'Given all the fuss they made when they found out Jack had ditched Oxford to go and study art instead, I think it might be a jolly good idea for us to go elsewhere. Otherwise, I have a horrid suspicion that we'd probably end up spending Christmas having a big row. *Not* awfully festive.'

'What about you, Sophie?' asked Leo.

Sophie had been staring at her letter, a thoughtful expression on her face. At this question, she looked up suddenly.

'I think it sounds like a wonderful idea,' she said. 'Winter Hall is somewhere near Norchester, isn't it?'

'That's right,' said Leo, looking delighted. 'It's quite easy to get to. You can catch a train to the station in a village called Alwick, about ten miles away from the house. You really will come? How wonderful!'

It was a very merry tea. With the prospect of a jolly Christmas ahead of her, Leo was more animated than usual, her pale cheeks quite bright with excitement. Lil had a great many questions to ask – largely about what clothes they ought to bring with them, and what sort of things they would be having to eat. Meanwhile, Billy and Joe were curious to know what happened at a high society country house party at Christmas. 'You're bound to meet all sorts of important people,' Billy said pragmatically. 'It could be very useful for Taylor & Rose.'

Only Sophie was quiet, once or twice looking down at the letter again. At last, Leo said that she must go: she still had to pack before travelling to Winter Hall the next morning. It was agreed that Lil, Jack and Sophie would follow her once the office of Taylor & Rose had closed for Christmas, on the day before Christmas Eve.

As the door closed behind Leo, Lil looked at Sophie. 'I wasn't certain if you would want to go,' she said frankly. 'What happened to your plan for a quiet Christmas?'

'Oh, I *absolutely* want to go,' said Sophie. She pushed the letter over towards the other three. 'Pour yourselves another cup of tea – and read this,' she said.

CHAPTER FOUR

Lil took the thin sheet of writing paper, very much intrigued. She saw that it was covered in rather old-fashioned handwriting.

'Read it out loud,' urged Joe, and she began:

Calcutta, India
November 1909

My dearest Sophie,

I hope this finds you well – I have thought of you often, and I was very glad indeed to receive your letter. Thank you for your kind enquiries as to my health & situation. I am quite well, although I must say that my new home here in India is quite unbearably hot, and I cannot accustom myself to the presence of so many Snakes and Insects and other Unpleasant Creatures. Mary, my new young charge is a little girl of seven years – rather sulky and spoilt by the servants of the house, but beginning to show signs of improvement.

I have been very eager to write to you my dear, as I believe I have some information of importance to impart. As you know, your Dear Papa had no living relations, and most of his friends were military gentlemen, serving abroad. However, I remembered that your Dear Papa did tell me once of the name of a friend that we should contact in the event that anything should <u>happen</u> to him. This gentleman, he told me, was an old and trusted friend, now retired from Army life, and could be relied upon absolutely for help in his absence.

It was a long time ago, and it was rather a fleeting conversation. What is more, I must say that I did not care at all for the notion that anything Unfortunate might happen to your Dear Papa. However I wrote down the gentleman's name, and then I must confess, I put it quite out of my mind. But the moment that I recalled this conversation, I went at once to look in my portmanteau, and at last, I found the name of the gentleman - a <u>Colonel Fairley</u>, of Alwick House, near Norchester.

Of course, I felt most urgently the importance of communicating this discovery to you - but when I wrote to you at Mrs MacDuff's boarding house (I must say, not at all a reputable-seeming establishment) my letter was returned to me in a quite deplorable condition, marked NOT KNOWN. As you can well imagine, I was very anxious for you. I had all but given up hope of tracing you until at last, your letter reached me. (As it happened by chance, the very next day I had sight of The Times of India, in which I was astonished to see a photograph of you. I was a little shocked and alarmed to hear that you are mixed up in such an extraordinary enterprise as a detective agency - although I, more than anyone, can understand that <u>needs must</u>.)

My dear, I can quite understand your eagerness to learn more of your Dear Papa's affairs. But I am afraid he told me little about his career - I know he had travelled widely, but he never once mentioned anything of <u>Egypt</u>.

I cannot tell you, my dearest Sophie, of how dreadfully I felt – and still do feel – at having to leave you to fend for yourself in such a manner. I shudder to think what your Dear Papa would have said at such a situation. I do hope that Colonel Fairley may be of some help to you. I can only hope that you will forgive me for my forgetfulness, and that this information may prove useful.

I beg of you to write to me again my dear, and I remain most affectionately yours,

Millicent Emily Pennyfeather

'Millicent Pennyfeather – but who's that?' asked Lil, looking up from the letter, her eyes bright with interest.

'My old governess,' explained Sophie. 'I wrote to her a few months ago, before we got mixed up in the theft of the dragon painting, but the letter must have taken a long time to reach her out in India. I really wanted to know whether she knew anything about Papa spending time in Egypt: remember that photograph of him in Cairo? It doesn't sound like she knows anything about that – but she has remembered something else that could be important.'

'This Colonel Fairley?' asked Lil.

'Yes – and look where he lives.'

'Alwick House near Norchester – but that's –' began Billy.

'*Exactly*,' said Sophie. 'Alwick is the name of the village close to Winter Hall. If we go there for Christmas, then I could pay him a visit!'

'And *he* might know something – perhaps about your father's time in Egypt, or even how the Baron knew your parents!' finished Lil, her voice ringing with excitement.

Sophie nodded vigorously. What she did not say was that even if Colonel Fairley proved to know nothing at all about her father's time in Egypt, and had never even heard of the Baron, it would be enough just to speak to someone who had been Papa's friend. It was a long time since she had been able to talk to anyone who had known him. As

Miss Pennyfeather reminded her in her letter, she had no relations at all that she knew of, and sometimes she felt very alone. Looking at the others, sitting across from her in the cosy office – Lil, bursting with excitement at this new discovery, Billy carefully examining the letter, Joe sitting quietly, scratching Daisy's ears, and thinking it all through – she felt very grateful indeed for her friends.

At that moment, Lil glanced up at the clock on the mantelpiece and gave a little squeak of alarm. 'Golly, Sophie – just look at the time! We ought to go, or we'll be dreadfully late.'

'Late? Where are you off to in such a rush?' said Joe, as the two girls hustled into their coats and hats.

'Oh – only our Sewing Society.'

Billy dropped the letter. '*Sewing Society!*' he exclaimed in a disgusted tone. He had made it quite clear that he couldn't imagine why Sophie and Lil would waste their evenings, sitting around with a lot of girls, fussing over silly bits of stitching, when they could be doing something really interesting – like working on new cases, or at the least reading an exciting detective story, like one of his favourite Montgomery Baxter tales.

'Whatever you may think, it's jolly important,' said Lil primly. 'We're helping Connie and the suffragettes. And as a matter of fact, you might find it more interesting than you'd think.' She smirked slightly at Sophie as she said this, then, in a different tone of voice, she went on: 'You two wouldn't mind just quickly tidying away these tea things before you go, would you? We have to dash, and I know it's important to keep the office tidy and smart and all that sort of thing. Oh, I say, thanks awfully.'

With that, she sailed out of the door. Sophie grinned at the two boys, and then followed behind her.

Billy and Joe exchanged glances over the mess of tea things they had left behind them.

'Typical,' muttered Billy, shaking his head. 'That's just absolutely *typical*.'

Far from London, the snow was also falling on Winter Hall. When Tilly peeped out into the dark, she could see that the flakes were coming down thick and fast. She let the curtain fall back across her bedroom window, and scrambled gladly into bed under the weight of the heavy blankets.

Her room was at the top of the house and was almost always cold, especially at this time of year. It was a very plain room, like all the maids' bedrooms: simply furnished with two little beds, a chest of drawers, and a washstand. She shared with Sarah; under-housemaids and scullery maids were not considered important enough to have rooms to themselves. Now, she could hear the heavy sound of Sarah's breathing in the next bed: she was already fast asleep after a long day of scrubbing and washing in the scullery. Tilly didn't mind that; some nights she felt like talking, but tonight she wanted to *think*. She snuggled down under the covers, tucking her cold feet up underneath her, and thought back to that moment in the East Wing when her candle had snuffed out, and she'd been plunged into darkness.

She admitted it to herself now: she had been frightened out of her life when that awful shadow had reached out towards her. She had even screamed – thank goodness no one had been around to hear her! But she'd managed to get up and scramble away, back down the passage. She hadn't dared stop to catch her breath until she was back in the dazzling light of the hallway, with the door to the East Wing closed firmly behind her. She hadn't even had the nerve to take a peep and see if that dark shape – whatever it was – had tried to follow her. Instead, she'd walked back as swiftly as she could to the servants' quarters, trying to look cool and calm when a footman came by with the coffee tray for the Drawing Room.

Of course, she hadn't breathed so much as a word about what had happened to the others. She knew that Lizzie would crow over her about it for weeks if she did. Besides, she felt quite sure now that whatever it was she had seen, it must have a rational explanation. She knew there were no such things as ghosts – and that meant she had seen a *person*, someone who was trying to frighten her.

Strolling back into the Servants' Hall as though nothing

unusual had happened, she'd carelessly tossed the duster over in Lizzie's direction – but it didn't have at all the effect she had expected. In fact, the other housemaid paid her no attention whatsoever. William, His Lordship's valet, had come in with news about the Christmas house party, and everyone was gathered round him, hanging on to his every word. Christmas at Winter Hall was always a grand affair, and the servants were all eager to know who would be attending this year.

As Tilly joined the little circle, she saw that Charlie, the under-footman was there, and she stared at him through narrowed eyes. There was no doubt that frightening the life out of her and Lizzie was exactly the sort of idiotic thing he'd find hilarious. But if he'd been pretending to be a ghost in the East Wing five minutes ago, however had he managed to get back below stairs before her? At that moment, Charlie caught her staring and gave her a cheeky wink. What was that supposed to mean, she wondered indignantly? Was it meant to be some kind of acknowledgement of what he had done?

'It's such a shame that Miss Helen won't be joining us for Christmas,' Lizzie was saying.

'She's Mrs Godwin now,' William corrected her. 'And of course, she'll be spending Christmas with her husband and children. That's quite right and proper. But Mr Vincent is here – and Miss Leonora will be coming home from Town tomorrow.'

Miss Leo! Tilly forgot all about the ghost for a second, as her stomach gave an excited flip of gladness. It would be wonderful to have Miss Leo home again.

'Also arriving tomorrow is the Countess of Alconborough, and with her, the Whiteley family – Mr Charles Whiteley, Mrs Isabel Whiteley and Miss Veronica Whiteley,' announced William importantly. There was an interested murmur at this. The Dowager Countess of Alconborough was a familiar face at Winter Hall – but the Whiteley family were new.

'That's three ladies' maids, then – and likely a valet too, for the gentleman,' said Emma, the head housemaid, whose mind ran on very practical lines. 'Who are they, these Whiteleys?'

'Mr Whiteley is in the mining business,' went on William, his tone making it evident that *business* was to be considered a little coarse and improper. 'Mrs Whiteley is his second wife – and before she married, she was Miss Isabel Hampton-Lacey, of the Staffordshire Hampton-Laceys.'

They all nodded approvingly at this. Knowing the ins and outs of all the society families was an important part of working at Winter Hall: Mrs Dawes' copy of *Debrett's* was even more well-thumbed than Her Ladyship's own.

'Miss Veronica is his daughter from his first marriage,' William explained. 'She is about Miss Leonora's age – or perhaps a little older – and she made her debut this

46

summer. I believe she is a very pretty young lady, with a large fortune.'

Lizzie pounced on this at once: 'I'll bet you they're thinking about a match for Mr Vincent!'

'Surely they'll not be thinking of marrying him off just yet, poor fellow,' said Charlie.

Ella giggled. 'Ooh – I wish they'd marry him off to *me!*' she exclaimed. 'I think Mr Vincent is ever so handsome!'

Ma came bustling in from the kitchen, just in time to overhear this last remark. 'That's quite enough of that sort of thing,' she said at once. 'Mrs Dawes would have your guts for garters if she heard you talking like that, miss – and well you know it. Besides, we've got plenty to do without standing around gossiping. William, you'd better finish clearing the Dining Room – and Sarah, there's a stack of washing-up waiting for you in the scullery. Give her a hand with the drying, will you, Tilly love? I don't want butterfingers here breaking His Lordship's best brandy glasses.' But she patted Sarah gently on the shoulder as she said it: Ma's bark was generally much worse than her bite.

Tilly followed Sarah through into the kitchen, rather glad to have an excuse to get away and think. But as she carefully dried the glasses and put them away in their proper place, all she felt sure of was that the apparition in the passageway couldn't possibly have been a prank of Charlie's. He was only a lad – he might be tall, but he was too much like a beanpole to have been that big threatening figure, with its heavy plodding footsteps. Besides, he'd never have been able to beat her back to the Servants' Hall.

Now, as she lay in bed, she decided three things. First of all, she would go back to the East Wing tomorrow morning, and have a good look around. Secondly, when she was dusting the Library later, she'd pinch that book she'd read before – the one about ghosts. She wasn't supposed to take books from the Library, of course – she couldn't even imagine the dressing-down Mr Stokes the butler would give her, if he ever caught her at it. But she'd been doing it for as long as she could remember, and she'd never been caught yet. After all, it wasn't as though His Lordship would miss them. In spite of having all those hundreds of books, Tilly had never seen him read much besides the newspaper.

Thirdly, and most importantly, she decided she would tell Miss Leo all about it when she came home tomorrow. Whilst she didn't fancy talking to Sarah or any of the others – she'd likely work them up into even more of a tizz about ghosts if she did – Tilly knew that she could confide in Miss Leo.

She snuggled down further under the blankets, hugging the thought that her friend would soon be home. Miss Leo, or to give her her proper name, Miss Leonora, was three years older than Tilly, but, perhaps because she had been very ill with polio as a child, and had spent so much time

48

in bed, she had always seemed younger than she really was. She was quite different from her older sister and brother – and not only because of the crutch she had used ever since her illness. She was the only one of the family ever to be seen in the Servants' Hall. She had been everyone's pet when she was small: Ma would always let her scrape out the mixing bowl, or give her a bun hot from the oven. 'Poor little mite,' she'd say, when Miss Leo had gone.

In those days, Tilly and Miss Leo had played together, just as if they were sisters. Miss Leo had been Tilly's best friend in the world. They understood each other: Miss Leo knew that Tilly would prefer tinkering with the workings of a clock or reading a book about scientific inventions than sewing or polishing; just as Tilly knew that Miss Leo would rather paint or draw than sit primly in the Nursery embroidering in a pretty dress.

Tilly knew too that Miss Leo's life was a lonely one. She'd never been to school or spent much time with other children – and when she did, she had to put up with their whispers and giggles, all because she had a bad leg. Tilly knew how that felt – she'd spent enough time at school being taunted and jeered at because she didn't look like the other girls. She knew how to deal with that: she just put her head in the air and ignored them, knowing that they'd be laughing on the other side of their faces when she came out top of the class. But Miss Leo had never had the chance to toughen up. When she wasn't with Tilly, she was always by herself.

What was worse, as they got older, Ma and Nanny, who ruled the Nursery, did not seem to approve of their friendship any longer. They wanted to keep Tilly and Miss Leo shut up in their separate boxes: Leo in the Nursery, all dressed up in a velvet frock with a frilly white petticoat; Tilly in the kitchen, shelling peas or doing a bit of mending for Mrs Dawes. It was as if they were two dolls, Tilly used to think, neatly tidied into their rightful places like the porcelain figures in Miss Leo's big doll's house.

'Know your place,' Ma told her, but Tilly had found ways to make sure she and Miss Leo could keep being friends. After school, she made sure she was always on hand to hang up Miss Leo's clothes or run her bath or stoke up the Nursery fire. 'She's getting to be a good little maid, isn't she?' Ma said proudly to Nanny, but Tilly and Miss Leo just grinned at each other, knowing they had found a way to make sure they could still spend time together.

Ma approved of Tilly waiting on Miss Leo. 'You're a bright girl,' she'd say, as she rolled out pastry for a game pie, or stuffed the mutton for a luncheon party. 'Quick and handy – and so sharp you'll cut yourself one of these days. Miss Leo's of an age to be needing her own lady's maid soon, and if you play your cards right . . .'

She hadn't needed to finish the sentence. Tilly knew

exactly the picture that was in Ma's head. She was imagining Tilly as a proper lady's maid in a black frock with a lace collar, permitted to sit up at the top of the table in the Servants' Hall, and to take her tea in the housekeeper's room. Only a housekeeper or a butler ranked higher than a lady's maid, and Ma had grand ambitions for Tilly. But what Tilly had never admitted to Ma is that she wasn't so sure that she really wanted to be a lady's maid at all. Waiting on Miss Leo was a good way to make sure they could spend time together, but there were so many more interesting things that Tilly could do than fuss about with hairstyles and dresses. His Lordship had recently bought his first motor car, and Tilly hung about the garage whenever she had a free moment, breathing in the wonderful petrol smell, and staring at the big shiny machine with its roaring engine. She wondered how it would feel to drive it. Could girls be chauffeurs, she wondered? She'd much rather do that.

Then Miss Leo had managed to persuade Her Ladyship and His Lordship that she should be allowed to go off to London to study art. Tilly couldn't even imagine what London might be like, though she'd seen photographs of it in the newspapers that His Lordship left scattered about the Library. Fascinating pictures of big new buildings and busy streets jammed with people and bicycles and automobiles and motor buses. She wondered what it would be like to live somewhere like that - London or maybe Oxford, where Mr Vincent had gone to university. Tilly knew from Miss Leo that young ladies could study there too, although they wouldn't be awarded a proper degree, as the young gentlemen were. But they could still learn Latin and Greek and science and mathematics. For a moment, she imagined going there herself. She'd study mechanical sciences, she thought, so she could learn all about how machines worked.

Ma always said that these kinds of thoughts did her no good, and that Tilly oughtn't to 'get ideas above her station'. It didn't matter tuppence to her that Tilly had always been top of the class at the village school, nor that Alf, His Lordship's chauffeur, said he'd never known any lad get his head round the workings of a motor engine half so quick as Tilly. There would be no thought of any more schooling for a girl like her. Even spending too much time in the garage was frowned upon. 'You keep your feet on the ground, my girl,' Ma said. Tilly sighed to herself in the dark.

But at least Miss Leo would be back tomorrow – and Tilly could hear all about what London was really like. Thinking of tomorrow, she rolled over and blew out the candle in one sharp breath. She'd have to be up before six to sweep the grates and make the fires and take up the early morning tea trays. Putting all thoughts of ghosts – and Miss Leo – firmly out of her head, Tilly closed her eyes and made up her mind to sleep.

CHAPTER FIVE

Mr Lim raised his eyebrows as he peered at the newspaper. 'A New Year's Eve Ball? So this is Mr Sinclair's latest scheme!'

'It's going to be his grandest yet!' said Lil. 'There are all kinds of special entertainments planned – but the best part will be the fireworks on Piccadilly Circus at midnight.'

Mei Lim was looking over her father's shoulder at the newspaper, her long black plait falling forward as she did so. 'Is it really true that the King is going to be there?' she asked, her eyes wide.

'It sounds unlikely, I know,' admitted Sophie. 'But apparently the Queen is a great admirer of Monsieur Chevalier – and the King knows Mr Sinclair too, of course.'

'Mr Sinclair knows *everybody*,' added Lil. 'The King is even going to make a special appearance to the crowds outside, from the balcony of the Marble Court Restaurant. It's supposed to be a secret but of course, everyone knows about it.'

Sophie smiled, knowing exactly what she meant: a secret was never a secret for very long at Sinclair's.

'Well, I s'pose the King does have good reason to think well of Sinclair's,' said Mei's older brother Song, from where he stood at the stove, stirring a big iron pot that smelled deliciously of ginger and spices. 'After all, it's thanks to Sinclair's very own detective agency that he got back the painting that was stolen from him,' he went on, with a grin.

The rest of them were crowded around the table in the little back room of the Lim family grocer's shop. *L.LIM & SONS* couldn't have been more different from the grand Sinclair's department store, but it was one of Sophie's favourite places in the world. Tonight, the back room felt even cosier than usual, in the light of the flickering gas lamp, with the snow still coming down outside. At one end of the table, Mei and Song's younger brothers – the twins, Shen and Jian – were drawing with a new packet of coloured chalks that Leo had sent them as a Christmas present. Whilst Lil regaled Mr Lim with a lively account of one of Taylor & Rose's recent cases, Mei and Sophie helped Song bring the dishes over to the table, and a few moments later, Mrs Lim came bustling through from the shop to join them for the evening meal.

'So how did it go this evening?' she asked, squeezing in between Lil and Mr Lim, adding to the twins: 'Boys, put those away – it's time to eat.'

'Do you know, I really think it might have been our best session yet,' declared Mr Lim proudly. 'Some of our young ladies are proving themselves very talented.'

Song chuckled as he took his seat on a stool next to Sophie. 'Maybe some of them are a bit *too* talented. I was worried that Miss Clifton was going to do Lil an injury!'

'Huh – that's what you think!' declared Lil, brandishing her fork. 'I could get the better of Connie any day you like.'

'And are you girls still telling people that you all belong to a sewing society?' asked Mrs Lim.

Lil grinned. 'Of course. We say we're sewing banners for the suffragettes to carry in their parades. Even Billy and Joe don't know what we're really up to.'

'I still don't understand why it has to be such a secret,' said Song.

'We promised that we'd keep it quiet,' Sophie explained. 'Some of the girls are worried that their parents wouldn't like it. They'd think it improper.'

'And a sewing society sounds so frightfully *innocent*,' said Lil with satisfaction. 'Not even the most prim mama could possibly object to that!'

Mr Lim frowned. 'I hope that none of the girls' parents would have any serious objections to the classes,' he said in a worried tone. 'I wouldn't want any of them to find themselves in trouble at home.'

'Trouble at home isn't the half of it!' exclaimed Lil at once. 'Why, some of these girls are doing awfully dangerous things – taking part in rowdy protests, and chaining themselves to railings, and goodness knows what else! It's fearfully important that they can defend themselves properly.'

'It's a good thing we're doing, Dad,' Song reassured his father.

'I think so too,' agreed Mrs Lim decisively. 'The way I see it, a young girl should know a little about how to defend herself. With any luck, most of them won't need it – but there's certainly no harm in being prepared.'

Sophie nodded. It had been her own desire to *be prepared* that had begun all this. Ever since she had come face to face with the Baron, she had felt frustrated and worried by her own weakness. She knew that if she ever encountered him again, she did not want to feel so vulnerable. She felt certain that if she were prepared, she would be able to sleep more soundly at night.

It was to Song that she had finally confided this. Over the past few months, he had become a particular friend. Sophie enjoyed his company, and admired his ambition of becoming a chef in a big London restaurant one day. She knew she could rely on him for a common-sense perspective. Song was always sensible and practical, and this had been a case in point: he had understood how she had felt, and had come up with a solution. 'You ought to talk to Dad,' he had said. 'Kung fu is exactly what you need. It's not about being big and strong, but using your opponent's strength against them. You know Dad learned a bit from the monks, when he was a boy – and he's been teaching me some, since the summer when we had that run-in with the Baron's Boys. Maybe he could teach you too?'

As soon as she had heard of Sophie's plan, Lil had at once said that she wanted to join in too. 'That sort of thing is tremendously useful for actors. Awfully good for flexibility and posture. Besides, we've got ourselves into some tricky situations in the past. In our line of work, I can't help thinking that it would be a jolly good idea for us to know a bit about how to defend ourselves.'

Of course, Mei wasn't going to be left out, and next had come Connie Clifton, a friend of Leo's from art school and a committed suffragette. 'This is exactly what we need!' she had exclaimed. 'We heard that some of the other suffragette groups had been learning ju-jitsu – suffrajitsu, they're calling it. We're dying to learn something like that too. Could some of us join your class? We'll pay, of course. Mrs St James will be thrilled!'

Now their practice sessions had become a weekly event. Mrs St James, the leader of Connie's group of suffragettes, had arranged for them to have access to the basement of an East End Mission Hall, where Mr Lim, with Song acting as his assistant, could teach a dozen young ladies at a time. She even provided tea and buns for them all afterwards. Each girl paid a little for her lesson, and Mr Lim had been heard to say that at this rate, teaching would soon earn him as much as his grocer's shop.

Sophie still wasn't sure that what she had learned would help her if she was to come face to face with the Baron in another dark alleyway – but the sessions certainly made her feel better. She liked the challenge of learning something new, and for once, being small wasn't necessarily a disadvantage – she might not be as tall or strong as Lil, but in spite of the encumbrance of skirts and petticoats, she was quick and light on her feet. The lessons were fun too: she felt quite certain that the sombre East End Mission Hall had never heard anything like so much giggling and shrieking. Best of all, afterwards, she and Lil would come back to the Lims', where Song would make them all supper. Now, as Lil told the others about their planned visit to Winter Hall, she sat back and listened, letting their words wash over her and enjoying the familiar sound of their voices.

After supper she went through into the little scullery to help Song clear away the dishes.

'You'll be away for Christmas, then?' he said. 'We were going to ask whether you'd like to come here.'

'I'd have loved that,' said Sophie, as she stacked up the

plates beside the sink. 'But I couldn't pass up the chance to go to Winter Hall.' She quickly explained about the letter from Miss Pennyfeather, and Song listened with interest.

'No wonder you want to go and find out. Well – I suppose we'll see you after New Year.'

'You might see me sooner than that,' said Sophie, with a sudden smile. 'I've got a kind of Christmas present for you. Well, I suppose it's not exactly a present – it's really more of an *opportunity*.'

Song looked at her quizzically as she explained: 'They're bringing in lots of extra staff to help with the Sinclair's New Year's Eve Ball. Waiters, mainly – but there will be people needed in the kitchens too. I spoke to Mr Betteredge and – well, there's a place open for you, if you'd like it.'

Song stared at her. 'Do you mean the kitchens of the *Marble Court Restaurant*?' he breathed in awe. It was considered to be one of the best restaurants in London, with its famous head chef, Monsieur Bernard.

'It would be temporary, of course – just for a few days before the party, and on the evening itself. You'd only be working as a kitchen porter, but it would give you the chance to meet Monsieur Bernard – and for him to see what you can do.'

Song wasn't the sort of person who got over-excited, but now he looked like he could hardly speak. 'But . . . but . . . that's incredible!' he burst out incoherently. 'Sophie –

thank you – this means so much to me! It's terrific!' He took a step towards her, as if he was going to grab her hands, but just then, Lil came bouncing through the door.

'What are you two gabbling about in here? Sophie, we ought to make tracks. The snow's coming down awfully fast now. We should get a cab.'

Soon the two girls were sitting cosily in the back of a hansom cab, the horses picking their way carefully along the snowy streets towards home. They were both tired, and even Lil was quiet now, gazing out of the window at the ghostly blur of the snow, illuminated here and there by the glow of the street lamps.

Sophie was thinking how pleased Song had been by the chance of a job at the Marble Court Restaurant. Not so very long ago, it had been a struggle to find decent paid work for herself: now, it was very pleasant to be able to help others. As the cab made its way slowly past the shimmering lights and advertisements of Piccadilly Circus and on to Piccadilly, the brightly lit facade of Sinclair's glittered out of the dark. She remembered how last winter she had stood in the snow looking up at it, feeling certain that this building held promise for her. Now, the Christmas trees sparkled in the windows, and high above, the lights of Mr Sinclair's private apartments gleamed, and she was surprised to feel a sudden prickle of festive excitement. Perhaps she was looking forward to Christmas, after all.

CHAPTER SIX

'**W**e need more linen for the Blue Room. Quick, girls! Don't dawdle.'

'Mr Stokes, the cases of claret have arrived – where would you like them?'

'Hurry and ring the gong. We mustn't be a minute late with luncheon. You know how particular Her Ladyship is about punctuality when there are guests in the house.'

Below stairs at Winter Hall was all a-fluster with activity. The stone-flagged passageways rang with the sound of footsteps. With so many extra people in the house, guest bedrooms to be arranged, and meals to be prepared, there was a great deal to do – and yet Mrs Dawes was not too busy to notice the sound of the motor pulling up on the drive.

Tilly left the bed linen to the other housemaids and followed her outside into the cold, shivering in her thin frock and apron. A small, familiar figure in a plain woollen coat was being helped out of the motor by Alf.

'Hello, Mrs Dawes! Hello, Tilly! How nice to see you!' she called out.

Tilly stared in surprise. Miss Leo's quiet voice was the same, but there seemed to be something different about her. It wasn't that she had grown any taller or that she was dressed differently – in spite of all the frilly frocks Nanny always wanted her to wear, Miss Leo had never given a pin for how she looked. But she seemed older somehow, and what was more, Tilly noticed that her bulky crutch was gone, replaced by a handsome walking stick.

She wanted to leap forward and ask a dozen questions, but she knew that this was one of the occasions when she was supposed to 'know her place' and so she hung back, whilst Mrs Dawes stepped forward. 'Welcome home, Miss Leonora,' she said warmly. 'We're glad to see you. Now, hurry inside and get warm. Charlie will bring up your trunks and Tilly can unpack for you. You've missed luncheon but Nanny will have something ready for you in the Nursery.'

'Oh, but I don't need any help,' said Miss Leo eagerly. 'I'm quite used to looking after myself now, and being independent.' But catching Tilly's expression, she added swiftly: 'Though actually, it would be nice to have Tilly help me. I'm rather tired after the journey.'

As she came up the steps and through the doors, Tilly saw that Miss Leo was staring all around her, quite as if she was seeing Winter Hall for the first time. She couldn't imagine why, for it wasn't as if anything had changed. The big hallway looked exactly as it always did, with the grandfather clock and the portraits on the panelled walls. The door to the Ballroom was open: Tilly noticed Miss Leo peep through at the big Christmas tree that the maids had decorated the day before, with all the usual ornaments, and little red candles. They ought to have waited until Miss Leo came home to do that, Tilly thought. Miss Leo had always loved helping to dress the Christmas tree, and it had always been her job to place the fairy doll in the very top branches. When she had been very little, Tilly had once cried because she wanted to be the one to do that: Ma had scolded and threatened a spanking, but Miss Leo had looked astonished and then put the fairy doll straight into Tilly's small hands.

Now, in the hallway, they could hear the sounds of the family at luncheon in the Dining Room. Miss Leo hesitated for a moment, as though wondering if someone might come out to greet her. But the voices and the clink of china went on without interruption, and Miss Leo blew out a faint little sigh, and began to trudge up the stairs. Her shoulders hunched, and all at once, she looked smaller and younger again.

Tilly ran up the stairs after her. 'I'm so glad you're back,' she whispered.

'I wish I wasn't,' said Miss Leo in a flat voice. 'But I

am awfully glad to see *you*, Tilly. Let's go upstairs – I've got heaps to tell you.'

The railway station was noisy and smoky, and damp with melting snow. Porters with trunks swung by, whilst gentlemen in bowler hats hurried for their trains and messenger boys pushed their way through the throng, with brown-paper parcels tucked under their arms. Everyone seemed to be in a terrific hurry, and for a moment, Sophie was buffeted amongst the crowd. Then she caught sight of Lil, waving to her excitedly from beside the station book stall, and a moment later, Jack emerged from the ticket office and strolled over to join them.

Sophie couldn't help smiling at how effortlessly he seemed to swing through the crowd. Like his younger sister, Jack was tall and good-looking. He had dark hair, which had a habit of flopping over his eyes, and a remarkable ability to charm everyone he met. Today, he was wearing a thick overcoat and carrying a small suitcase, as well as a little leather case that Sophie supposed must contain his painting things – for like Leo, Jack was studying at the Spencer Institute of Fine Art.

He grinned at her in welcome. 'I say, this is a lark, isn't it? Splendid that you could come!'

Sophie found herself blushing. Jack had made no secret of the fact that he thought her a fine girl, and when he smiled at her, she was conscious of feeling excited and embarrassed and flustered in a way that was not in the least like her usual self. She was rather glad that Lil was chattering away, insisting that they make a stop in the Refreshment Rooms to buy some chocolate for the journey.

Together, they made their way to the platform, and clambered on to the train, where they found themselves an empty compartment and settled down.

'I do like train journeys,' said Lil, peering out at the steamy station platform as though she were willing the guard to blow his whistle, so the train could be on its way. 'And I'm glad we've got our own compartment. It's so much nicer being able to talk properly without having to worry about being quiet and minding our manners for strangers.'

But the words were scarcely out of her mouth when the door to their compartment opened, and someone else came in – a small, elderly lady, with white hair, a pince-nez on a long, glittering chain, and a velvet hat with a bunch of very purple violets in it. She smiled around at them all benevolently, as the guard blew his whistle, and the train began its slow chug out of the station.

'Excuse me, young man, would you put my suitcase up into the luggage rack please?' she asked in a high, quavering voice. Jack smiled charmingly, and did as she asked, whilst Lil made a face at Sophie. So much for their own private compartment!

'And might I trouble you for that corner seat, my dear?' the old lady asked Sophie, clutching a white lacy handkerchief in a thin, lace-gloved hand. 'I mustn't travel with my back to the engine. Oh, thank you. How kind.'

Sophie politely moved seats, allowing the old lady to position herself into the corner. She carefully set down an enormous carpet bag, before removing a succession of articles from inside it. First was a novel in a yellow paper cover, then a small tin of lozenges, marked 'for coughs', then some complicated-looking knitting, a little brown medicine bottle, a lacy shawl, an illustrated magazine, and finally, a packet of hairpins. She then systematically returned all the items back into the bag, with the exception of the magazine and the tin of lozenges, which she opened, releasing a sickly medicinal aroma into the compartment.

'H-hem,' she coughed, before popping a lozenge into her mouth.

Lil was staring in obvious fascination. Sophie guessed that she was already picturing this old lady as a character in a play. 'Where are you travelling to, ma'am?' she asked in a polite tone.

'I'm going to Alwick, dear,' the old lady replied.

'Oh – that's where we're going too,' said Lil, trying to sound bright and cheerful, but her voice falling a little flat at the news that their new companion would be with them for the whole of their journey.

Resigning themselves to the inevitable, they all settled down quietly. Lil pulled out her *Theatrical News*, and Jack took a small sketchbook and a handful of pencils out of his pocket. Meanwhile, Sophie opened a book – a collection of Montgomery Baxter tales, which Billy had loaned her – but the boy detective's intrepid adventures did not really catch her attention. Instead, as the train gathered speed, rattling and bumping its way through the London suburbs, she stared out of the window as streets and the untidy backs of houses gave way to a landscape of bare trees and empty fields. It was a long time since she had been out of the city, and she found herself gazing at the black silhouettes of birds swooping against pebble-grey clouds and rough brown hedgerows, dusted with glittering frost like sugar on a cake.

The light was already ebbing out of the day, the sky heavy with the promise of more snow to come. Their compartment was only dimly lit and it was quiet too, with no sounds but the rattle of the train, the scratch of Jack's pencil and the occasional soft flicker of pages turning. After an hour or more had passed, Sophie heard a decorous little snore, and glanced over to see that the old lady had nodded off to sleep over her magazine, her pince-nez still perched on the end of her nose.

They felt more able to talk in low voices after that, and Lil passed around the packet of chocolate, which had got rather warm and squashy from being in the pocket of her coat. Between them, the two girls quickly told Jack all about Miss Pennyfeather's mysterious letter – and their plan to pay a visit to Colonel Fairley.

Jack listened with great interest. 'Do you suppose this fellow was someone your father knew in the Army?' he asked.

'I suppose so,' said Sophie. 'I know he had a lot of Army friends – they used to come and visit us sometimes. But I don't remember ever meeting a Colonel Fairley.' She paused for a moment. 'The thing I can't help thinking is – if they really were such awfully good friends, if he was the person we were supposed to go to if we found ourselves in trouble – then, why didn't he contact us when Papa died? Or come to his funeral? There were notices in all the newspapers, so he must have known about it.'

'Maybe he was away – travelling perhaps?' suggested Lil.

'Perhaps,' said Sophie. 'But then why wouldn't he have tried to get in touch when he got back home? It all seems so odd.'

Jack had a sudden thought: 'Do you suppose – well, it couldn't have anything to do with your father's connection to *the Baron*, could it?'

Sophie opened her mouth to reply – and then closed it abruptly. She had caught a sudden gleam from behind the old lady's pince-nez. Her eyes were no longer quite closed, and she suddenly had the peculiar sense that the old lady was *listening*. Not idly eavesdropping on a conversation, but alert, actively paying attention to every word they said.

Just then, the train hurtled into a tunnel, and the compartment was plunged into darkness. When the greyish light seeped back in, the old lady was simply drowsing once more, her eyes shut. Sophie frowned. With the other two watching her curiously, she tilted her head in the direction of the old lady and then put her finger to her lips. After a quick, surprised glance, Lil began to talk airily about the new play she would be rehearsing in January. For the rest of the journey they all kept their conversation carefully general, as the train rattled onwards towards Alwick, and Winter Hall.

PART II
The Case of the Hidden Passage

Montgomery Baxter tapped the panelled wall sharply with his knuckles. The sound was hollow. 'I thought as much. Gentlemen – this room conceals a secret passage!'

CHAPTER SEVEN

Sophie had realised that Winter Hall would be grand, but she did not realise just how grand until she first glimpsed it from the big motor car that had met them at the station. Built of fierce grey stone, its stern lines and tall Gothic windows were forbidding – even frightening. As they drove through great iron gates on to the estate, she glimpsed the flash of a frozen lake, a herd of deer, galloping across the snowy moors towards the shelter of a dark pine wood. Before them, the house sat, perfectly still but for the blue columns of smoke rising from its tall chimneys. A moment later, they were pulling up on a gravel driveway and the big doors were opening – and there was Leo, leaning on her cane and waving to them.

Sophie had never been anywhere like this before. Even Lord Beaucastle's riverside mansion had been nothing to compare with these immense dark-panelled rooms, long passageways, vast fireplaces and magnificent staircases. Then there was the army of servants: the uniformed chauffeur who met them at the station; the footmen who whisked away their suitcases; the butler who bowed gravely; the maids who unpacked for them before they had even reached their rooms.

Sophie found herself watching the maids with an especially strange feeling. Less than a year ago, she had thought she might have to take a job in service herself. Now, it seemed only the smallest twist of fate that had brought her here to Winter Hall as a guest for the grand Christmas house party.

Leo told them about the history of the house as she showed them around. 'The oldest parts date back to the 1500s. It's been partly rebuilt and extended since then, of course – but originally it was built during the reign of Queen Elizabeth. She gave the land as a gift to one of her advisers, Sir Frances Walsingham. Walsingham was her spymaster, you know – and they say that's why the older parts of the house have so many hidden rooms, and secret passages.'

'Secret passages!' exclaimed Lil. 'How frightfully exciting!'

Leo laughed. 'I'll show you one if you like,' she said, pausing in the hallway and pushing back a heavy tapestry, worked with designs of lions and unicorns. Behind it was a small door built into the panelled wall.

'This is one of my secret places,' she explained, leading

them through into a dusty corridor, and beckoning them up a narrow flight of stairs. Leo led the way onwards to a little room, furnished with a few bits of old furniture, with some of her own drawings pinned up around the walls. 'No one ever comes here except me. I don't have any idea what the room was originally for – I suppose it must have been a kind of hiding place.'

'How mysterious!' exclaimed Jack.

'Oh, there are plenty of mysterious things at Winter Hall,' said Leo, looking pleased at their enthusiasm. 'I'll give you a tour of the grounds tomorrow – there's an old folly there that you'll like to see. Then there's the East Wing – that's the very oldest part of the house. I've got a nice little mystery there, all ready and waiting for you to solve.'

'A mystery for us – here at Winter Hall?' Sophie repeated, surprised.

'That's right,' said Leo. 'Tilly – one of the maids, who is a particular friend of mine – told me that the servants are quite convinced that the East Wing is haunted. Just recently they've begun to see peculiar lights moving around at night – and to hear queer noises – and Tilly even caught a glimpse of the ghost herself.'

'A *ghost*?' asked Lil, most intrigued.

'Well, Tilly doesn't think it is a ghost at all,' Leo explained. 'She thinks it might be someone playing a trick

– trying to scare her and the other servants. We thought you might help us work out who's really behind the "haunting".'

'Of course!' said Lil. 'I don't think we've ever investigated a ghost before! Can you ask Tilly to come and talk to us about it?'

Leo grinned. 'Of course I will.' They heard the distant clash of a gong, and she went on: 'But for now we mustn't be late for afternoon tea – and you can meet the rest of the house party.'

It was half past six on the day before Christmas Eve, and Billy was the last person left in the Sinclair's offices. There had been a festive mood in the air all day, and as soon as five o'clock had struck, the clerks had begun departing, calling cheery Christmas greetings over their shoulders.

The three clerks whose desks were nearest to his own – Davies, O'Donnell and Crawley – were amongst the last to leave, bundling themselves up into overcoats, and Crawley even ornamenting his hat with a sprig of holly. One after another, they shook his hand, and earnestly wished him a very merry Christmas, before departing for the nearest public house to raise a glass to the season.

'Sorry you'll be stuck here tomorrow, Parker,' said O'Donnell, as he followed the other two out of the door. As the most junior clerk – and Miss Atwood's assistant

– Billy had drawn the short straw of having to work on Christmas Eve.

But actually, he didn't mind being the last person left in the office. In fact, he felt rather proud that Miss Atwood had entrusted him to hold down the fort. Now, with no one else around, he settled back to wait for Uncle Sid to finish work and lock up the store. He drew out the bumper festive edition of *Boys of Empire* – his Christmas gift to himself – and turned to the latest instalment of his favourite Montgomery Baxter serial, entitled 'Montgomery Baxter's Casebook'. This new story was only just beginning, but Billy felt sure it would be an exciting one, pitting the brave boy detective once more against his most dangerous adversary – a mysterious criminal known only as Number One.

Before he began to read, he leaned back in his chair and glanced out of the window beside his desk. From where he sat, he could see straight across the street, directly into the windows of the big building that stood opposite. At this time of the evening, the lights were all blazing, but the blinds were not yet closed – allowing him to look into what appeared to be half a dozen different stage sets, each brilliantly lit.

Billy had always been curious. *Nosy Parker*, one girl at school had called him. But it *wasn't* nosiness, he thought indignantly now. He was just someone who noticed things, that was all. As a matter of fact, his ability to notice things had helped them several times during their cases. Most recently, of course, it had helped them to discover who was really behind the theft of the painting from Sinclair's, when he had observed how oddly Mr Randolph Lyle had been behaving on the telephone. Billy had always loved stories, and he liked to find out the stories behind things. The building opposite was no exception.

The ground and first floors were entirely given over to a restaurant. Billy could not see very much that went on down there, but he enjoyed watching the comings and goings of the building's upper storeys. The tall windows of the second and third floors were swathed in tasselled curtains, and printed with the words 'Miss Henrietta Beauville's Ladies' Dress Agency'. Miss Beauville was one of the most fashionable dressmakers in London, and there was always a great deal going on in this part of the building: ladies rushing in for their dress fittings; delivery men unloading bolts of cloth; groups of models arriving; and sketch artists, busily illustrating the latest styles for the fashion papers. The highlight of it all was catching a glimpse of Miss Beauville herself, who was almost as much of a celebrity as Mr Sinclair. She cut a glamorous figure as she strode up and down, barking out orders to her staff. From where he sat, Billy could even see into her own private workroom, where she would sometimes shut herself up for hours with yards of silk and tulle, working on extraordinary new creations.

One floor above Miss Beauville's was a bustling office. Billy had never quite been able to work out exactly what business they did there, but it seemed to involve a great many books and important-looking documents. It was a very lively place, with lots of smart young gentlemen answering telephones, and busy young ladies tapping away on typewriters. Billy thought they looked a jolly set, and had sometimes reflected that if he wasn't at Sinclair's, he wouldn't mind working there himself. He had even identified some favourites amongst them, including the red-haired office boy, who Billy had noticed liked to take a moment now and then to catch up on the latest *Boys of Empire*.

At the very top of the building, he could see into another office. Here, four or five serious young men spent their days squinting over drawing boards, wielding pencils and technical instruments. The atmosphere was usually quite solemn, but on that particular day, even the top floor seemed to have been infused with festive jollity. In fact, all through the building, Christmas celebrations of one kind or another were under way. Miss Beauville was giving a sherry party for her seamstresses: dressed in crimson velvet, she was holding up a glass, making a toast. Meanwhile, the floor above was decked with paper chains, someone had set up a gramophone and a few people were dancing. Above them, the serious young men of the top floor had laid down their pencils and instruments to enjoy mugs of tea and a big plate of mince pies.

Only the fifth-floor office stood empty, just as it always did, the windows darkened. Large notices, printed with OFFICE TO LET in big black capitals that might be glimpsed from the top of an omnibus, had been stuck up in the windows for as long as Billy could remember. Now, he saw that the notices had gone. Had someone taken the vacant office at last? Leaning forward, he tried to see if he could glimpse anything behind the windows, but there were no lights on, and everything looked quite dark.

He turned back to the *Boys of Empire* lying on his desk – but just as he opened it, a little movement caught his eye. Glancing up, he saw that he had been wrong. There *was* someone moving around in the dark, empty office. He could see a shadowy figure, moving furtively to and fro. Just then, a small lamp was lit somewhere in the room, illuminating the silhouette of a man, stacking up a number of large wooden crates. Billy strained his eyes, trying to see what was printed on the side of the boxes. Perhaps the contents would be a clue to the new occupant's business? Whatever it was they did, they must be keen to get started. He couldn't imagine many people would be bothering with work at half past six on the day before Christmas Eve.

The man lifted one of the crates, and carried it over towards the window. As he did so, Billy caught sight of his face – and instinctively, he shrank back. The man had a shock of black hair streaked with white, and an extraordinary expression – fierce and threatening. With a sudden flash, like a spark of electricity, Billy realised that he had seen his face somewhere before.

What was more, now that one of the crates had been set down before the window, Billy could see it clearly. He gasped. Printed on the side of it was a symbol that was very familiar to him: in fact, it was documented several times in the folder in the Taylor & Rose office labelled 'The Baron' in Sophie's neat handwriting. They had first seen it drawn on a coded message, looking rather like an ink blot. They had come upon it stamped on the cover of a leather folder on the Baron's desk in his secret office. They had observed it again on a gold lapel pin, worn by members of the *Fraternitas Draconum*. Now, he stared and stared at the shape stamped in black on the surface of the wooden crate. It was the twisting form of a dragon.

CHAPTER EIGHT

Lady Lucy Fitzgerald, Leo's mother, looked around the Winter Hall Drawing Room after dinner, feeling rather vexed.

She *ought* to have been perfectly contented. Here she was, hosting her famous Christmas house party, wearing one of the exquisite new dresses Miss Beauville had made for her – a cerise evening gown shot with glacé silk in which she knew she looked at least ten years younger than she really was. She was surrounded by an array of impressive guests: the Countess of Alconborough, who attended only the best society gatherings; her dear friend Lady Viola Tremayne, very elegant in a new *Maison Chevalier* ensemble; Mr Pendleton – Eliza Pendleton's youngest boy, such a nice young man about town, and a far better companion for Vincent than those rakish fellows he persisted on racketing about with. Then there were the Whiteleys, and especially young Miss Veronica Whiteley. What a suitable wife she would make for Vincent! Though she might be only the daughter of a businessman, she had the manners of a lady – and with a great fortune like hers, there need never be any concern for Winter Hall's future, even given Vincent's unfortunate tendency to extravagance.

Best of all, of course, there was Mr Edward Sinclair himself. Now he truly was a feather in her cap! She glanced over at him now as he sat back easily in his chair, sipping coffee and being divinely charming to everyone – even tiresome old Great-Aunt Selina. Lady Fitzgerald bestowed upon him her most engaging and grateful smile.

But the smile faded quickly as she glanced over to where the younger members of the party were playing cards. When she had told Leonora she might invite a few friends for Christmas, she had imagined one or two young ladies of good families. She had even dared to hope for someone as well connected as the Duke of Roehampton's sister, who she knew had attended the Spencer. But instead, she had turned up with these two girls who did not really seem like *ladies* at all and had turned out to be in some sort of *job* at Mr Sinclair's store!

The young man did not matter so much: he had nice manners, and was at least a student at the Spencer. Indeed, it sounded as though he was doing rather well: she had heard him telling Viola that he was soon to start an apprenticeship with the painter Max Kamensky. That made him interesting and perhaps one day important –

and there was nothing Lady Fitzgerald liked better than interesting, important people.

But those girls – well! They were not at all the type of people that she would ever choose to invite to such a select gathering at Winter Hall. Really, it was a good thing that Mr Sinclair had not objected to the presence of two of his *employees* amongst the party: the whole thing could have been terribly embarrassing. Fortunately he'd taken it in good part, laughing over it in a good-natured manner.

Leonora did not understand how things were done, Lady Fitzgerald thought now. She was clearly getting into unsuitable habits living all alone in Town. Perhaps Viola would spend more time with her to keep her in line – she had always been so good and patient with Leo. Or perhaps they ought to send a maid back with her – for goodness knows how she lived in London. She stared in disapproval at her youngest daughter, with her obstinately straight hair, and pale cheeks – and that silly cane beside her. As if it wasn't enough that Leonora had an *infirmity*, she insisted on drawing attention to it with that ridiculous thing with the lion's head. And wherever had she got that frightful plain frock she was wearing?

Beside her, the dark-haired girl in the pink evening dress laughed. Lady Fitzgerald had taken a particular dislike to that girl, who had been monopolising Vincent since the second she had stepped through the door. Just look at him staring at her! He was supposed to be entertaining Miss Whiteley – but clearly he was completely taken in by this newcomer – undoubtedly a fortune-hunter. Lady Fitzgerald was disconcerted to realise that the other girl – the little fair one – was watching her with a shrewd look in her eye, and she looked away, affronted. Why – in her day, a young unmarried girl would never have dared to look so boldly at her hostess. It was quite brazen!

The door opened and the maid came in bearing a fresh coffee pot, and Lady Fitzgerald gathered herself. Despite Leonora's unsuitable guests, the Christmas house party must be a success. Forcing herself to smile, she said in a bright voice: 'Who would care for a little more coffee?'

Tilly filled the cups carefully from the silver pot, taking in the scene as she did so. Housemaids were not supposed to look around them, but Tilly had long since learned how to take a sneaky look without being noticed. She was eager to see Miss Leo's friends – especially the young lady detectives.

She still found their existence rather astonishing. She had read about detectives, of course: on the whole Tilly preferred books to be about facts, but she did enjoy stories sometimes, and she knew about Sherlock Holmes, and Inspector Bucket in *Bleak House* and Montgomery Baxter in those *Boys of Empire* papers that the under-footmen were always reading. Montgomery Baxter got on her nerves though: he was a show-off and thought himself too clever by half. She preferred Sherlock Holmes: she liked the precise, scientific way he approached things. But never in any of those books had any of the detectives been a *girl*.

Yet Miss Leo had told her that her friends had just opened a detective agency in London and that they were very good at solving mysteries. 'They helped me out of a fearfully sticky situation at the beginning of term,' she had explained, suggesting that they might be able to help solve the puzzle of the ghost in the East Wing. Miss Leo had been intrigued by Tilly's story, though no more able to make sense of it than Tilly herself. 'But I'm certain that Sophie and Lil will be able to work it out. They're clever about this kind of thing.'

Glancing at them now, Tilly had to admit that Miss Leo's friends didn't look particularly clever. In their evening dresses, they could have been any young ladies, sitting in the Drawing Room after dinner – although it was true she had never known young ladies of their age to arrive at Winter Hall by themselves, without a mama or a chaperone or even a maid to accompany them.

Instead, there was a young man with them – a good-looking young man that Tilly knew all the housemaids were sure to be in a flutter about. He was Jack, the young gentleman studying with Miss Leo at art school. 'Jack's an awfully good sort,' Miss Leo had told her. 'He took me under his wing when I first arrived at the Spencer, and I didn't have any idea how to make friends.'

Now, Miss Leo flashed her a quick smile as Tilly refilled her cup. She was sitting at the card table with her three friends, as well as the debutante, Miss Veronica Whiteley, and a fair, ruddy-faced young gentleman called Mr Pendleton. They were all talking and laughing as though they were very good friends. As Tilly poured the coffee she caught a few snippets of their conversation:

'Of course, Phyllis is very busy getting all her wedding clothes. Her wedding dress is going to be made by Miss Beauville herself.'

'Mother was supposed to come too, but she didn't fancy the journey from our country place in this fearful weather. But I was already in Town helping old Hugo with some preparations for the wedding so I thought I'd toddle along by myself. I say, Miss Rose, it is topping to see you again!'

They certainly seemed to be having a better time than anyone else in the room, Tilly thought, as she continued her rounds with the coffee pot. His Lordship was talking politely to Mr Whiteley about his farms and the estate. They both took more coffee, but Miss Selina – His Lordship's great-aunt, a large old lady with several chins, shook her head. 'Of course I have to be *very careful* about what I eat and drink,' she said in a loud, fretful voice to Mr Edward Sinclair – terribly smart in his stylish dinner jacket. 'My doctor tells me I must take great care of my digestion. I can have only the best food – and the best medicinal wines. It costs a *great deal* – which is trying for a person in my circumstances – but it is simply essential for my health.'

Beside them, Lady Tremayne and Mrs Whiteley were talking about fashions. Tilly had already heard the maids exclaiming over their beautiful gowns, and now she glanced quickly at them, knowing that Lizzie and the others would want a full report when she was back in the Servants' Hall. Mrs Whiteley was wearing a silver satin dress, with a collar of diamonds, whilst Lady Tremayne looked sleek in embroidered velvet and a long string of pearls.

Mr Vincent was lounging against the mantelpiece, looking bad-tempered. He waved Tilly away like she was an irritating insect when she approached with the coffee pot.

'I don't know why you're bothering with these kids' games,' he said brusquely to the card players. 'Why don't we have a game of something decent – like whist or baccarat?'

Miss Leo looked up, surprised. 'Oh, I don't think anyone cares to play for money!'

Mr Vincent sneered at her. He was certainly handsome, but his face was quite spoilt by his expression, Tilly thought. 'Well perhaps *you* wouldn't, but I am sure these gentlemen would prefer a proper entertainment.' He eyed Jack and Mr Pendleton speculatively. 'I'm quite certain they won't refuse a little flutter – eh?'

Miss Leo looked worried, and Tilly could guess why. Everyone in the Servants' Hall knew that Mr Vincent had a taste for gambling. When he'd had those London friends of his to visit they'd been up half the night playing cards. Now she feared he was setting out to leave their guests with empty pockets. Neither of the young gentlemen seemed in the least bit worried though: Mr Pendleton was smiling, whilst Jack shrugged easily.

Mr Vincent was already taking a seat at the table. 'You ladies can watch,' he told the rest. 'Miss Rose, you sit by me. I believe you'll bring me luck.'

Across the room, Tilly saw Her Ladyship stiffen and purse her lips as Mr Vincent flashed a snarling grin in Miss Rose's direction. Across from him, Miss Whiteley rolled her eyes disdainfully. So much for making an impression on the wealthy debutante, Tilly thought!

Mr Vincent was shuffling the cards with swift, practised ease. 'Now to set the stakes – let's make things interesting, shall we?' he said, reaching into his pocket.

'Allow me,' said Jack. He produced a handful of Christmas bonbons wrapped in shiny paper.

'What are those?' demanded Mr Vincent in disgust.

'This is what we're going to play for,' said Jack, cheerfully. 'Thought it'd be a bit of fun.'

'Oh – jolly fine idea – those are my favourites!' agreed Mr Pendleton enthusiastically.

Mr Vincent stared at them both in disbelief.

'Go on, Vincent, deal the cards,' said Miss Leo, giggling.

Muttering under his breath, Mr Vincent had no choice but to go ahead and deal. Miss Leo caught Tilly's eye and winked at her, as the housemaid slipped quietly back out of the room.

An hour later, Sophie closed her bedroom door behind her with a sigh of relief. The evening seemed to have gone on for a very long time: dinner alone had lasted for what felt like hours. Every time she had thought that they must have finished, another round of dishes had appeared – soup or cheese or petits fours. It had felt very strange, sitting at the long polished table, as powdered footmen presented her with each new plate, and carefully filled up her crystal glass. In the light and shadows cast by the candles, she felt almost as though she had been transported into one of the old oil paintings that hung upon the walls. The people around her were like figures from an oil painting too, she thought, glancing up the table at the craggy silhouette of Leo's father, Lord Fitzgerald, speaking to the Countess of Alconborough, stately in ostrich plumes, and then down to the other end, where Lady Fitzgerald was scrutinising the table with a sharp eye.

Sophie knew that she was watching them. She had given them a frosty reception, and the other guests had followed suit. Leo's old Great-Aunt Selina had stared at them with undisguised curiosity, whilst the Countess of Alconborough had actually lifted up her lorgnette to peer at them. Only Leo's godmother, the elegant Lady Tremayne, had been polite and welcoming, taking the time to make conversation. It was obvious that she and Leo were fond of each other, and she seemed to be genuinely pleased to meet her goddaughter's friends. Otherwise, it had all been rather embarrassing: indeed, at the worst moment, it had seemed that she and Lil would not even be allowed to come down to dine with the rest of the party, but instead would be dismissed to the Nursery for a bread-and-milk supper with Leo's old Nanny.

'These girls are not *out*!' Lady Fitzgerald had exclaimed disapprovingly. 'Really, Leonora! If they have not yet been presented at court, then they cannot possibly dine in company!'

Leo looked embarrassed. Spots of colour appeared on her pale cheeks. 'I'm sorry, Mother. I – I didn't think – I mean, no one cares a bit about any of that sort of thing any more,' she mumbled.

Lady Fitzgerald arched her eyebrows. 'Indeed?' she said in a cool voice. 'Well, I suppose that may be the way things are at *art school*, Leonora, but we still abide by the proper rules of society here.'

It was Mr Sinclair who had resolved that. Fixing Lady

Fitzgerald with his warm smile, he had gently suggested that on this occasion, perhaps her daughter might be right? 'Of course, all your traditions are so wonderfully charming. But they can't apply to girls like Miss Taylor and Miss Rose, here. Why – they're new women! They don't have a bit of time for anything as delightful as a court presentation. I work them much too hard for that!'

There was a polite titter of laughter, the tension faded, and Leo's hands unclenched.

They had certainly never expected to find Mr Sinclair at the Winter Hall house party. They had all been astonished when he had arrived late that afternoon, having driven himself up from London in his Rolls-Royce automobile. He had strolled in as they were taking afternoon tea in the Drawing Room.

'Sorry I'm late,' he had said, casting his motoring goggles, cap and gloves easily into the waiting hands of a footman. 'You know how it is with motoring. There's always something that goes wrong.'

Sophie had feared he would be displeased to find that they were at the party, as though they were his equals and not merely his employees. But to her relief, he had seemed only tickled to find that Sophie and Lil were amongst the guests. 'I never know where you girls are going to turn up next,' he had said, with a grin.

As it happened, Mr Sinclair was not the only familiar

figure at the house party. Amongst the haughty ladies and gentlemen, she had been relieved to spot two friendly faces – Mr Pendleton, and Miss Veronica Whiteley, both of whom they had met through their adventures earlier that year. Mr Pendleton was enraptured to see them, and perhaps more surprisingly, Miss Whiteley looked delighted too. 'Which is really something,' Lil had muttered to Sophie later. 'I never thought I'd see the day when Veronica would be pleased to see *me*!'

Yet even in spite of their company, Sophie felt very relieved now that the evening was over, and she was able to relax in the quiet of her room. Her bedroom was situated on the first floor, not far from the mysterious East Wing that Leo had told them about. Lil's room was next door, with an interconnecting door that linked it to her own; whilst Jack was a little way along the passage. Each of their names had been carefully handwritten on a small card that was ceremonially displayed on the front of their bedroom door: *Miss Sophie Taylor; Miss Lilian Rose; Mr Jack Rose.*

'I'm awfully sorry that I couldn't give you the best guest rooms,' Leo had said. 'The Indian Room and the Rose Room are the nicest, I think – but of course, Mother always keeps those for her friends.'

Surveying it now, Sophie wondered again how any room could possibly be more luxurious than this one. It seemed full of wonderful comfort – from the blue silk paper on the walls, to the dressing table with its vase of hothouse flowers, to the little writing desk ready laid out with writing paper headed *WINTER HALL*. As for the bed, a vast four-poster with draped curtains, it seemed far too grand to actually sleep in. The sheets were deliciously soft and smelled of lavender, but even after she had climbed between them, Sophie felt restless. She was not used to lying in such an enormous bed – nor to eating such an extraordinary dinner in the company of so many strange people.

What was more, she could not stop thinking about Colonel Fairley. She had decided she would set out to visit him first thing in the morning, and the thought made her both nervous and excited. What would he be like? Would he be pleased to see her? Would he really be able to help unravel any of the secrets that puzzled her about her father's past?

Somewhere in the big house, she heard the low, hollow sound of a clock chiming midnight – then a door opening and closing somewhere, and footsteps on the stairs. Everyone must be going to bed, she thought. She turned over under the heavy weight of the blankets and closed her eyes – but then, all at once, they snapped open again.

There was a noise coming from across the room: she was sure of it. She could hear the faint creak of a door opening very slowly. Then the soft pad of footsteps. Someone or something was tiptoeing across the room – coming closer and closer towards the bed! She lay flat and still, frozen with dread as the tall, dark shape grew closer. A shadow loomed over her.

'Sophie . . .!' came a voice, tremulously out of the dark.

'*Lil!*' exploded Sophie in a furious whisper. 'What are you doing? You almost frightened me to death!'

'I'm sorry! I couldn't sleep! I know it's stupid – but I kept thinking about Leo's story of the East Wing being haunted, and it's only just down the passageway. And it's so dark here, and I kept hearing all these queer noises and . . . well, I wondered if I could just stay here with you for a little while?'

'Of course you can,' said Sophie, as Lil clambered up on to the bed. 'There's certainly more than enough room. This bed is big enough for half a dozen people. But you'll have to be *quiet*.'

'All right,' said Lil obediently, nestling down under the sheets and pulling up the blankets. For a few moments, there was silence, and then she spoke again:

'I say, Sophie . . . You don't think that there really could be a ghost at Winter Hall . . . do you?'

'Of course not,' said Sophie decidedly. 'Now stop being an idiot, and go to sleep.'

CHAPTER NINE

The first thing that Sophie wanted to do on Christmas Eve was to go back to Alwick to visit Colonel Fairley. But it soon became clear there would be no possibility of doing so that day.

'I'm afraid Father has gone out in the motor,' said Leo apologetically. 'He's driven over to see one of the tenants right on the other side of the estate and he won't be back until later. I'm awfully sorry.'

'Oh well – perhaps I could walk to Alwick instead?' suggested Sophie.

But Leo looked worried. 'I don't think that would be a very good idea. It's almost ten miles from here, you know. Besides, it looks like there might be more snow coming. But don't worry – I'll make sure you can drive over to Alwick first thing on Boxing Day.'

The four of them were tucking into big plates of kedgeree and hot coffee, all by themselves in the Breakfast Room. 'Mother and the other ladies probably won't come down for hours yet,' Leo explained. 'They mostly take breakfast in bed.'

In spite of the fact that she had not yet come downstairs, Lady Fitzgerald had made very definite plans about how the younger members of the party were to spend their morning. Vincent had been told to take the young gentlemen out riding, whilst Leo took the young ladies on a tour of the grounds – a plan that Sophie guessed had been devised specifically to keep Vincent as far away from Lil as possible.

She felt frustrated as she put on her hat, coat and gloves, and followed the other girls into the gardens. She didn't think Leo understood just how important this visit was. Suppose the Colonel wasn't at home on Boxing Day? Suppose they missed him altogether? She was so impatient to meet the Colonel that she felt more than ready to contemplate a ten-mile walk through the snow.

But once she stepped out into the garden, her disappointment began to lift. Winter Hall lay under a thick white blanket of snow, and her breath puffed out in little clouds, as the four of them picked their way carefully down the stone steps. In the formal gardens, they found the ponds were thick with ice, and the sculpted hedges and trees were laced with frost. Birds twittered and scurried in the undergrowth as Leo pushed open a door in the wall, and led them out on to the lawns – a great expanse of perfect whiteness.

The snow was so different here, Sophie thought, enjoying the satisfying *whumph* it made when she set her boot down into it. It was fun to tramp through as Leo led them up towards a small stone building standing at the top of a little hill.

'I wanted to show you the old folly,' she said. 'It was built in 1760 by one of my ancestors – Henry Fitzgerald. He was a great traveller and he was inspired by old buildings he had seen in Italy and Greece. He called it the Temple of Birds.'

They floundered through some deeper snow and clambered up the stone steps. Inside, Sophie saw that it did look rather like a classical temple on a miniature scale: its curving roof was supported by a circle of elegant columns, now crumbling with age. There was nothing inside, but the floor was laid with a beautiful mosaic in blue, green and white tiles, forming the picture of a tree with birds perched upon its branches.

'How pretty!' exclaimed Lil. 'And I say – what a splendid view!'

Leo smiled with pride: she looked happier out here, away from the house, her eyes bright and her cheeks pink with the cold. They all stood still for a moment, taking in deep breaths of frosty air, and gazed out over the perfect winter landscape that was spread before them: a silent vista of pale hills and silvery woods. At that moment, Sophie felt as though the hustle and bustle of Piccadilly and Sinclair's could have been in another world.

As it happened, on Christmas Eve, the offices of Sinclair's were significantly less hustling and bustling than usual. The desks were empty, the typewriters were silent, and Billy was the only one there to witness the earnest conference that was taking place between Miss Atwood, Claudine and Mr Betteredge about the latest plans for New Year's Eve.

'Whatever Monsieur Chevalier may wish, we cannot possibly have live peacocks wandering about the store!' declared Miss Atwood.

'You do not have to tell me that!' Claudine snapped back, sounding twice as French as usual in her agitation. 'I know quite well we cannot! That is what I have been saying all morning. But he says he must have his peacocks – that the Captain has promised –'

'There, there,' said Mr Betteredge, patting Claudine's arm. 'Don't upset yourself, my dear. I know Monsieur Chevalier has been rather *demanding*. But I am quite sure that we will find a way to keep him happy.'

'But that is not even the worst of it!' exclaimed Claudine. 'Monsieur Chevalier is now saying that he wishes to fill the Entrance Hall with water – and transform it into a Venetian canal – with gondolas!'

Mr Betteredge was a good-natured gentleman given

to making the best of things, but even he paled at this suggestion. 'Dear dear – what a pity Mr Sinclair insisted on going away to this country house party!' he said anxiously. 'I am sure he would have been able to talk Monsieur Chevalier round.'

'Mr Sinclair has a very busy social calendar,' Miss Atwood informed Mr Betteredge. 'He can't be expected to be here all the time, you know.'

'Well, we shall have to come up with something. Perhaps if we agree to the peacocks we can persuade him to give up the gondola idea?'

'Could we tell him we will have the peacocks up on the roof garden?' suggested Claudine.

'A splendid idea! But oh – what about the weather?' Mr Betteredge glanced out of the window at the frozen street. 'Might peacocks mind the snow?' he mused.

Miss Atwood turned to Billy. 'Parker,' she instructed briskly. 'Go down to the Pet Department and ask Mr Shanahan to come up at once. We need his expertise on birds. And while you are about it, I suppose you may as well take That Dog out for its exercise.'

'That Dog' – Mr Sinclair's pug, Lucky, who had been left behind with Miss Atwood as she disliked going anywhere in Mr Sinclair's motor car – was currently snuffling about under Billy's desk. As Billy got to his feet, and she heard the jingle of her lead, she began wriggling her little tail in a frenzy of excitement. A moment later, after having passed on Miss Atwood's message to Mr Shanahan on the first floor, the two of them were outside in the weak morning sunlight, heading towards the stables – and Daisy and Joe.

Billy had been keen to talk to Joe ever since the previous evening, and wasted no time in relating what he had seen from the office window. Whilst Lucky and Daisy pranced around each other in the stable-yard, Joe listened attentively.

'Righto – so let me get this straight,' he said at last. 'Yesterday evening, you're the last one in the offices. You take a dekko out of the window, and you see that an empty office in that big place over the road has just been let. You see a fellow in there, moving crates about – and when you see his face, you think you recognise him.'

'I *know* I recognised him,' Billy corrected. 'It's just that for the life of me, I can't think from where.'

'Then you notice that the boxes he's been shifting are stamped with the symbol of a dragon,' Joe went on.

'That's about the long and short of it,' Billy agreed.

'But that doesn't necessarily mean it's anything *dodgy*,' said Joe. 'This fellow you recognised – he could have been anyone. Some customer who's been knocking about the store, perhaps?'

Billy shook his head decisively. 'It wasn't a customer. There was something awful about that chap's face . . . I'm sure I've seen him before. He looked *sinister*.'

Joe shrugged. 'All right – so the fellow you saw seemed a bit off. But the picture of the dragon – that could mean anything. There'll be all kinds of folks using that symbol. After all, almost every pub you see is called *The Red Dragon* or *The Green Dragon*, isn't it? It doesn't necessarily mean the secret society.'

There was a hopeful note in his voice. Joe had grown up in the East End, with the shadow of the Baron looming over him, he'd even once worked for him, as a member of his gang, the Baron's Boys. Whilst none of them were keen to cross swords with the Baron again, Joe more than anyone, hoped that he had gone for good.

But Billy had to shake his head again. 'It wasn't just a picture of *any* dragon though,' he said doggedly. 'It was exactly the same symbol – the symbol of the *Fraternitas Draconum*. I'm certain of it.'

Joe frowned anxiously. 'All right – so you saw the symbol, and what happened then?'

'Nothing at all. The fellow put the lamp out and then he left. I've been keeping a close eye out since then, but the office has been empty all morning.' Billy heaved a sigh. 'I dunno, maybe I am making a fuss about nothing – but it seemed peculiar. I think we ought to go over there and see if we can find out who's taken that office.'

Still looking uneasy, Joe nonetheless nodded agreement, and accompanied by Lucky and Daisy, the two of them made their way across Piccadilly. Although it was Christmas Eve, the street was as busy as ever, with a hurry-scurry of last-minute shoppers, delivery boys with parcels, one or two brave souls on bicycles and an old fellow selling bunches of holly and mistletoe.

As they approached, they could see the waiters laying the tables for luncheon behind the shiny plate-glass windows of the big restaurant. Just around the corner was the entrance to Miss Beauville's Dress Agency and the offices that occupied the upper storeys. As luck would have it, Billy saw that the office boy from the fourth floor was standing in the doorway, sorting through a bundle of letters. He was a stout lad, with freckles and a thatch of ginger hair. A folded Christmas edition of *Boys of Empire*, open to the new Montgomery Baxter story, was poking out of his pocket.

'Here – d'you work here, mate?' Joe called out.

The boy turned warily. He took in Joe – a tall, strong young fellow, dressed in rough stable-clothes, with a big Alsatian at his side – and stepped involuntarily backwards.

'What's it to you?' he demanded.

'Just wanted to know about that fifth-floor office up there,' said Joe casually. 'Still to let, is it?'

'How should I know?' the boy shot back. 'Don't look like no letting agent, do I?' He made as if he was going to go inside and close the door, but Billy stepped forward.

'The sign's come down,' he said earnestly. 'Someone

must have taken it.'

The boy stared at Billy – his office clothes, the little black pug that was nosing around in the grey slush at his feet. 'Not any of my business, is it?' he said uncertainly. 'Not yours either, I suppose.'

Eyeing the *Boys of Empire* peeping out of his pocket, Billy tried a different tack. 'All right. No need to get shirty. Look – we need information. You see.' He lowered his voice meaningfully. 'We work for a detective agency.'

The boy's eyes widened. 'A *detective agency?*' he repeated. 'Don't make me laugh. The two of you? That's a likely story!'

Billy held up his hands. 'It's true. I give you my word. We're gathering information. Think of us as – well, something like the Baker Street Irregulars. I s'pose that'd really make us the Piccadilly Irregulars, though,' he added in a sudden burst of invention. 'I'm Billy and this is Joe.'

Still looking unsure, although obviously intrigued too, the boy introduced himself as Stanley.

'The thing is, Stan, we're working on an investigation at the moment, and we need to know who's moved into that office. Could be important,' explained Joe, tapping his nose and nodding at Stanley, as if to indicate that they were both men of the world who knew what was what. 'Help us out and we'll make it worth your while.'

Stanley wrinkled up his forehead. 'Well – look – I can't

really tell you much. We don't know who's moved into the office yet. We haven't seen much of anyone. There was someone up there last night, moving in a whole lot of crates. But I haven't seen anyone today.'

Billy and Joe exchanged glances. They knew all this already. But Stanley was now rifling through the letters he was holding. 'But hang on a sec. Got the post for the whole building here, haven't I? I'm sure I just saw something. Let's see – this one's Miss Beauville's . . .' He flipped through the envelopes quickly. Billy looked over his shoulder with interest. Between those addressed to *Miss Henrietta Beauville's Ladies' Dress Agency* he glimpsed one or two addressed to *Douglas Webber Publishing*. So *that* was what they did in the office on the fourth floor.

'You work for a publisher,' he declared.

Stanley looked up at him, surprised. 'Blimey! How did you know which office I work in?' he demanded. 'Is that one of them Sherlock Holmes tricks?'

Joe grinned at him. 'We said we worked for a detective agency, didn't we?'

Stanley stared at them both suspiciously, but turned back to the envelopes. After a moment, he held one out. 'Here it is,' he said.

Billy took it eagerly. There was no name on the envelope, which was addressed simply to *Lindwurm Enterprises, 5th floor.*

'Lindwurm Enterprises,' Stanley said. 'Funny sort of name, ain't it?'

'There can't be many businesses out there called that,' agreed Joe.

Billy nodded thoughtfully. It was certainly a strange name, but it gave no clue to what the company actually did – or who the man was that Billy had seen the night before. He turned the envelope over, and found a return address. 'Look. It's come from Albert Works in Silvertown. Where's that?'

'Silvertown? It's out East – along the river, towards Woolwich,' explained Joe. 'There are lots of factories out there. Great big sugar refineries – and a place that makes India rubber.'

That was interesting, Billy thought. If Albert Works was a factory, then could it perhaps be the place that all those stamped crates had come from?

He was still pondering this as Joe tipped Stanley sixpence for his trouble, but then on an impulse, he pulled out a card from his pocket, and scribbled on it with the stub of a pencil.

'If you find anything out about this *Lindwurm Enterprises* – or if you see anything queer going on – ask for me here,' he said, tapping the card. 'But mind you don't tell anyone else about it.'

Stanley turned the card over. 'Taylor & Rose,' he read.

'Ain't that the young ladies' detective agency?'

'That's right,' said Billy with dignity.

Stanley raised his eyebrows but said nothing. He was still eyeing the card as the two boys headed in the direction of the park.

'Well I s'pose we know where to look next,' said Joe.

Billy nodded, decisively. 'In Silvertown.'

CHAPTER TEN

'Tell us exactly what you saw,' said Lil eagerly. 'What did the ghost look like?'

Leo had arranged for Tilly to come and meet them in the old Nursery. It felt rather peculiar to be doing detective work with a doll's house on one side, a rocking horse on the other, and a collection of china dolls watching them from up on a shelf – but at least here they knew that they would be quite private, far away from the rest of the Winter Hall house party.

Sophie had recognised Tilly at once as the maid who had served coffee in the Drawing Room on the previous night. She was a tall girl with curly black hair, and a straightforward, no-nonsense manner that Sophie liked immediately.

'Jolly good to meet you, Tilly,' Lil had said, holding out her hand. 'I'm Lil – and this is my brother Jack – and this is Sophie.'

Tilly had stared at her, confused. It was obvious that

most Winter Hall guests did not introduce themselves, nor try to shake her hand. But after gazing in surprise for a long moment, she took Lil's hand and gave it a firm shake. Now, she was telling them all that she could remember about the ghost:

'It was spooky all right – but it didn't really look like a ghost at all. Not the sort you read about in books anyway – floating apparitions and clanking chains, and all that. It was more like a big dark figure.'

'And you heard footsteps?' asked Lil.

'That's right – heavy footsteps. At first, I thought it might be one of the under-footmen, Charlie, trying to scare me for a joke. He's always playing silly tricks. But it couldn't have been him. He isn't big enough.'

'What about any of the other servants?'

Tilly shook her head. 'I can't think who else it could have been. Most of the servants would think a prank like that was a waste of time. We're most of us too busy for playing jokes.'

Sophie leaned forward. 'Apart from you, who else has seen – or heard – this ghost?'

'I did a bit of asking around,' explained Tilly, pulling a folded piece of paper out of her apron pocket. 'The problem is that it's hard to get proper *facts* out of people. They aren't very logical. But this is what I found out – I've written it all down.'

Sophie and Lil examined the paper:

17th December – 10.00pm or Later
Mary (Washerwoman) hears 'strange noises in the night'
        coming from the East Wing.

18th December – 19th December 10.00pm – 12.00 Midnight (approx)
Jamie (gardener's boy) reports seeing 'lights floating about
up high' in the windows of the East Wing.

20th December – 8.30pm (approx)
Lizzie (Under-housemaid) experiences a strange chill
while dusting in the East Wing and hears the sound
of footsteps.

20th December – 9.30pm
Tilly (under-housemaid) experiences strange phenomena in
the East Wing – chill, footsteps and sighting of
a tall dark figure.

22nd December – 9.45pm (approx)
Emma (head housemaid) notices curious 'thumping sounds'
above in the East Wing whilst in the cellar
– possibly footsteps?

'I must say, you've been very thorough,' said Lil approvingly. 'Our friend Billy, who works with us – well, I think he would be rather impressed.'

'There's something else I wanted to show you too,' said Tilly, looking pleased. 'The morning after I saw the ghost, I went to the East Wing to have a look around.'

'Very smart,' declared Lil. 'Examining the scene of the crime! What did you find?'

'Nothing out of the ordinary at all – except for this.' Tilly produced a small blue and white matchbox.

Lil took it and turned it over between her fingers. 'Could one of the other servants have dropped it?' she asked. 'Lizzie, maybe – when she was in there dusting?'

Tilly shook her head decidedly. 'We always use Bryant & May matches,' she explained. 'I've never even seen a matchbox like this before.'

'It's French,' Sophie said, pointing to the word *Allumettes* written on the side of the box. 'I don't suppose there have been any French guests in the house – or anyone who has recently been to France?'

Tilly shook her head. 'Not so far as I know,' she said. 'Although I suppose Her Ladyship did go abroad in the autumn.'

'But she went to Germany. She always goes to Baden-Baden to take the waters,' Leo explained.

Sophie eyed the matchbox speculatively. 'Well it's

certainly interesting,' she said. She turned back to look at Tilly's notes. 'The other thing is that every time anyone has seen or heard anything suspicious in the East Wing it's been at more or less the same time of day. All these incidents have happened in the evening – between 8.30 p.m. and midnight.'

'Did anyone see or hear anything peculiar before this date?' asked Lil, tapping the first item on Tilly's list.

Tilly shook her head. 'There have always been tales about the house – and rumours about the East Wing especially. That's only to be expected I suppose, with it being so old. But actually seeing or hearing a ghost? That's never happened before.'

'Which means that this "haunting" has only been going on for about ten days,' mused Lil.

'When did the house party guests first arrive?' asked Sophie suddenly.

Tilly frowned, remembering. 'His Lordship and Her Ladyship came home from a visit to friends about a fortnight ago. Mr Vincent arrived the next day – he'd been in Town. The first guests, Lady Tremayne and Miss Selina, arrived two days afterwards. After that – well, Miss Leo came home on the 22nd, which was also when the Whiteley family and the Countess arrived. They travelled together. And Mr Pendleton motored up from London in his own auto on the same day. It's a beauty – a lovely new

Austin with a four-cylinder 2.5 litre engine,' she added reflectively.

'Never mind that now,' said Leo hurriedly. She knew Tilly could be rather boring when she got on to the subject of engines. 'So that was the 22nd – and then the three of you and Mr Sinclair arrived the next afternoon.'

'That's rather interesting, isn't it?' said Lil thoughtfully.

'I say!' Jack interjected. 'You don't mean to suggest that someone from the house party could be behind this?'

'Don't you think it's quite a coincidence that it began at exactly the same time?'

'But why would any of the guests bother to masquerade as a ghost – just to frighten the servants? That's a silly school-boy prank.'

'But what if it isn't just a silly prank?' pondered Sophie. 'What if the "ghost" has some other reason to secretly visit the East Wing at night – and to keep others away? By frightening the servants, and making it appear that the East Wing is haunted, they would be able to keep everyone away from that part of the house. The only question is why someone would want to do that.'

'What about burglary?' suggested Lil. She turned to Tilly and Leo. 'You said that the East Wing is a kind of show place. It must be full of valuable things.'

Leo nodded vigorously. 'That's right! Lots of terribly old antique furniture, and paintings.'

'But why would any of the house party guests stoop to petty theft?' asked Jack. 'I mean, they're all fearfully well off.'

'Apart from us,' said Lil with a giggle. 'Yes I suppose they are. But I know – what about Miss Selina? I sat beside her at luncheon and she hardly stopped talking about how terribly short of money she is. Perhaps she's been pinching a few things from the East Wing? She is family, after all – perhaps she thinks it's fair game?'

'And Miss Selina is tall,' said Sophie thoughtfully. 'Do you think she might have been the figure you saw, Tilly?'

'I suppose she could have been,' said Tilly, scrunching up her face in the effort to imagine elderly Miss Selina as the terrifying East Wing ghost.

But Leo was shaking her head. 'Great-Aunt Selina is perfectly well off. She has plenty of her own money, and Father gives her an allowance too. She's just greedy. All that talk about her health and how she's a poor old woman is simply to make him feel guilty and give her more money.'

'Still – it's a possibility,' said Lil. 'If she's greedy, maybe she can't resist the idea of all those treasures in the East Wing. But is there anyone else?'

'I can't think of anyone in need of money,' said Sophie. 'We all know that the Whiteleys are very wealthy – and Mr Sinclair is a millionaire. Besides, they all arrived *after* the peculiar noises and lights began. So did Mr Pendleton and the Countess.'

'There is one person,' said Leo. Her face had gone rather red. 'It could be – well, I suppose it could be Vincent.'

'Vincent!' exclaimed Lil in astonishment.

Leo's face went redder than ever. 'I know it's awful to accuse your own brother. But he's had money troubles before – and remember how keen he was to try and play cards for money last night?'

'Do you think he's got himself into debt?' asked Jack.

'I'm not sure. But I know he's been gambling and spending lots of money in London with his friends.'

'But surely he must have a frightfully good allowance? He can't really have got himself into too much of a fix.'

Leo shrugged. 'Father keeps him on rather a tight rein. He had to bail Vincent out of some trouble once before, when he was at Oxford. He didn't mind so much then – he said it was different when Vincent was a student. But now Vincent's supposed to be being responsible, learning how to run the Estate and all that sort of thing.'

'But still – he wouldn't go plundering his own home, just to settle a few gaming debts?'

'I wouldn't put it past him,' said Leo blackly.

'Well that's two possible suspects,' said Sophie. 'Miss Selina and Vincent. Both of them may have a motive for robbery. Both of them are probably tall enough to be the figure Tilly saw. And both of them were here in the house ten days ago, when people started to notice funny things happening in the East Wing.'

'But they weren't the only ones here,' Lil reminded Sophie. 'Leo's parents and Lady Tremayne were here too – although I suppose Lord and Lady Fitzgerald would scarcely steal things *from themselves*.'

'And Lady Tremayne is very wealthy,' said Leo, flying to her godmother's defence. 'There's no reason she would need to steal from anyone!'

'That's assuming this is about theft, of course,' reasoned Sophie. 'But of course, Lady Tremayne is also rather slender. She doesn't quite fit in with the large figure you saw, Tilly.'

'We ought not to forget about the servants,' Lil reminded them. 'Might there be a reason any of them would urgently need money? Or perhaps there's someone new that has joined the staff who has light fingers?'

'Oh no!' exclaimed Leo. 'I'm sure none of the servants would ever steal from us!'

But Tilly was more thoughtful. 'I can't think of anyone who has fallen on hard times, if that's the kind of thing you mean,' she mused. 'Most of the servants have been here for years. Sarah, the scullery maid, is new, but she's scared to death of the East Wing and she's so small I could just about pop her into my apron pocket – so I don't think there's any chance she's our ghost.'

'What about the servants who've come to the house with the house party guests?' suggested Sophie. 'Mr Sinclair has travelled here with his valet, for instance – and Veronica and Mrs Whiteley both have their own ladies' maids with them. I suppose Miss Selina will be travelling with a maid too?'

But Leo shook her head. 'Great-Aunt Selina never brings a lady's maid with her when she comes to Winter Hall. It's another way for her to show Father how dreadfully poor she is.'

'What about Lady Tremayne?'

Tilly shook her head. 'She usually brings her maid with her but she didn't this time. Our head housemaid Emma has been looking after her.'

Lil, who had been jotting down the names of the possible suspects, now paused suddenly. 'We've been assuming this is about theft – but what if it isn't that at all? Why else might someone want to creep about in the East Wing at night?'

'To talk secretly to someone?' offered Leo.

'To *hide* something?' volunteered Tilly. 'Something they didn't want anyone to find?'

'Could it be something as ordinary as . . . a tramp coming in at night, looking for somewhere warm to sleep?' suggested Jack.

Tilly shook her head. 'It can't be anyone coming in

from outside. Not at night, anyway. Mr Stokes always locks the house up after dinner. There's no windows left open at this time of the year, and there's been no sign of any break-in – so it must be someone from *inside* the house.'

'Besides, it isn't like London here,' added Leo. 'Someone like that passing through the area would be allowed to sleep in one of the farmer's barns. There wouldn't be any need to go creeping about.'

'And there were no signs of anyone hiding out there,' Sophie reminded them. 'Well – except for that matchbox you found, Tilly.'

'Are you quite sure that you didn't notice anything else peculiar – or different?' Lil quizzed her. 'Or anything missing?'

Tilly frowned. 'No,' she said, but then she admitted: 'I wasn't really looking for missing things. And there are so *many* old things in the East Wing that I'm not certain I'd notice if something was gone.'

Lil snapped the notebook shut and got to her feet in a businesslike manner. 'Well, in that case – why don't we all go and have a look now?'

Tilly and Leo led the way: down the stairs, along several passageways, and finally through the door that led into the East Wing. It was easy to see that this was the oldest part of the house, Sophie thought: the ceilings were lower, and the stone-flagged floor was wobbly and uneven in places. What was more, it felt very empty – as though no one had lived in this part of the house for a long time.

Leo pointed out the Queen's Bedchamber with the big, carved wooden bed. Peeping inside, Sophie could see that the room was crammed with old furniture, and dozens of paintings and curious objects. She could see now what Tilly had meant when she had said it would be difficult to be certain if anything was missing.

Back in the passageway, she asked Tilly to pinpoint exactly where she had seen the 'ghost'. Tilly pointed to a spot about halfway along the passage. 'I was just about here,' she said. 'The figure came towards me, moving quite slowly. Then my candle went out.'

'Do you know which direction it came from? Out of one of these rooms to the side, perhaps?'

Tilly frowned. 'I don't think so,' she said, shaking her head. 'It came from directly ahead of me.'

'So most likely from the room at the very end of the passage?'

'Yes, I suppose so – and it was just beside the door that I found the matchbox,' said Tilly, indicating the place.

Sophie went through into the room at the end of the corridor, the others close at her heels. She felt the tingle of excitement she always experienced when a puzzle was being laid out before her. A quick glance around the room revealed an old cabinet filled with silver and china, several chairs, a side table, and a tapestry footstool. The stone floor was partially covered with a large rug, worked with a pattern of flowers. But the most noticeable thing about the room was the fireplace, which was surrounded by a large and very beautiful carved chimney-piece in three panels. Two of the panels were decorated with a pretty design of intertwining vines, leaves and fruit, whilst the central panel showed a splendid tree, with birds perched upon its branches. The paintwork had once been brightly coloured, and richly gilded, but it was fading now, and the gold decorations had lost their sparkle.

'How beautiful,' said Jack in admiration.

'This room is supposed to have been Walsingham's private study,' Leo explained. 'He commissioned this chimney-piece himself.'

'It's rather like the mosaic on the floor of the folly,' said Lil.

'That's right,' said Leo. 'Supposedly Henry Fitzgerald took the idea for the design from this old chimney-piece.'

Sophie stepped forward to examine the birds perching in the tree: an eagle, an owl, a pheasant. There was even a little brown sparrow perched on a top branch. She ran her finger thoughtfully along the top of the bare mantelshelf. It came away thick with grey dust.

Tilly looked disconcerted. 'Mrs Dawes would have a fit if she saw that. P'raps I ought to fetch a duster?'

'Don't do that,' said Sophie. 'Not yet anyway. The dust is useful. Look . . .'

She pointed to the floor beside the fireplace. Beside the edge of the rug, on the stone floor, the shape of a footprint could be seen in the dust. Only the front part of the foot was visible – the heel was indistinct – but it was enough to see that it had been made by a large foot.

'That's got to be a man's footprint – surely?' exclaimed Jack.

'Not necessarily,' said Lil, bending down. 'It's a bit bigger than mine – but not much.' She stretched out her own foot for comparison, and Jack was forced to agree that it could possibly be the footmark of a tall woman wearing a stout shoe. He carefully outlined the shape of it in his sketchbook, whilst Tilly and Leo scouted around, looking for any more footprints, and Lil began examining the objects on the side table – a jumble of marquetry boxes, bronze ink stands, china figurines and ornate clocks.

Sophie stayed where she was beside the fireplace. There was something odd about it. Apart from anything else, it seemed rather strange that the mantelshelf had been left completely bare, whilst the side table and cabinet were crammed with trinkets. She examined the chimney-piece once again, tracing the sweeping shape of a tree branch, outlined in peeling gilt paint. Glancing down at her fingertips, she saw that they were quite clean.

'The chimney-piece isn't dusty,' she said aloud.

Tilly came over to look. 'How queer,' she said in surprise. 'The central panel has hardly a speck of dust on it!'

'Do you suppose one of the maids has been here?' suggested Leo.

Tilly shook her head. 'Lizzie didn't get this far – remember? I found the duster she'd dropped back there, along the passage.'

Sophie was still examining the chimney-piece. She had noticed that the picture of the owl appeared to be slightly raised. She felt its curved shape with the tip of a finger, and almost without thinking, pressed it gently. It clicked: there was a sudden loud whirring sound, like cogs turning; and then a heavy clunk.

'Oh golly!' exclaimed Lil.

Before their very eyes, the central panel of the chimney-piece had swung open like a door. Beyond it was darkness, a chill draught of air swept into the room, bringing with it a dank smell.

Sophie turned to stare at the others. 'It's a secret door!' she said.

CHAPTER ELEVEN

ven Leo was astounded. 'I thought I knew every hidden door and passage in Winter Hall,' she said, staring into the dark space beyond. 'But I had no idea about this one!'

Lil fetched the footstool, and pulling it towards the fireplace, clambered up to get a better look inside. 'I say – I can see some stone steps going down!' she exclaimed. 'A secret staircase!'

'I wonder where it leads?' said Jack excitedly.

'Can't you guess?' said Lil. She looked around at the others eagerly. 'Surely the passage must connect the East Wing to the old folly in the grounds? It can't be a coincidence that it's exactly the same design as the mosaic. Maybe there's a hidden entrance there too? And that means there could be a secret way *into the house from the outside!*'

'Heavens!' exclaimed Leo. 'So that means the ghost could be someone who has been using the secret passage as a way to creep into the house – not someone from *inside* the house at all!'

'Yes – and if they were creeping along that passage, they'd need a lamp or candle, wouldn't they? That could explain the matchbox – and maybe the lights that Jamie said he saw floating, high up,' said Tilly. 'After all, if someone was coming through that door up there with a lantern, it might look like a floating light!'

'What's more, it makes sense of the cold feeling you and Lizzie both experienced,' Sophie added. 'We can all feel it now, can't we? There's a cold draught blowing along the passageway – so when the panel is opened, you feel a sudden whoosh of ice-cold air.'

'Of course!' Tilly exclaimed. '*Terrible chill* indeed,' she muttered, half to herself.

'Well come on, then,' said Lil, dancing from one foot to another in anticipation, 'We *are* going to explore the passage, aren't we?'

But at that moment there came the clang of a gong somewhere in the house.

'Time for tea,' said Leo. 'We can't miss it – or we'll be in frightful trouble with Mother.'

Lil climbed sadly off the footstool. 'I never thought I'd say this,' she murmured. 'But I rather think that in this house there are just *too many* meals.'

For the rest of Christmas Eve, they were kept very busy indeed. There was afternoon tea, with Cook's mince pies, the lighting of the candles on the Christmas tree, dressing for dinner, drinks in the Drawing Room, the long meal itself, and finally brandy, cigars and billiards for the gentlemen, and coffee and bridge for the ladies. Sophie and Lil did not know how to play bridge and were rather glad to be able to excuse themselves. Lil whispered that perhaps they could go and take another look at the secret passage, but Sophie shook her head. It was late, and exploring could wait. For now, they slipped up to Sophie's room to discuss the mystery of the ghost.

'I still think it all has something to do with the house party,' mused Lil, sitting cross-legged on Sophie's bed in her nightgown, her hair in two long plaits. She had announced that she was definitely not sleeping in her own room tonight ('I know perfectly well that there are no such things as ghosts, but I don't like it in there all by myself') and now her brow was furrowed, as she sat, trying to make sense of what they had discovered. 'Great-Aunt Selina and Vincent are still our best suspects. But if it is one of them, I don't really understand why they'd bother sneaking through a secret entrance.'

Sophie was brushing her hair at the dressing table. Now she put down the brush and turned to face Lil. 'That's right. Why go to all that trouble – when they could just go into the East Wing in the ordinary way?'

'Unless they're using the secret door to smuggle away

the stolen goods, perhaps?'

Sophie nodded, thinking it was going to be rather difficult – and uncomfortable – if they really did discover that one of Leo's relations was stealing valuables from Winter Hall. Yet at the same time, she was glad to have a mystery to occupy her. It was a good distraction from thinking about Colonel Fairley.

'Well – there's one way we could try and find out what's really going on,' Lil said speculatively. 'We could lie in wait for the ghost ourselves. We know from Tilly's notes that the ghost has appeared almost every evening at sometime between 8.30 p.m. and midnight. So, perhaps we could lurk somewhere nearby after dinner – and then catch them in the act!'

'That's an idea! They may not turn up, of course – but if they do, we'll know for sure who the ghost really is.'

'Let's talk to the others about it in the morning.' Lil yawned. 'I say – isn't it funny that it's Christmas Day tomorrow? It doesn't really feel like Christmas. Oh, I know there are all the proper things – Christmas trees and mince pies and so on – but Winter Hall is such a peculiar place. So many servants – and gongs ringing – and having to dress up all the time . . .'

Sophie nodded. 'I don't blame Leo for preferring London. I can't say I like any of her family very much. Lord Fitzgerald ignores us, Lady Fitzgerald obviously loathes us, and Vincent is always glowering – and he's so horrid to Leo.'

Lil shrugged. 'I feel a bit sorry for him. I can't think of anything worse than having all those people deciding what you're going to do with your life. Why, imagine someone else choosing who you were going to marry! That's why the Whiteleys are here, of course. They're cooking up a match between Veronica and Vincent.'

Sophie grimaced. 'Poor Veronica. She doesn't look very pleased with the idea. After she was almost forced to marry the Baron, you'd think that they would at least let her choose her husband for herself. And as for Vincent, he looks like he'd rather pay his attentions to *you*.' She giggled. 'Mr Pendleton's nose is quite out of joint.'

Lil clambered into bed. 'Well that's just *silly*,' she said decidedly. 'I think Vincent's a cad. If he can't even behave decently to his own *sister*, then I'm certain I don't want any more to do with him than I have to. Besides, it's not as if he would ever marry me.' She gave a little gurgle of laughter. 'Just imagine – his parents would have a fit! Although Lady Lilian Fitzgerald does have a certain ring to it, don't you think?' she finished with a grin.

Sophie laughed, as she climbed into bed too.

'You know, it's rather interesting to see what high society people are like, but I think I'd loathe this kind of life,' Lil reflected. 'Apart from anything else, I don't even *want* to get married.'

'Don't you?' asked Sophie in surprise.

'No fear! I'd rather be an independent woman of means,' declared Lil grandly, snuggling down under the counterpane. 'Travelling the world – and performing on the stages of Paris and Vienna and New York – and solving mysteries of course. I shan't have time for romance.'

Sophie chuckled. 'But what about poor Joe? You know he's always had a soft spot for you.'

'Joe's a terribly good sort – I like him awfully. But as a *chum*, not as a husband. Besides, what about you? You're the one with two different suitors dangling after you!'

'Whatever are you talking about?' said Sophie with an embarrassed laugh.

'Oh *please*,' said Lil, enjoying herself immensely. 'You know quite well that Jack thinks you're wonderful.' She snorted. 'Probably because you're about the first girl that hasn't swooned at his feet the second he met them. And don't think I didn't see Song looking all gooey-eyed at you the other night after our Sewing Society meeting. So which one of them is it going to be?'

Sophie leaned over to blow out the candle. 'Well . . .' she said in the dark, with the air of one about to confide a great secret. 'Actually . . . I don't think I'm too bothered about suitors either.'

'No?'

'No. As it happens, I think I'd rather be an independent

woman of means, travelling the world and solving mysteries.'

Lil gave a delighted giggle. They were both still smiling when they fell asleep.

Tilly woke early the next morning, when her room was still in darkness. For a moment she felt as thrilled as she used to on Christmas morning when she was very small, and could glimpse the shadowy lump of a stocking at the foot of her bed, crammed with treats – an orange, a shiny red apple, a handful of nuts.

Now of course she was too grown-up for a stocking, but in spite of the cold, she jumped out of bed, and went over to the window and peeped outside. There was a fresh dusting of snow on the rooftops, and she felt a bubble of excitement in her stomach. It would be a busy day below stairs, but Christmas was always fun. There would be presents to exchange with Ma – hopefully she would have got the book Tilly had hinted at, and not something dull like a new apron. Then a walk across the frosty estate to church for the Christmas service, the housemaids all rigged out in their Sunday best with ribbons on their hats. At teatime, there was always a party for the children on the estate, officially hosted by Her Ladyship, but really organised by Mrs Dawes and the maids with Miss Leo's help. There would be crackers and party games and presents – and then after the party and once the family had dined, there would be a big Christmas supper in the Servants' Hall with a bowl of punch, and Mr Stokes would make a toast.

The only thing to spoil it was that Miss Leo would be leaving again once Christmas was over. She'd confided to Tilly that she wanted to go back to London as soon as she could.

'I can't bear it here any longer. It's all right while Jack and the others are here. It's been rather fun. But once they've gone, it will be simply horrid – especially as I don't get very much time with you.'

Tilly had stared back at her unhappily. Of course, she was glad Miss Leo was happy in her new life in London – but she hated the thought of her vanishing away again.

Above stairs, the house party also had a busy day ahead of them. After breakfast, they attended the service at the pretty old church on the estate. As the congregation stood to sing a carol, Sophie was a little disconcerted to spot a familiar-looking velvet hat with very purple violets several rows ahead of her; but when she looked for the old lady after the service, she was nowhere to be seen.

Afterwards, they walked back to the house for a large luncheon, followed by the exchange of presents in the Drawing Room. Sophie watched as Leo opened her presents – a fashionable frilly gown from her mother, for which she tried to look pleased and stumbled out awkward thanks, followed by a beautiful set of oil paints from Lady

Tremayne which clearly thrilled her. Sophie had only brought little gifts for Lil, Jack and Leo, but Mr Sinclair surprised them all by presenting each of them with a very large and magnificent box of Sinclair's chocolates.

Next came skating on the frozen lake, and then the children's party, when all of them – even prim Veronica – joined in with noisy games of pass the parcel and hunt the slipper and blind man's buff. Only Vincent stood apart, smirking from the sidelines as Sophie carefully tied the blindfold over a little girl's eyes, and first Leo, then Mr Pendleton and then Lil obligingly allowed themselves to be caught. He wouldn't even take part in the country dancing that followed, rudely refusing when Mrs Dawes gently suggested he could be partners with Veronica, and leaving her looking quite offended. From where she was whirling about with Jack, Lil and three of the estate children, Sophie was glad to see Mr Pendleton swiftly stepping in and volunteering himself as Veronica's partner instead.

After that of course, it was time to dress for dinner, and for another meal – and so it was not until they were sitting in the Drawing Room later that evening that Sophie and Lil had the chance to explain Lil's plan to the others. For the plan to work they would need plenty of helpers, so they had decided to recruit Mr Pendleton and Veronica to assist. Unfortunately, they both seemed rather baffled by Lil's excited explanations, whilst even Jack and Leo frowned, looking uncertain. Sophie found herself wishing very much that Billy and Joe were there. She knew that they would have been quick to understand the plan! She wondered how the two boys had been spending Christmas Day, and made up her mind to write them a letter to tell them all about the new mystery. Perhaps she could write it before she went to sleep – but no, she thought, if she waited until tomorrow afternoon, she'd be able to write about the visit to Colonel Fairley too. She felt a quick flutter of nervousness and excitement at the thought.

'Surely you don't really think that anyone from the house party could be stealing things from the house?' Veronica was asking.

'We don't know for sure – but Tilly must have seen *someone*,' said Lil impatiently. 'We have to find out who. Listen, it's all quite straightforward,' she went on, folding her hands with an important air. 'Tomorrow night, after dinner, we divide ourselves up into three groups. The first waits out of sight, somewhere close to the door that leads into the East Wing. Meanwhile, the second group hides *outside* near the folly. Whether our "ghost" gets in through the door into the house, or uses the secret entrance – we can't miss them. Do you see?'

'I think so,' said Mr Pendleton. 'We get the blighter surrounded – catch him in the act – and then bop him on the head!' he finished, illustrating this with a dramatic gesture.

'I really don't think we'll need to go bopping anyone on the head,' said Sophie hurriedly.

'Absolutely *not*,' said Lil. 'We just want to find out who they are. Then we will *confront* them – and let them know that it's simply not decent to go around pinching things, and pretending to be a ghost!'

'What about the third group?' asked Veronica, frowning.

'Well, the third group go to the Drawing Room after dinner as usual and keep a sharp eye out for Miss Selina and Vincent, as they are our main suspects. That's your job – and Mr Pendleton's.'

Veronica looked relieved. 'So all we need to do is stay in the Drawing Room and watch them?'

'That's right. Stick to them like glue, and if they show any signs of sneaking off to the East Wing, then follow them. Mr Pendleton had better watch Vincent, since he'll be with the gentlemen after dinner. You can keep an eye on Miss Selina.' Lil turned to Leo. 'You and Tilly can watch the East Wing door. That leaves Jack, Sophie and I outside watching the folly.'

'Jolly good!' said Mr Pendleton cheerfully. He turned to Sophie. 'I say, this detective business is rather a lark, what?'

Sophie smiled and nodded absently, but for once her mind was not really on detecting – or even the mysterious Winter Hall ghost. She couldn't stop thinking about tomorrow's visit to Colonel Fairley.

PART III
The Body in the Library

'This was no accident,' said Montgomery Baxter, as he
scrutinised the scene through his magnifying glass.
'There can be no doubt that this is a case of foul play!'

CHAPTER TWELVE

'This must be it,' said Sophie nervously. The gate opened with a creak, and she, Lil and Jack picked their way carefully up the icy footpath through the garden.

She had been determined to set out to Alwick promptly that morning and had asked Leo about it at breakfast before she had eaten so much as a bite.

'Of course,' said Leo. 'I'll ask Alf to bring the motor round as soon as possible.'

'But you can't go alone,' said Lil, helping herself to more toast and spreading it liberally with butter.

'Of course not. After all, we don't know a thing about this fellow,' agreed Jack. 'Lil and I will come with you.'

The Fitzgeralds' chauffeur had driven the three of them slowly along the icy roads back to Alwick. He would wait for them in the old inn on the village green, while they traipsed up the path through the snow towards the large, pleasant-looking residence that the innkeeper had pointed out as Alwick House.

A small, white-haired lady in a rustling black silk dress and an old-fashioned lace cap answered their ring. Sophie felt almost too apprehensive to speak, so it was Lil who said: 'Good morning – is this the Fairley residence?'

The lady – who must be the housekeeper, judging by the bunch of keys at her waist – beamed at them. 'Oh yes,' she said warmly. 'And you'll be here to see the master, I suppose? Come in – you'll find him in the Library.'

They looked at each other in surprise at this warm welcome. It was almost as though she had known they were coming, Sophie thought. While they took off their coats and wiped the snow from their boots, she glanced quickly around the pleasant hall, full of books and pictures. Her heart was thumping with anticipation as the housekeeper led the way along the hall.

'And here's the master,' she announced, as she opened the Library door.

Before them was a cosy, comfortable room, the walls lined with rows of old leather-bound books, and a fire roaring in the grate. The windows looked over a pretty walled garden, which lay under a blanket of snow. Under the window, a large desk was laid out with pen, ink stand and blotter: but the big leather chair behind it was empty. The room appeared to be totally unoccupied, with the exception of a very large Persian cat curled up on the hearthrug.

Jack was the first one to speak. 'Er – I do beg your pardon,' he said, very politely. 'But where *is* Colonel Fairley?'

The housekeeper looked taken aback. 'Oh dear – I thought you *knew!*'

'Knew what?' asked Lil at once.

Her smile had faded; her face was concerned now. 'I'm terribly sorry, but if you're looking for the Colonel – well, you won't find him here.'

Sophie's heart sank. 'Where is he?'

'I'm afraid Colonel Fairley has passed on.'

Lil gaped at her. 'Do you mean to say he's *dead?*'

'I'm afraid so. The poor gentleman. About this time last year it was, in this very room.' She shook her head sorrowfully, and explained: 'He was cleaning one of his revolvers, and it went off in his hands. He was killed at once. Such a sad accident! And the Colonel ever such a kind gentleman.'

'He died? He died this time last year?' Sophie repeated in a quivering voice. She could scarcely believe her ears.

'That's right, miss. A sad Christmas it was, for all of us. I am sorry – I didn't know that you wanted to see the old master. I assumed you must be here to see the *new* master. That's Mr Marmaduke, here. We get a lot of young folks coming to pay a call upon him, thinking it amusing.'

To all of their amazement, she gestured to the cat dozing

regally on the rug.

'This – *he* – is your new master?' repeated Jack incredulously.

'That's right,' the housekeeper said, nodding earnestly. 'Folks think it's a little queer, and I must say, I never thought I'd see the day when I was housekeeper to a cat! But the Colonel was a bachelor gentleman – he had no wife or child. Mr Marmaduke here was his nearest and dearest. After he died, when they looked at his will, they found that the Colonel had named Mr Marmaduke as his heir. It was just the sort of odd thing he might do, for he was what you might call an eccentric gentleman.'

'But . . . is that even legal?' asked Jack.

'Well it would seem that it is,' said the housekeeper. 'Though it caused a few ructions, I can tell you. Lawyers up from London and quite a to-do. But they said it was all perfectly right and proper, so Mr Marmaduke is the master here now.'

Sophie said nothing: she couldn't speak. She had spent days anticipating this meeting and imagining it – but Colonel Fairley was *dead*. She found herself blinking back tears.

Lil was staring in rapt fascination at the cat, so Jack was left to do his best to reply. 'How – very interesting!' he said gamely. 'Well, ma'am, perhaps we should explain our business with the Colonel, and maybe you can help us.

Miss Taylor here recently discovered that her late father was a close personal friend of the Colonel, which is why she wanted to meet him.'

The housekeeper looked thoughtful. 'A Mr Taylor? I don't remember a gentleman of that name. But then, the Colonel had a great many friends. Very sociable gentleman, he was.'

'Do you think he might have had any mementos of Miss Taylor's father? Photographs or letters or anything of that sort?'

'Well now, I suppose there could be,' said the housekeeper readily. 'All the Colonel's papers are here. The relations were very particular about that. There's a great-nephew in Harrogate who is next in line to inherit and he made quite a fuss about making sure all the Colonel's papers and business effects are kept in order.'

'Mr Marmaduke doesn't have any children, then?' Jack asked. 'They wouldn't be – er – next in line?'

'Well between you and me, I expect he probably *does* have a few offspring,' said the housekeeper confidentially. 'But it's a bit difficult to prove for sure. That's what the legal gentlemen said, at any rate.'

Jack looked like he was trying very hard not to laugh, but Lil had seen what he had been driving at. 'Do you think we could perhaps have a look through those papers?' she suggested quickly. 'Just in case there might be any photographs of Sophie's papa – or anything like that?'

The housekeeper beamed at them. 'Well now – I don't see why you shouldn't – and take what you like too! The Harrogate great-nephew doesn't care a button for the Colonel's personal things – it's only the business papers and the old books and paintings he's interested in! Only the things that might be *worth* something,' she said disapprovingly. 'Terribly particular he is about those! But you help yourselves to any personal photographs or letters, my dears. We'd rather see them go to someone who will value them, wouldn't we, Mr Marmaduke?' At the fireside, the big cat gave a throaty meow and stretched out one paw, quite as if he were answering her.

She showed them over to a cabinet where the Colonel's papers had been kept, and then bustled out to fetch some refreshments. 'You need something to keep out the cold on a day like this.' After bringing them a jug of cocoa and a plate of currant buns, she departed again, murmuring something about needing to prepare Mr Marmaduke's luncheon.

'I say, how peculiar! I don't believe I've ever heard anything like it in my life!' burst out Lil as soon as she had left the room. 'Who would leave their fortune to a *cat*?'

'*Ssshhhh!* Make sure you don't offend Mr Marmaduke,' said Jack, chuckling. 'He might throw us out of his house.'

The cat blinked his large green eyes at them reproachfully.

'It's an awful shame about Colonel Fairley,' said Lil in a more serious voice. 'I am sorry, Sophie. I suppose that explains why you never heard from him when your papa died.'

Sophie had bent down to Mr Marmaduke, who was regally consenting to be stroked. Now, she had to swallow before she could answer: 'I suppose it does. He died a year ago too – that's the same time as Papa.'

'Come on,' said Jack, in an effort to be cheerful. 'Let's take a look at those papers. You never know what we might find.'

They spent the next half hour busily searching through Colonel Fairley's cabinet, with occasional breaks to sip cocoa and nibble buns. There was a great deal to look at: the Colonel had obviously been a man with considerable involvement in local affairs and, as the housekeeper had told them, a great many friends. There were plenty of letters, but nothing from Sophie's father – though after picking over a few old photographs, Sophie at last uncovered a picture of a group of military gentlemen in dress uniforms, and spotted amongst them the figure of her papa.

Staring at the photograph, a new wave of sadness swept over her. He was slipping away from her so fast, she thought, looking at the indistinct black and white figure. She had really hoped that she was going to at last find someone who had known him, someone who she could talk to about him and would help her remember. Instead, the Colonel had gone too.

'He was rather an antiquarian chap, wasn't he?' Jack was saying. 'Lots of these seem to be receipts for purchases of books or paintings. Some jolly interesting stuff too.'

'Yes – just look at all these books,' said Lil, who had lost patience with searching through old letters, and had begun to roam around the room. She ran a finger along some leather-bound spines. 'Half the titles are in Latin, and some of them look awfully old.' She lifted down a big volume and flicked through the old pages, growing brown at the edges. 'I don't know how anyone could actually read this. Such funny old-fashioned printing.'

Jack got up to join her. 'Look at this one,' he began, removing another volume from the shelves, its crimson cover richly gilded with a design of three winged lions. As he did so, a folded piece of paper that seemed to have been wedged inside fell to the floor.

Lil picked it up and unfolded it. 'Oh! But whatever is *this* doing here?' she said, her voice shocked. 'Sophie –!'

She held it out, and with the photograph still in her hand, Sophie scrambled up from where she had been sitting on the rug. She took the paper; it was an old envelope, addressed in a neat hand:

Mr. L. Lim
L. Lim & Sons
limehouse
London E14

Sophie looked from the envelope, to Lil's baffled face, and then back again, but just then the door opened and the housekeeper came bustling in again. Lil thrust the envelope quickly into the pocket of her frock.

'Well, then – and did you find what you were looking for?' asked the housekeeper.

Sophie held out the photograph that she was still holding, and the housekeeper took it. 'Bless my soul. That's Captain Cavendish! You don't mean to say *he* was your father, my dear?'

'That's right – Captain Robert Taylor-Cavendish was his full name,' she explained.

'Fancy that! I knew him as Captain Cavendish. He'd been in the Colonel's regiment, and the two of them were thick as thieves. Of course, we hadn't seen much of him for a few years, not since the Colonel retired. The Captain was always busy with all those travels to foreign parts. And so the poor gentleman is gone too, is he? Well, I'm sorry for your loss, my dear. You take the picture, by all means.' She pressed the photograph into Sophie's hands, and seemed inclined to say more, but her sympathetic face was more than Sophie could bear. All at once, she wanted very much to get out of the house and away.

'Thank you,' she managed to say to the housekeeper. 'You've been very kind. If you're sure it's really all right, I'll take the photograph. But we'd better be going now. They're expecting us back at Winter Hall for luncheon.'

They said their goodbyes and hurried together down the snowy path, back towards the inn and the village green.

'What on earth could a letter to the Lim family be doing in Colonel Fairley's study?' demanded Lil in a low, urgent voice.

'Sssshhh!' hissed Sophie. 'Let's wait until we're alone.'

In spite of her warm coat, she found that she was suddenly very cold. For as they climbed into the back of the Fitzgerald's motor, she had seen that watching them from the snowy village green was the familiar figure of a little old lady, wearing a bunch of purple violets in her velvet hat.

CHAPTER THIRTEEN

'**Y**ou really found this in Colonel Fairley's library?'

Leo gazed at the envelope in fascination, turning it over between her long, thin fingers. Back at Winter Hall, the four of them were sitting before the fire in the Nursery – supposedly playing at paper games, but the pencils and paper were quite abandoned while they all pored over the envelope addressed to *Mr L Lim*.

They had known at once who that was, of course. There was only one *L.LIM & SONS* in Limehouse. *L Lim* was Mei and Song's grandfather, who had died earlier that year, and whose name was above the door of the shop. None of them had ever met Grandfather Lim, but they knew that Mei and Song had been very close to him. What was more, Sophie had always thought of him as an ally – for they had discovered that he too had been on the trail of the Baron.

Now, they examined the envelope in detail. It was an ordinary stamped envelope, a little yellowed now, as though it had been wedged inside the book for some time.

The flap of the envelope had been secured with a red wax seal stamped with the shape of a lion's head, but the seal had been broken, and whatever letter or note might once have been inside, the envelope was now completely empty.

'It must have been written by Colonel Fairley,' said Jack. 'The handwriting matches the writing on those letters we were looking at in that cabinet.'

'But it was never actually posted,' said Sophie. 'There's no postmark.'

'Do you suppose the Colonel wrote this letter and then thought better of it?' suggested Lil. 'Or could someone else have found it before he had a chance to post it – and taken out the letter inside?'

'I say – look at the seal,' said Leo, turning the envelope over and touching the red wax with a gentle fingertip. 'Doesn't it remind you of anything?' She held out her cane. 'Look.'

Sophie stared from the lion's head on the red wax seal, to the lion's head on the handle of Leo's cane. She remembered that cane had first been given to Leo by the Lims when her old crutch had been broken. 'It used to belong to Grandfather Lim,' she said slowly. 'Both lions . . . do you suppose there is some kind of a connection between them?'

'Maybe Colonel Fairley was the one who gave Grandfather Lim the cane in the first place,' said Leo, her eyes widening. 'But what on earth could a retired Army Colonel living in Alwick possibly have to do with an elderly man in a grocer's shop in Limehouse?'

Sophie got up and went over to the fire. 'My papa was a friend of Colonel Fairley's – and Colonel Fairley knew Grandfather Lim,' she mused slowly. 'What's the one thing that Grandfather Lim and my papa have in common?'

It was Lil who answered her. 'The Baron,' she said.

They stared at each other for a few moments, puzzled and alarmed. Sophie felt startled when the gong sounded, reminding them that it was time to dress for dinner. Her fingers felt stiff and awkward as she hurried once more into her evening dress.

Downstairs in the Drawing Room, they discovered that a number of extra guests had been invited to join them for a Boxing Day dinner, including a group of ladies and gentlemen from a neighbouring estate, and several people who lived locally, including the vicar and the doctor.

'Of course, I wouldn't usually invite a *doctor* to dine,' Sophie heard Lady Fitzgerald murmuring discreetly to the Countess. 'But it's one of our traditions to have some of the local people here on Boxing Day.'

'One never knows *who* one might be expected to dine with *these days*,' said the Countess, with a poisonous glance in Sophie's direction.

At the head of the table, Lord Fitzgerald had been

seated once more between the Countess and Mrs Whiteley, whilst Lady Fitzgerald had Mr Sinclair on one side, and a gentleman from the neighbouring estate on the other. Her charming smile was briefly interrupted by an irritated glance at Vincent, who had casually swapped his name card in order to seat himself beside Lil.

The other guests were ranged around the table: Sophie found herself between Mr Pendleton and an elderly gentleman who spent most of the soup and fish courses relating his experience of shooting wild game in India in his youth. It might not be very interesting, but by arranging her face into a polite expression and nodding occasionally, Sophie managed to give the impression she was listening, while allowing his words to wash over her. She was still thinking hard about their discoveries. Besides the Baron of course, the other connection between Papa and Colonel Fairley and Grandfather Lim was that they had all died within a month or two of each other. No one had suggested that there was anything at all suspicious about Grandfather Lim's death – he had, after all, been very elderly. But what about Colonel Fairley? She had a sudden idea:

'My trusty old Lee-Enfield rifle would have done the job of course,' the old gentleman was saying, squinting fiercely through his monocle. 'But this fellow had only a feeble little Browning. And at those distances, you absolutely *must* have a long-range rifle if you want to achieve any degree of accuracy.'

Sophie smiled and nodded, and then tentatively changed the subject: 'This seems to be a very beautiful part of the countryside. Have you lived here long?'

'Long? I've lived here most of my life!' said the old gentleman, scowling as though she had insulted him.

'In that case, I suppose you must know everyone hereabouts,' she went on hurriedly. 'I wonder – did you know Colonel Fairley?'

'Fairley? Of course I did! Known him for years. Acquainted with him, were you?'

Sophie murmured something about him having been a friend of her late father's.

The old gentleman's stern face softened. 'Poor fellow,' he said, sighing as he dabbed his walrus moustache with a napkin. 'Eccentric old buffer, of course – that mad business of leaving everything to a *cat*. Perfectly idiotic, if you ask me! But he was a decent sort, for all that – and a damn fine shot. Of course, he took a scholarly fit after he retired from the Army, always shut up in that Library poring over old books and fussing over paintings. Can't see the appeal myself. But Fairley was well liked around here. People were quite cut-up when he died.'

'It was an accident with a revolver, wasn't it?' asked Sophie.

'That's right. Dashed unpleasant business.' The old gentleman leaned forward, and addressed the doctor, who

151

was sitting opposite him.

'Hi – Bates – you attended poor Fairley, didn't you? What was it that happened to him?'

The doctor looked up from his fish. 'Oh, he'd been cleaning one of his little revolvers, and the thing had gone off in his hands. Poor fellow was killed instantly.'

'You know, I'd never have believed it of Fairley,' said the old gentleman, shaking his head. 'Very thorough, steady sort – not the type to make a mistake, especially a dashed stupid mishap like letting his gun go off like that. And by Jove, he knew his way around a firearm. Well of course he did – he'd been a military man. Showed me his medals once – a dozen of them, he had. And do you know, he had one of the finest gun collections in the county . . .'

Sensing that her companion was about to revert to his favourite topic of shooting, Sophie hastily interrupted: 'Do you mean to say that there might have been something – well – *unusual* about his death?' she asked.

The old man raised his eyebrows, and then squinted at her again through his monocle. 'Unusual? I'm not sure what you mean, my dear.'

Across the table, the doctor grinned at her. He had already heard a little about Taylor & Rose, and now he said: 'Foul play, do you mean? The body in the library, and all that sort of thing? I suppose that would be very much in your line.'

Sophie blushed. 'All I meant to say is that if the Colonel really was so careful and so knowledgeable about guns, it seems rather surprising that he could have been the victim of an accident of that sort.'

Dr Bates nodded. 'Well yes, you're quite right there. It's true that we might have asked some questions about Fairley's death – were it not for one very simple thing.'

'What was that?' asked Sophie.

'Colonel Fairley died in the Library,' explained the doctor. 'At the time of his death, the door of the Library was locked from the inside, and the windows were shut and locked too. He couldn't possibly have been shot through a locked door now, could he?' He grinned and took a sip of his wine. 'Besides I can't imagine a fellow less likely to be murdered than old Fairley. I never knew someone so universally liked – I don't think I ever heard a word said against him.'

'Very true, very true,' murmured the old gentleman.

'And Fairley was getting on, you know,' said the doctor, warming to his subject. 'His sight was beginning to fail – his hands not as steady as they once were – and he was becoming forgetful as he got older. These things do happen as people age.'

'Yes *thank you*, doctor,' said the old gentleman tartly. 'Some of us are still in full possession of all our faculties. Why, I can tell you my dear, that –'

But Sophie never did hear what the old gentleman had to tell her about his faculties. Their hostess had turned away from her right-hand neighbour, to Mr Sinclair, who was sitting on her other side. This was the signal for the other guests to 'turn' too, and all down the table, everyone followed suit.

Opposite her, Sophie saw Veronica turn, and look expectantly at Vincent, but in direct opposition to correct dinner etiquette, he was still talking to Lil. Veronica looked annoyed, and down the table, Sophie's keen eyes saw that Lady Fitzgerald looked annoyed too.

Before the doctor turned to address Miss Selina, who was seated on his own other side, he leaned forward across the table, and spoke again to Sophie. 'Do you know, there was one rather queer thing about Colonel Fairley's death that no one could ever fathom. Of course, there was an awful fuss when the will was read. Fairley was a rich fellow, and there were noses out of joint. There was a great-nephew who stood to inherit the majority, and he had lawyers brought in to look into it all. He kicked up quite a stink, insisted on all of Fairley's assets being properly inventoried – antiques, art, books, the silver, the whole of his gun collection. And do you know, there wasn't so much as a single pearl-headed pin missing – except for one thing.'

'What was it?' asked Sophie, growing more intrigued by the minute.

'A small painting that hung in the library. Oh, it wasn't anything special. A rather dirty old thing, that no one knew much about – likely some piece that he'd picked up in a saleroom somewhere. It had completely vanished. It was quite the mystery,' he said with a wink.

Sophie's heart began to thump. 'Oh – how peculiar! Did they know who painted it?' she asked, trying to keep her voice light and casual.

The doctor shrugged. 'No idea, I'm afraid. But I don't believe it was anything of value. I daresay perhaps the old chap gave it away to someone before he died – or simply got tired of it and threw it away.'

He grinned at her again and turned to Miss Selina, but Sophie had to ask one more question.

'Excuse me – I don't suppose you remember what it was a painting *of*, do you?'

'Oh, didn't I say?' The doctor took a sip of his wine. 'It was a dragon – a sort of gold-coloured dragon.'

Sophie sat back in her seat, stunned. Beside her, Mr Pendleton had turned in her direction, but he wasn't looking at her: he was staring at Vincent. Even the plate of roast chicken with bread sauce that had been set down in front of him by a footman did not distract him.

'I say, Miss Taylor,' he began. 'I know it's not the *done thing* to criticise when you're the guest and all that, but I can't help thinking that's rather bad form. I know Miss

Rose is jolly good fun, but dash it all, Miss Whiteley is a fine girl too. It's simply not cricket to leave her languishing like that.'

Sophie only half heard him. Her thoughts were in a tangle. Across the table, Great-Aunt Selina was talking loudly to the doctor.

'Of course, I do struggle . . .' She raised her voice a little further, and cast a quick, sharp eye along the table towards Lord Fitzgerald. 'My medical bills cost me a *good deal*. My doctor insists on regular trips to the seaside. Fresh air, he tells me, is *essential*. But the costs mount up – the expense is so difficult for a person in *my* position. I may even have to curtail my visit to Brighton this year,' she said with a regretful little sigh.

Along the table, Lord Fitzgerald was talking to his neighbour, clearly not listening to a word that Great-Aunt Selina had said. Nettled, she looked over at Sophie.

'Miss Taylor, I hope you don't mind me saying so but you are extremely pale,' she said, attacking her chicken viciously with her knife and fork. 'Are you sickly? I hope you are not *outgrowing your strength*. That can happen to young girls, of course. Especially if they are not getting enough fresh air and exercise.' She glared at Sophie. 'I daresay you would benefit from a good *strengthening tonic*. That would give you a little more colour. A young girl ought to be *hearty and healthy*.'

'Oh, I say – I think Miss Taylor looks in absolutely splendid health,' insisted Mr Pendleton gallantly.

But Sophie only smiled at him absently. She could hardly tell Great-Aunt Selina the truth about why her face was drained of colour: the sudden realisation that Colonel Fairley's death had been no innocent accident. The doctor might well grin at the notion of foul play, but from everything he had told her, Sophie now felt certain that the Colonel had been murdered by the man who called himself the Baron.

CHAPTER FIFTEEN

'Why did I ever think this was a good idea?' complained Lil, as she, Jack and Sophie stood in a huddle in the darkened grounds of Winter Hall. It was bitterly cold, and in spite of having bundled themselves up in as many warm clothes as possible, they were all shivering. It did not help that in the silent winter moonlight, everything in the grounds looked strange – the shapes of ordinary trees transformed into something eerie and peculiar. Beyond, a little distance away from them, the old folly loomed like an unearthly apparition in the dark.

'For all we know the ghost isn't even planning to make an appearance tonight,' Lil went on. 'If they've got any sense they'll be tucked up nice and toasty in bed.'

Sophie rubbed her hands together in an effort to try and warm up. 'Never mind,' she said. 'Listen. I've got to tell you about what I found out at dinner.'

Lil and Jack listened in astonishment, as Sophie unravelled the doctor's story. 'If Papa and Colonel Fairley died at the same time, and Papa was murdered by the Baron – I think perhaps Colonel Fairley was too,' she finished up. 'The accident was unlikely and out of character. And *then* there's the business of the missing painting.'

'Do you really think it could have been one of Casselli's dragon paintings?' asked Lil eagerly.

'The doctor said it was a painting of a golden dragon – small and rather old. That sounds *exactly* like one of the dragon paintings to me.'

'There was a golden dragon in the original sequence,' said Jack, getting quite excited now. 'Though no one knew what had become of it.'

'Well perhaps the Colonel had it – and was keeping it secret,' suggested Sophie. 'We know the Baron was obsessed with those paintings. There's some kind of secret information in them that he wants very badly. I don't doubt that he – or one of his men – would have killed the Colonel to get hold of one of them.'

'But what about the locked Library door?' said Lil.

'You know as well as I do that the locked door means nothing. This is the Baron we're talking about. A locked door is hardly going to pose a challenge to him.'

Lil nodded. 'He might have got hold of a key,' she mused. 'Or what about this? At first the door *wasn't* locked. The Baron came in, shot the Colonel and then left, locking the door behind him. It would be a simple thing for him to push the key back under the door into the room. Then, when people arrived on the scene, they'd all be desperately trying to get through the door. When they finally broke through, they would assume the door had been locked all along – and the key had fallen out of the lock when they'd been jiggling at the door handle.'

'Yes – there are half a dozen ways he could have done it,' agreed Sophie. 'The point is that the Baron – or even one of his men – could easily have murdered the Colonel and then set the whole thing up to look like an accident.'

Her thoughts were whirling: it had been a long day, and all at once she felt very tired. She wished that she was tucked up in her big bed with its lavender-scented sheets, not standing out here in the dark and cold, waiting for a mysterious person who was up to no good – and who possibly wouldn't turn up at all. But just then she felt a sharp dig in her ribs.

'Look!' Lil murmured. 'I think I can see someone!'

They all stared ahead of them, and Sophie had to swallow a gasp. A figure could be seen picking its way down the path. In the dark, it was impossible to tell whether it was a man or a woman – but there was no mistaking that they were headed straight for the folly. A moment later, the figure went up the steps and disappeared inside.

Sophie felt wide awake at once. 'Come on!' she whispered, and the three began to hurry over the snowy grass. But when they had climbed up the steps, they saw that there was no one inside the folly.

'I told you!' said Lil excitedly. 'They've disappeared! They must have gone into the secret passage – we have to find it and follow them!'

But finding it was not quite as easy as they had anticipated. Tilly had provided them each with a small candle lantern and matches – but even once the lanterns had been lit and were shone carefully over the floor, it was not at all easy to identify a secret entrance in the dark. At last, Jack's keen eyes spotted a small metal ring set into the mosaic. Prising it upwards carefully, they saw to their excitement that it opened a small trapdoor in the floor.

Sophie peered down into the darkness, listening for the echo of footsteps. But there was no sound to be heard, and one by one, they crept carefully down some stone steps. They found themselves standing in a tunnel: wide enough and tall enough for them to stand upright, stone-flagged and with walls of roughly hewn stone.

'It's the secret passage. I knew it!' whispered Lil. Her face looked unearthly in the dark, lit up by the light from her candle-lantern. 'Come on!'

'But what about the trapdoor?' murmured Jack. 'Should we leave it open? Or might that give us away?'

'Let's leave it as it is,' whispered Sophie. 'The last thing we want is to get trapped down here.'

She shivered as she spoke. It was very cold in the tunnel, and she did not like the look of the dark passage looming before them. For a minute, she looked longingly back at the steps leading towards the folly. Then she remembered the shadowy figure they had seen, and squared her shoulders. They were detectives, after all – and they had a job to do.

Lil's teeth had begun to chatter. 'I jolly well hope this ghost is worth it,' she muttered, as they stepped forward into the dark.

For several minutes, they walked in silence, listening intently, but all remained silent. Lil shone her lamp into all the dark corners, but there wasn't so much as a footprint on the stone floor.

'What a peculiar place,' said Jack at last in a low voice. 'Do you suppose this was built by Walsingham too?'

'That would make sense,' said Lil. 'After all, Walsingham was a spymaster? I suppose a secret way in and out of the house must have been awfully useful for all his clandestine business. Then perhaps the other man, Henry Fitzgerald, added the folly later to mark the entrance to the passage?' She broke off. 'I say – look ahead. What shall we do now?'

Ahead of them the wide passage divided into three narrower branches, each heading in a different direction.

'Three of us – and three passages,' said Jack. 'I suppose we'll have to split up. That way at least *one* of us will find the way to the East Wing and have the chance of catching our ghost.'

'Very well – but we'd better take care,' said Sophie cautiously. 'We mustn't lose our way. We have no idea how far these passages go – or where they might lead.'

Lil nodded too. 'And don't forget – we're to meet with the others back in the Nursery at midnight.'

A few moments later Sophie was creeping alone down the left-hand passageway. Although she would never have admitted it to the others, she had not been at all keen on the idea of splitting up. She had learned from experience that she could keep her head in frightening situations, but that did not mean that she was not scared, and there were some things that always made her anxious. Being up high was one; the closed-in, pressing darkness of this underground tunnel was another. She took a few deep breaths and walked on, listening to the reassuring sound of her own feet padding along.

Perhaps it was no bad thing to be on her own, she told herself. She had a lot to think about after the visit to Colonel Fairley – and indeed, for several minutes, she was so lost in thought that she did not notice she was approaching a short flight of steps. Then, shining her lamp upwards, she realised in excitement that these were the steps that led up to the door in the chimney-piece. She had found it – this was the secret route into the house!

Excitedly, she started up the steps, but halfway up, she paused again. It occurred to her that whilst Lil's idea of confronting the 'ghost' had been all very well when there were three of them, it might not be quite such a good plan now that she was alone. It seemed unlikely that the elderly Miss Selina would be capable of clambering about in the snow at night, through trapdoors and along underground passages, which meant that their most likely suspect was Vincent. Sophie found she did not much like the idea of catching him in the act of stealing from his own house. She could not imagine he would take kindly to her interference, and for a moment, she hung back. But she did not need to actually *confront* Vincent, she realised. If she could just glimpse what he was up to, they would at least know for sure that he was the ghost. Otherwise, all their night-time exploring would be for nothing.

She crept forward up the stairs – but before she reached the door, she heard something that made her stop in her tracks.

It was a voice, quite close to her. To her astonishment, she realised that someone was speaking in the room on the other side of the chimney-piece door.

'You didn't come last night,' it said.

Sophie froze. Somewhere beyond she heard the low buzz of another voice, though she could not hear the words. Then the first voice replied, in a more jovial tone: 'You aren't seriously worried about *them* are you? Well you needn't. In any case, I'm clearing out of here tomorrow. If you know what's good for you, you'll do the same.'

The world seemed to tip and slide. It couldn't possibly be real, Sophie told herself. She was dreaming it – she must be.

'I won't skulk about here any longer, like a rat in a hole,' said the voice, stronger now and with a sharper edge to it. 'Besides, I must see that everything is ready for New Year's Eve.'

She would know that voice anywhere. Not even just the sound of it but the words – the way it shaped sentences – its rise and fall.

'Don't think I'm not grateful for all you've done. I know we've had our differences in the past but that's set aside now. I knew that you would be the one I could count on for this.'

She could not possibly mistake that voice. She had heard it before, standing like this listening, icy cold in the darkness – her throat dry, her heart pounding in her chest. Hiding behind a thick, velvet curtain in a box at the theatre, darting in a breathless panic into the bedroom of Mr Lyle's apartment, standing on the end of the East End docks in the middle of the night. She had heard it in a dark alleyway in Chelsea, and in the very depths of her own nightmares. It had whispered to her: *This time I know I'll see you again.*

The voice she could hear through the secret door of the East Wing was the voice of the man that – try as she might – she had been wondering about for the last two months. It was a voice that she would know anywhere, and that she would never forget – the voice of the man who had killed her parents, and who she believed had killed Colonel Fairley. It was the voice of the Baron.

CHAPTER SIXTEEN

As the footsteps of the two girls faded into the distance, Jack set out boldly along the right-hand passage. He found that he was rather enjoying himself. All right, so this wasn't quite what he had expected from a country house party – but he had always enjoyed an adventure. All in all, it had been a jolly interesting Christmas, he reflected. Winter Hall was such a strange place – and as for the people, they were stranger still. He'd come across plenty of well-off upper-crust chaps before, but they'd mostly been good sorts – whereas you couldn't say that of scowling, sulky-faced Vincent. He'd managed to draw him out a little, chatting about Oxford and one or two fellows they both knew there, but it was obvious he looked down on artists. He sneered at his guests and barely had a word to say to his own sister. Jack certainly wouldn't fancy spending much time with him.

Mr Pendleton was a different kettle of fish: he seemed a decent sort for a fellow who wouldn't know one side of a painting from the other; and he rather thought Miss Whiteley might turn out to be quite good fun if she had the chance to relax and let her hair down. As for Lady Tremayne, she had been jolly kind. It was obvious that she knew more than a bit about art, and Jack was practical enough to realise that having a few wealthy patrons like her could be beneficial to his career.

Then there had been all this business about ghosts, and hauntings, and secret passages, and mysterious murders in libraries. Jack grinned to himself, thinking that things did always seem to become rather eventful when Sophie and Lil were around. He didn't mind that; in fact he rather liked it. He thought of the determined look on Sophie's face whenever she was getting her teeth into a problem. He had never known a girl quite like her before. She might be small and dainty, but she was strong enough to handle anything – even the shock of discovering Colonel Fairley's death.

Now he turned his mind to the task at hand, shining the lamp before him. He noticed that the passage, which had at first seemed to curve to the right, was now curling back on itself, twisting towards the left. Was it carrying him back towards the house itself, he wondered? Or towards some other secret spot of Walsingham's?

For a moment, he cast himself into the role of the Elizabethan spymaster, dressed in a long, swirling cloak, a dashing sort of hat with a feather in it, and possibly a moustache. He tried to imagine what it would have been like to go creeping down the passageway on a secret mission to protect the Queen from treachery . . . In reality, of course, Queen Elizabeth had had red hair but in Jack's version of events she had suddenly become small and fair – and rather determined-looking.

Just then, he became aware of faint sounds in the tunnel ahead of him and stiffened. They were footsteps – and they were moving rapidly in his direction. Could it be the 'ghost' coming back down the passage?

He paused, unsure what to do. The footsteps came closer and closer, an urgent tap-tap-tap against the stone. Surely they couldn't be the footsteps of an elderly lady – they were far too vigorous for that. Vincent, then? A tall figure with a lamp appeared around the corner, and he made up his mind to confront the fellow. He stepped forward boldly, and the glare from the lamp dazzled him.

There was a very familiar yell.

'*Jack!*' proclaimed a cross voice. 'You scared me! Why did you jump out at me like that?'

Squinting in the light, he realised that his sister was standing before him, her hands on her hips.

'I thought you were the ghost!' he protested. 'But I suppose our two passages must have linked up.'

Walking a little way along the passage, Lil showed him

that the path she had followed had led to another fork. 'I turned right – and joined up with your passage. That means we'll have to take the other branch. Well at least we're together now. It isn't much fun wandering around down here all alone. These tunnels are creepy!'

But they had not walked on for much more than two minutes before they found that the passage led to a stout, wood-panelled door.

'Where do you suppose this leads?' asked Jack.

Lil tentatively pushed it. The door opened at once, and they found themselves in a small, square room – windowless, and covered from floor to ceiling in dark wooden panelling. What was more, it was obvious that someone was living here. A wide wooden bench against the wall was being used as an improvised bed, with rumpled sheets, pillows and blankets. There was a makeshift washing area in the corner: a cloth spread over a table, a small looking glass, some shaving things, and a bowl and a jug of water. A table was strewn with papers, books and the remains of a meal: some bread, a piece of cheese wrapped in paper, a bottle of brandy and an empty glass.

A large oil lamp stood in the centre of the table, together with an ashtray containing the remains of a cigar, and a blue and white box of matches. Jack picked it up and turned it over in his hands. '*Allumettes*,' he said aloud.

'It's another hidden room – like the one Leo showed

us,' whispered Lil. 'I say – do you suppose this could be the hideout of the ghost?'

Together, they looked quickly around the room. Jack examined the mess of papers on the desk: to his surprise, he saw that amongst them was a London newspaper, dated from only a few days before Christmas, with Mr Sinclair's ball on the front page. Beside it was two or three handwritten letters, written in what he at first assumed was a foreign language, but on closer inspection, seemed more like a nonsensical muddle of letters and numbers and peculiar characters. Lying beneath was a thin sheet of paper, showing a diagram of a strange symbol, drawn in red and black ink. He picked it up and studied it with interest.

'What do you suppose this is?' he said.

Lil's hand grabbed suddenly at his arm.

'I don't like this,' she said, her face serious. 'Look – do you see this?' She pointed to one of the square boxes on the map, which was clearly marked with the twisting shape of something that might have been a serpent, or perhaps a dragon. Jack realised it was vaguely familiar.

'What is it?'

'Don't you remember? It's the symbol of the *Fraternitas Draconum!*' she hissed, her voice heavy with meaning.

Jack stared at her. He remembered who the *Fraternitas Draconum* were, of course – they were the sinister organisation who had been behind the theft of the dragon paintings. Sophie had once even eavesdropped on one of their secret meetings in a private room at the exclusive gentlemen's club Wyvern House. Their members were all rich men like the crooked art collector Randolph Lyle – and one of their most senior members was the Baron himself. But what could those men possibly have to do with this strange secret room at Winter Hall?

Lil was examining the document, her dark eyebrows drawn into a stark frown. 'We've got to take this,' she began, but almost at once changed her mind. 'No – no – we'd better not. We don't want anyone to know that we've been here. Do you have your sketchbook with you?'

Jack nodded, feeling for the square shape of it in the pocket of his coat. He rarely went anywhere without a sketchbook and a few pencils – you simply never knew when an opportunity to draw might come up.

'*Copy it*,' Lil instructed him. 'And do it quickly. Then we need to get out.'

Sophie stood motionless at the top of the stone steps. The tunnel was silent; in the room beyond, she could hear once more the faint buzz of another person speaking. Only the Baron's words were distinct: she could even hear his impatient intake of breath. He must be standing right beside the fireplace, she realised – maybe even leaning upon the mantelpiece. He was mere inches away from her. The thought of it made her shrink back.

'I shan't contact you again, not until this is over,' he said. 'It's better that way. Of course, if I have to, I'll send a message but I hope it won't be necessary. After all, you know what you have to do.'

But his voice *was* different, she thought suddenly. The Baron had always spoken in the smooth, confident tones of a wealthy, educated gentleman. Now his voice sounded hoarse and there was an urgent note in it that she had not heard before.

'Make sure the King is in position exactly as we've discussed. He must be in our sights. I will take care of all the rest. It's going to be quite a show. A New Year's spectacular, right enough.' He gave a hard little laugh and his voice

swelled with pride. 'The city will burn. The assassination –
that will be only the beginning. There will be chaos on the
streets. And when the society sees all that I have achieved
– when the Master sees what I can do – he will be *begging*
me to return to them. He will see that everything I have
sacrificed has been for a *reason*. I will show him – all of
them – what I can accomplish.'

In the passageway, Sophie found that she was quivering.
The Baron was talking about an *assassination*, she told
herself in disbelief. He was talking about murdering the
King.

'I have left a careful trail – the authorities will be in no
doubt that our German friends are responsible. We will be
at war in a matter of days! Of course, the Society is perfectly
positioned to benefit. Our funds will be restored; we will
prosper. We can stabilise, rebuild – and turn our attention
back to the missing paintings. Getting them back will be
short work, of course. The government won't give them a
second thought with the King assassinated, and a war in
Europe on their hands. Once we have the paintings and
we have their secrets – a new Age of the Dragon will be
upon us!'

His voice had risen in excitement, now there was a tense
silence. When he spoke again, he sounded more like his
usual smooth self. 'Just make sure you have your motor
waiting. It's going to be dangerous on the streets. And

whatever you do, don't go near Piccadilly Circus.'

She listened intently, hardly daring to breathe. Then the Baron said briskly: 'I should go – I need to be on my way. Farewell – and make sure you do exactly as I have told you.'

It was only as she heard the grating sound that she realised what was happening. The secret panel was opening, and the Baron was about to step through into the passageway – exactly where Sophie now stood.

Leo and Tilly stood side by side behind the tapestry in the hall. Leo had known it would make a good place to hide: after all, she'd crept behind it and through the secret door that lay beyond dozens of times, whenever she'd wanted to escape from her parents, or Nanny – or to avoid Vincent in one of his nastier moods.

Now as she stood there, she felt very thoughtful. What would she do if she discovered her brother really was stealing from the East Wing to settle his gambling debts? She supposed she'd have to tell her parents: Vincent would be horrid about it, and she wasn't even sure that Mother would believe her. Or would she? After all, she'd noticed her disapproving gaze fasten upon her son several times in the last few days.

Her legs were beginning to ache, and she leaned a little more heavily against her cane. She found herself thinking longingly of London: of her cosy rooms, of the studio at the Spencer, of the streets and squares of Bloomsbury where no one cared what she wore or who she was friends with. She couldn't wait to go back – to go *home*.

Beside her, Tilly was listening intently. It was good to have Tilly back by her side again, and Leo thought with a pang of how unhappy the other girl had looked when Leo had confessed how much she was looking forward to returning to London. She wished now that she hadn't been so tactless. It was so unfair that she had managed to get away from this place and make a new life for herself, doing what she loved – whilst Tilly was left behind, pouring tea and poking fires. If only there was a way for Tilly to get away too, she thought.

But that gave her a sudden idea. Only that morning Mother had been harping on at her about the way she lived in London. The need to *dress* properly and *behave* properly and see the proper sort of *people*. Leo had not really been listening, but she did remember that Mother had said she should have a lady's maid with her. Now she gave a little squeak of excitement. What if that maid were to be Tilly?

'Tilly,' she whispered at once. 'What would you think about coming back with me to London – to be my lady's maid?'

Tilly stared at her. 'What?' she exclaimed, forgetting all about being quiet.

'It wouldn't be much of a job. I mean, I don't go to

175

CHAPTER SEVENTEEN

Veronica and Mr Pendleton were waiting for them when Lil and Jack came traipsing up the stairs. It had been snowing again when they had finally made their way out of the tunnels via the secret trapdoor in the folly and now they were cold, wet and tired.

'Did you catch the blighter?' asked Mr Pendleton in excitement.

'I'm afraid not,' said Jack, flopping down into Nanny's armchair. 'But Lil was right about the secret passage.' He quickly related the tale of the figure they had seen, the underground tunnels, and the discovery of the secret room. 'We found something jolly peculiar in there too,' he began, taking out his sketchbook, but Lil shook her head. 'Let's wait for the others and show everyone together.' She had wrapped a blanket round her shoulders for extra warmth, and now she looked up at the clock: it was already past midnight. 'They should be here any minute.'

While they waited, Mr Pendleton began explaining

what he and Veronica had found out: 'We did exactly what you said, didn't we, Miss Whiteley?'

Veronica nodded. 'But I don't see how either Vincent or Miss Selina could be the person you saw going into the folly. It certainly wasn't Miss Selina, anyway. She was in the Drawing Room until about half past ten, and then she went to bed, saying she had a headache. I said that I was tired too, and I followed her up there – my bedroom is only down the passage from hers. I sent my maid off to bed so she wouldn't know what I was up to – and then I just watched. There was a light under Miss Selina's door for about half an hour – and then, just after eleven, it went out. I didn't hear a peep after that. There's simply no way she could have left the room before midnight without me seeing her go,' she finished.

'Not unless she clambered out of the window and shinned down the drainpipe and then went racing off down a secret passage,' said Lil. 'And I can't imagine Miss Selina's capable of that. Not unless she's an awfully good actress and just pretending to be an invalid. But what about Vincent?'

Mr Pendleton looked uncertain. 'Well – I stuck to him like glue all evening. He looked pretty sick about it, I can tell you. He kept trying to shake me off – but I went on trotting after him. Eventually he gave it up and we played billiards until just after eleven. He won half a crown off me and that seemed to cheer him up, rather. Then he said he was turning in. But I never thought of following him up to bed. I'm afraid I'm not as smart as Miss Whiteley – so I suppose he could have slipped away after that.'

Lil shook her head. 'If he didn't leave you until after eleven, then it can't have been Vincent that we saw either,' she said. 'The person we saw went into the folly at about half past ten. What about everyone else? Did they all go to the Drawing Room after dinner?'

Veronica nodded. 'Yes. Lady Tremayne played the piano for a while. Lady Fitzgerald and Isabel and the Countess played a rubber of bridge – and you could see that they wanted Mr Sinclair to play with them, but Miss Selina made a fourth instead. Father and Lord Fitzgerald were having a terrifically boring conversation all about the House of Lords and the budget and the constitutional crisis or something like that – and Mr Sinclair was with them. After a bit, he started to talk to Lord Fitzgerald about some of the old books in the Library that he said he wanted to look at. Then, Miss Selina went up to bed, and Lady Tremayne said she was going up too – and so did I.'

'So everyone was accounted for in the Drawing Room until half past ten?' said Lil. 'I say – perhaps I was wrong. Perhaps our ghost isn't one of the house party at all.'

She glanced up at the clock again: it was almost half past twelve. She frowned anxiously. 'Wherever can Sophie be?

And Leo and Tilly too?'

Jack sat up, looking concerned. 'Do you think Sophie might be in some kind of trouble?' he asked. 'She's all alone. Ought we to go and look for her?'

Lil hesitated. She knew that Sophie was far from helpless: she had a sudden, vivid memory of the last Sewing Society meeting, when Sophie had cleverly outwitted Dora and Bunty – the two biggest and strongest of the suffragettes. Yet there was something about what had happened tonight – the mysterious figure, the dark passageway, the hidden room, and most of all that strange map with its familiar dragon symbol – that had made her feel deeply uneasy. 'We'll give them five minutes,' she said finally. 'If they're not back by then, let's go and look.'

Sophie stood trembling in the passageway. There had barely been time to blow out her candle and slip down the stairs into the shadows. Now, she stood with her back pressed against the wall, hardly daring to breathe.

She knew that if the Baron saw her she was lost. She was all alone, and everything she had learned at Sewing Society seemed to have deserted her. All she could do was stand still, her heart pounding in her chest, while the Baron's heavy footsteps clumped down the stairs towards her.

But he did not even glance towards where she was standing, and instead began walking swiftly away, back along the tunnel. Without meaning to, she let out a little breath of relief.

Almost at once, he paused. Sophie froze to the ground. Had he heard her? Was he about to turn and see her there, standing in the shadows? A wave of sickness washed over her – but then, without even turning around, he walked on, away from her down the passage, the sound of his echoing footsteps ringing loudly in her ears.

It was a long time before she allowed herself to move. She did not dare go through the secret door and risk coming face to face with the Baron's unknown companion: instead, she hurried as quietly as she could back along the tunnel. At the staircase she hesitated: what if the Baron was waiting for her out there, somewhere in the dark? It took all her courage to run up the stairs and back through the snowy grounds to Winter Hall.

In the Nursery, Lil looked up in relief as she entered. 'Sophie! Thank goodness – we were just about to come looking for you. Where have you *been*? And what's wrong?'

For a moment she felt dumb, and then the words began to spill out. The others listened in shocked silence – and then, all at once, the room was a babble of urgent conversation.

'The Baron?' repeated Veronica, her face white. 'Here – in this house?'

'The Baron is the one who's been using the secret

passage to get access to the house!' exclaimed Lil. '*He's* the ghost!'

'Yes – it all fits. The heavy footsteps – the lights – the footprint we found in the dust. The Baron was creeping in using the secret passage. When Tilly came into the East Wing he frightened her away – rather than be discovered there.'

'And he's the one who has been hiding in the secret room!' exclaimed Lil. In a very few words, she explained their discovery to Sophie. Jack took out his sketchbook, and for a moment, they all pored over the strange diagram in silence. Veronica was the first to speak:

'But *why* is he here? Why is he doing this?'

'It doesn't seem the least bit like the Baron we know,' said Lil. 'Hiding – and skulking about at night!'

Sophie looked up from the plan. 'But he's on the run from Scotland Yard, isn't he? And I think it all went wrong, after we got back the dragon painting. The *Fraternitas Draconum* were already annoyed with him, remember? They thought he was being reckless, drawing too much attention to them in his quest to get the paintings back. Then *we* got the paintings – and Mr Lyle was arrested – and the Baron himself barely escaped the police. From what I heard him say, the society isn't very happy with him at all. A year ago, he was the top man in the East End, with the Baron's Boys at his beck and call. He was masquerading as Lord Beaucastle, with all of this wealth – and even planning marriage to an heiress,' she said, nodding in Veronica's direction. 'There were layers and layers of people to protect him. Now all of that's been taken away. The Baron's Boys are gone, his Lord Beaucastle identity, his house and fortune – and now the society has gone too.'

'He's at rock bottom,' said Lil slowly.

Sophie nodded. 'But it sounds like he's got a plan to try and get it all back,' she went on. 'And from what I could hear it centres around New Year's Eve – and his plan to assassinate the King at the New Year's Eve Ball!'

Mr Pendleton nearly dropped his mince pie. 'I say!' he announced in astonishment.

'Assassinate the *King*?' Jack repeated, alarmed and baffled.

Sophie blew out a long slow breath of air, as she tried to sort out her thoughts. 'When the Baron and his allies planted the bomb at Sinclair's, he talked about using it to spark off a war in Europe,' she began. 'I think this is the same kind of thing. He plans to make it look as though Germany is responsible for the assassination. He said it would start a war – that there would be chaos on the streets – and that London would burn.'

'But why would anyone want that?' demanded Veronica.

'To profit from it,' said Sophie soberly. 'That's always what he's wanted, he and the society. He's doing this to impress them – to win back their respect. He talked about trying to get the paintings back too, and something about an Age of Dragons . . .' Her voice tailed away. She felt exhausted and wrung-out. The day that had begun with the hope of finding a new friend had ended only in coming face to face with an old enemy.

'So what do we do now?' asked Mr Pendleton, looking alarmed. 'Do we go to this secret room and confront the scoundrel?'

'No – no – we can't do that!' said Lil. 'The Baron is *dangerous.*'

'Besides, he said that he was about to leave. He may have gone already,' said Sophie. 'No, I think there's only one thing we can do. The advantage we have is that the Baron doesn't *know* we've discovered him.' She frowned for a moment. He must be laughing at her, she realised, turning up here in the same house for a cheerful Christmas party, without the first idea of how close he was: how easy it would have been for him to slip into her room at night with that long silver knife . . . She set her jaw. 'We have to let Scotland Yard know that the Baron is planning to assassinate the King on New Year's Eve – with the help of his accomplice,' she said firmly.

'Yes – his accomplice!' exclaimed Lil excitedly. 'So who was he was talking to?'

Sophie shook her head. 'I don't know. All I know is he

said they had disagreed in the past in some way. He talked about putting that aside and working on this together.'

'But whoever this person is – the Baron's accomplice – they must have been someone from *inside the house*,' persisted Lil. 'After all, we didn't see anyone else going into that tunnel.'

'What's more, they had obviously met there before,' said Sophie soberly. 'He said "you didn't come last night" as though it was a regular arrangement.'

'So do you think that the Baron's accomplice is someone from the house party, then?' said Jack in amazement. 'But who?'

It was Tilly who answered, as she and Leo came creeping in to join them in the nursery. 'We know that now – don't we? We've just seen someone sneaking out of the East Wing.'

'You'll never believe it,' said Leo, her face very grave. 'But it was Mr Sinclair.'

PART IV
The Clue in the Secret Plans

'We must obtain the blueprints,' Baxter informed his loyal companion. 'They – and only they – will provide us with the information we need to stop Number One's terrible scheme.'

CHAPTER EIGHTEEN

The train journey to Winter Hall had been exciting, but their return to town felt different – full of tense anticipation. Sophie almost expected the little old lady with violets in her hat to turn up again as they waited on the Alwick station platform, but she did not appear, instead, they had their compartment all to themselves – which was just as well, as they talked about what had happened all the way back to London.

Sophie had barely slept the previous night. Now she was very tired and her head was aching – but she remained quite clear in her mind about what they had to do:

'We must go to Scotland Yard at once. It's too important to delay for even a moment.'

'If only Mr McDermott wasn't away!' exclaimed Lil. 'He'd have come with us and explained everything. But at least we can go to Detective Inspector Worth. We know he'll listen to us.'

But as they rattled back towards London, Sophie did

not feel so certain. After all, Mr McDermott had worked for Mr Sinclair for as long as they had known him, and she was not at all sure that either he or the businesslike Detective Inspector Worth would be able to credit the idea that London's famous department store owner could possibly be working hand in glove with the Baron. She was still scarcely able to credit it herself.

They had talked it over for hours the previous night.

'Mr Sinclair?' Lil had repeated incredulously. 'The Baron's accomplice?'

'But Mr Pendleton and Miss Whiteley saw him in the Drawing Room!' exclaimed Jack.

'Yes but only until half past ten,' Veronica reminded him. 'We don't know what happened after that. But he did say he wanted to look at those old books in the Library. Perhaps he took a wrong turn – and went into the East Wing by mistake?'

Leo shook her head. 'It didn't look like a mistake. It looked like he was creeping about in secret.'

What Tilly and Leo had seen had only been reinforced by the events of the following morning. They had all slept rather late after the night's adventures, and when they had come down to the Breakfast Room, they had found Lady Fitzgerald, Lady Tremayne and the Countess already there, and had learned the surprising news that Mr Sinclair had left Winter Hall early that morning, without saying goodbye.

As the motor began to move, Sophie had turned back to look over her shoulder at the stern, grey shape of Winter Hall. She could still see the outline of Vincent, slouching in the doorway, and before him, the small figure of Leo, waving her handkerchief after them. For a moment, Sophie felt guilty for leaving her behind – but Leo would be back in London soon enough. Besides, it was not as though she was alone. Mr Pendleton and Veronica would be there for at least another day or two, and there was Tilly too, of course. They had agreed that Leo and Tilly would search the secret passage and secret room for more clues whilst the others went at once to report to Scotland Yard.

Back in London, amongst the smoke and noise of the railway station, Sophie and Lil said a quick farewell to Jack and hailed a cab to Victoria Embankment. Sophie had never been to the great headquarters of Scotland Yard before and was not sure what to expect, but when they drew up outside the big, red-brick building, they found it full of practical, everyday activity. At a large desk in the foyer they spoke to a clerk, explaining that they had urgent business with Detective Inspector Worth. After they had waited for a while on a hard wooden bench, feeling rather nervous, a young man appeared and called them into a small office.

He introduced himself at once, shaking each of their hands: 'My name is Detective Sergeant Thomas. I work with Detective Inspector Worth. I understand you wished to speak to him? I am afraid the Inspector is away for a few days, but I can assist you in his absence.'

Sophie was taken aback. She had counted on speaking to Detective Worth, and now she felt uncertain. But really, they had no choice. They would have to tell this young police detective what they knew. 'My name is Sophie Taylor. This is my colleague, Lilian Rose. We're from Taylor & Rose – the private detective agency at Sinclair's department store,' she began. She felt rather silly saying it – surely a real policeman would laugh at the idea of two girls being detectives?

But the Sergeant was listening quite seriously: 'Yes, I've heard about you both from the Inspector. That was some smart work you did over those stolen paintings. From what the Inspector tells me, you had a big part to play in exposing Lord Beaucastle too.'

Sophie felt a weight lift off her shoulders. Thank goodness he was actually treating them as though they knew what they were talking about – and not like a couple of silly little girls!

'We've just returned from Winter Hall, Lord and Lady Fitzgerald's country house. While we were there we discovered a secret entrance to the house, hidden in an old folly in the grounds,' Lil was explaining. 'We learned that someone had been using the entrance to get inside, where they had been hiding in a secret room!'

Sophie picked up the story. 'At first we assumed it was something straightforward – a thief at work, perhaps. But we discovered that the person using the secret entrance was the Baron.'

'The Baron?' The young man sat up very straight.

'I know your intelligence suggested that he had left the country – and perhaps he did,' Sophie explained, thinking of the French matchbox. 'But he's back now. I saw him myself and I overheard a conversation he had with an accomplice about a plan he intends to carry out on New Year's Eve at Sinclair's.'

'At Mr Sinclair's ball?'

Sophie nodded. 'It sounded very much as though he was planning an attack on His Majesty the King.' She hesitated for a moment and then blurted out: 'He talked of an *assassination*.'

'We came to report it at once,' said Lil.

The detective's face gave very little away. 'Tell me everything you heard,' he said at last, taking out pen, ink and paper.

Sophie related every detail she could remember of what the Baron had said, whilst the Sergeant made careful notes. Several times he stopped her and made her go over something again, trying to get as close as possible to the exact words she had heard. After he was satisfied, he asked: 'Do you know who he was talking to?'

The two girls looked at each other again. It seemed so impossibly far-fetched, Sophie thought. They'd been over and over it in the Nursery last night and again on the train today. How could it *possibly* be Mr Sinclair who was the Baron's accomplice? The Baron hated Mr Sinclair – he was his enemy. He had tried to blow up Sinclair's department store! But she could not keep from coming back to the Baron's words, as she had overheard them. *I know we've had our differences in the past but that's set aside now. I knew that you would be the one I could count on for this.*

It was Lil who spoke up at last: 'We don't know for certain – but it appears that his accomplice may be Mr Sinclair himself.'

The detective did not look as shocked as Sophie had expected. He merely raised his eyebrows and made a few more notes, as Lil went on, talking more urgently now:

'We have to stop the New Year's Eve Ball – either that or the King mustn't attend. The Baron plans to assassinate the King there. He wants to make it look like the work of German spies, with the aim of sparking off a war in Europe!'

The detective said nothing for a few moments, scribbling on his sheet of paper. Then he paused and gave a small bow and said: 'Thank you for coming to us so swiftly. We will deal with this at once.'

Sophie stared at him anxiously, but he seemed to

understand what she was thinking. 'Please, do not worry. You may be assured we will treat this very seriously indeed. It is a matter of national security. You can leave it safely in our hands.' He thought for a moment. 'Now, what I would like you to do is to go about your usual business exactly as normal – go back to your office and return to your work. Stay out of Mr Sinclair's way, if you can. We appreciate all you've done, but I must stress that there must be no further investigation on your part – this could be an extremely dangerous business. I would also ask that you please do not mention what you have told me to *anyone*. If we are to have the chance of apprehending the Baron, it is vital that he is not alerted to the fact that we know the truth. We will be in touch with you again if there is anything further we need.'

It felt very strange indeed to be walking back along Piccadilly as though everything was quite ordinary. The snow was beginning to melt, and the crossing-sweepers were clearing the dirty grey slush into piles. The festive season was at an end, and things were going back to normal all around them – but Sophie felt anything but that. Her heart was thumping as they trudged back into the familiar surroundings of Sinclair's stable-yard, where the porters and drivers were already at work. The Baron was back – and he could be here, at Sinclair's, in just a few days' time. What was more, now they knew that Mr Sinclair could be working with him. All at once, Sinclair's felt different – no longer a safe haven. Her stomach twisted as she looked up at the high windows of Mr Sinclair's top-floor apartments, wondering if he was there.

Lil led the way across the stable-yard. Of course, Sergeant Thomas might have told them not to tell anyone anything, but they couldn't possibly count Billy and Joe in that. They couldn't wait to tell the boys about everything that had happened. But when they called into the stables, Joe was not there.

Inside the store and up the stairs, they found the shop returning to life again after the Christmas break. But Billy was not to be found in Miss Atwood's office, and the door of Taylor & Rose was locked exactly as they had left it. The curtains were closed, the flowers in the vase had wilted – and neither Billy nor Joe were anywhere to be seen.

CHAPTER NINETEEN

'This must be it,' said Billy, spotting a sign which read ALBERT WORKS. Beyond the iron gates, they could see a long, rectangular building. Smoke streamed from its tall chimneys and there was a burning smell in the air.

'Look over there,' said Joe in a low voice.

From where the two boys stood, they could see that in the yard outside the factory building, a lorry was being loaded with wooden crates. As he stared, Billy saw that they were stamped with a distinctive black mark.

'That's it! Those are the same as the crates I saw in the office!' he exclaimed. 'See the dragon symbol?'

'So they really did come from here,' mused Joe. 'What d'you reckon is in them? Look – let's slip round this corner out of sight. If there really is any funny business going on here, we're best off not being seen.'

They slipped into the shadows beside the wall, watching while the big gates swung open, and the lorry loaded with crates rumbled out on to the road and away. Just then, a bell clanged in the depths of the factory buildings.

'What's that?' asked Billy, startled.

'End of the shift, I reckon,' said Joe, as the doors of the factory opened, and a stream of people emerged into the yard, heading for the gates. They were poor-looking folks, Billy thought, their shoulders stooped and their faces grey and tired. There were a few men, but most were women, and some were children – though surely they were far too young to be working? Some of them couldn't have been more than six or seven years old, dressed in ragged old clothes, and shivering in the damp, chilly air. As he watched, Billy noticed that several of the women, and many of the children had hands stained a curious yellow colour.

Joe was looking at them too. 'See that? They must've been dyed – probably by some kind of chemical they're using.'

'We should try and find out what they're making,' said Billy eagerly.

As the people began to filter through the gates, Joe took a step forward, and beckoned to one of the little girls. 'Come here a jiffy,' he said to her, speaking in the same gentle voice he used when he was calming down a nervous horse. 'Don't worry. We don't bite. We've just got a question for you. Tell us what you're making in there, and I'll give you a silver sixpence to take home to Mum.'

A bigger girl of ten or eleven stepped towards her and

took the small girl's hand. 'No good asking her,' she said in a hoarse voice. 'She don't have a clue what we're doing.' She looked at the sixpence Joe was holding out, and her eyes glittered. 'You want to know what we're making? Well I s'pose there's no harm in saying that. It's a chemical. New – and dangerous. Sets things on fire and makes 'em burn.' She looked back at the big building with dislike. 'Rotten place it is too. Worse 'n the sugar factory. Worse 'n the box maker's. Worse 'n just about anywhere else you can think of. Wouldn't stick it but we've got too many mouths to feed in our house. I'll have my sixpence now, thank you kindly, gents,' she said, reaching out a canary-yellow palm.

But Joe held it away. 'Wait,' he said quickly. 'Who d'you work for? Who's in charge here?'

The girl shrugged. 'Already gave you answers, didn't I? Give me my sixpence. Fair's fair.'

'We'll make it a shilling if you tell us,' said Billy boldly.

For a moment the girl looked him up and down, then she shrugged again. 'Couldn't tell you if I wanted to,' she said. 'I dunno who the big boss is, do I? It's the foreman who deals with us – ain't never seen anyone else round here. Well, apart from *her* that is.'

She jerked her head in the direction of the gates. While they had been standing there, a horse-drawn carriage had pulled up outside, and a smart lady was being helped out by the driver. She looked utterly out of place amongst the workers coming out of the factory gates. She could have been a customer at Sinclair's in her elegant fur-trimmed coat and matching hat. As they stared, she glanced around her, and then strode towards the factory entrance in her high-heeled boots. 'She generally comes in once a week or something like that,' said the girl, pausing to cough into a grubby rag that obviously served as a handkerchief. 'Haven't seen her for a while though. S'pose she must be the boss's wife or something. But that's all I know.' She took advantage of Joe being distracted by the woman to seize the sixpence. 'Come on,' she said to the little girl, and dragged her roughly away.

When Billy and Joe turned back towards the factory, they saw that the smart lady had disappeared inside – and the great gates were closed once more.

The offices of Taylor & Rose felt small and cold. They opened the curtains and lit the fire and threw away the dead flowers, and then Lil asked: 'What ought we to do now?'

Sophie shook her head. For once, she had absolutely no idea. After all that had happened, it seemed incredibly peculiar to be just sitting here, without anything particular to do. She was relieved that the Sergeant had taken them seriously, and very pleased indeed to know that Scotland Yard would even now be setting out to stop the Baron's plot. And yet, in spite of all that, she didn't know how she was supposed to go back to 'business as usual' when she knew an assassination was being planned for here in the store in just a few days' time – and that Mr Sinclair himself might be somehow mixed up in it. She felt on edge and every little sound of footsteps outside the office door made her jump.

In the end, she decided to try and read over the notes from the Abermarle case, whilst Lil made a half-hearted effort at tidying her desk. But they were both very glad when at last, the door opened and Billy and Joe came rushing in. 'We heard you were back!' exclaimed Billy. 'We've got something rather strange to tell you.'

Sophie and Lil exchanged glances. 'Rather strange doesn't even come close,' said Lil. 'Just wait until you hear what we have to tell *you*.'

The two boys listened in stunned silence to their story, Joe's face turning ashen when Sophie related how she had discovered the Baron hiding in the East Wing. But when Lil explained how Leo and Tilly had glimpsed Mr Sinclair sneaking furtively away, Billy could remain quiet no longer:

'They must've been mistaken! Whatever you saw or heard – it's completely mad! The Captain can't possibly be working with the Baron! You don't really believe that – do you?'

'I honestly don't know *what* to believe any longer,' said Sophie, shaking her head.

'But the Baron hates the Captain!' Billy exploded. 'Have you forgotten how he stole the Captain's jewels – and the painting from the store – and *oh yes, also the small matter of him trying to blow up Sinclair's* – with the Captain and all his friends in it?'

'Of course not,' said Lil. 'But –'

'The Captain has helped us every single time we've come up against the Baron! He's on *our* side!'

'That's what I thought too, at first,' said Sophie. She was wearing her mother's necklace again, and she fiddled with it as she tried to explain. 'But then I thought about it, and he didn't *actually* help us at all, did he? Not really.'

'What do you mean? Of course he helped us!'

'Think about it,' said Lil, growing impatient now. 'Remember when the Baron and his men followed us to the East End – and you and Song went to Mr Sinclair for help? Well it wasn't Mr Sinclair who helped you in the end – was it? It was Mr McDermott.'

'Mr Sinclair wasn't at home, *McDermott* was the one who got the police. And it was McDermott who helped us with the stolen paintings – and Detective Worth too.'

'In fact, even when I told Mr Sinclair about the bomb in the clock, it was *Mr McDermott* who actually stopped it going off,' Lil added.

'Now you're just being ridiculous!' Billy protested. 'You can't really think that Mr Sinclair *wanted* his store to be blown up?'

'No – of course not – but now I think about it there was something rather strange about the way he reacted. He didn't seem shocked, somehow. He just *stood there*. Surely that isn't how someone behaves when they discover there's a bomb about to go off, just a few yards away from them?'

Billy was gaping at her, but then Joe snapped his fingers. 'And remember when we were investigating the stolen dragon painting?' he said. 'We wondered about Mr Sinclair then too. He was supposed to be away in the country, but Leo and Jack saw him in that café, and we started to suspect that he might be somehow involved in the theft of the painting. That it could be – I dunno – a publicity stunt of some kind.'

Billy had turned to stare at him as though he had committed an act of treachery, but Lil's face had lit up. 'Yes! That's exactly it! Every single thing that's happened has made the store *front-page news*. They've made Sinclair's a place that jolly well everyone knows about. Somewhere that everyone wants to visit – out of sheer curiosity, if nothing else!'

Joe spoke up quietly: 'And if there's one thing that would be certain to grab the headlines – well, it'd be an attempt on the King's life, wouldn't it?'

'But no one would stoop to *murdering the King* just for a few newspaper headlines!' Billy almost shouted. 'You can't any of you seriously believe that!'

'I know it seems a bit far-fetched. But we've got to at least consider the possibility, haven't we?' said Joe in the same quiet voice. 'That's our job.'

Lil was nodding vigorously, and Billy looked from her to Joe in disgust. 'Oh, of course you agree with *her*,' he muttered angrily. 'You'll go along with anything she says!'

Joe looked a little embarrassed, and Sophie stepped in, trying to smooth things over. 'Joe's right,' she said. 'We have to at least consider all the options. After all, there have been plenty of occasions when we've thought something was absolutely impossible before – and we've been proved wrong.'

'Yes – we never would have guessed that Mr Cooper was really the one who stole the clockwork sparrow, nor that Lord Beaucastle was really the Baron, nor that respectable Mr Lyle was scheming to steal a priceless painting! But we can't afford to think like that any more,' said Lil sharply. 'And whichever way you look at it, you have to admit that jolly extraordinary things have been happening at Sinclair's ever since the day it opened.'

Billy looked angry. 'Well if you're so very clever, explain *this*,' he said in a cold voice. 'If all that's true, if Mr Sinclair has really been cooking up schemes to get publicity ever since the beginning – then why on earth would he want to set the two of you up as private detectives here in his store – where everything he's doing would be right under your noses?'

Lil opened her mouth to retort – and then closed it again. Billy looked triumphant.

But it was only too easy for Sophie to see the answer to his question. When she spoke, she found that her voice was wobbling slightly: 'Because he doesn't really think of us as proper detectives, of course. We're just part of his plan. The dear little girl detectives, on hand to save the day at exactly the right moment – and get even more attention for Sinclair's.' Suddenly she felt very sad, and more weary than ever. 'We're nothing but one of his publicity stunts.'

'*No we aren't!*' exclaimed Billy. 'I know the Captain better than any of you – and he just isn't like that. After everything he's done for us, you can't really believe that –'

'Look, this isn't one of your Montgomery Baxter stories,' Lil interrupted him. 'Mr Sinclair isn't some sort of *hero*. He's a businessman. You're being a . . . a . . . *mutton head*.'

'*I'm* being a mutton head?' Billy snorted incredulously. 'You don't know the first thing about it! You don't care two straws for the Captain – or Sinclair's! You never have. You're just passing time here – you can't wait to flit off to the theatre at the first chance you get, or to go off hobnobbing at country houses.'

'Oh, I say – that isn't fair!' Lil snapped back, but Billy wasn't listening. He was so offended that he stormed out of the room, slamming the door so hard that the glass panel rattled. Joe stared after him, and then back at Lil, who had flung herself down on the sofa with her arms crossed.

'He's being *stupid*,' she said angrily.

'It's just hard for him to get his head round the idea,' said Joe gently. 'He's loyal – that's all.'

'Oh, and I suppose I'm not? I suppose *you* think I'd just fly off to the theatre at the first opportunity too?'

Joe looked wounded. 'I'd better get back down to the stables,' he muttered. 'The Gaffer'll be looking for me.'

He sidled away, leaving Sophie raising her eyebrows at her friend.

'Oh, for goodness sake, stop looking at me like that,' said Lil crossly. Then her face softened. 'Oh dear – I really oughtn't to have called him a mutton head, should I? Oh – *bother*!'

Sophie was woken the next morning to the sound of rain against the window. Outside, the snow had been washed away and a bitter wind was blowing. She thought briefly of the comforts of Winter Hall: the warm fire, the lavender-scented sheets, the tray of tea brought by a maid – and then made herself hop out of bed into the sharp cold of her boarding-house room. She dressed quickly in a warm frock, thick woollen stockings and her buttoned boots, and put her mother's necklace around her neck. Her visit to Winter Hall was over now, she was back in London where she belonged – and it was back to business. Today, she had something very important to do.

She took out the Montgomery Baxter book that she had taken with her to Winter Hall and retrieved Colonel Fairley's envelope from where she had tucked it safely between the pages, and headed out into the rain to hail a cab to the East End.

The familiar windows of *L.LIM & SONS* looked very reassuring, lit up on the dark Limehouse street. Sophie hurried through the shop door, making the bell jangle loudly. Inside, she found not only Mr Lim, but all of the family at home: even Song was not due to start work at the Marble Court Restaurant until the following day. They gathered round the table in the back room to examine the envelope – quite as puzzled by it as Sophie was herself.

'You found this in that man's house?' repeated Mr Lim, after she had briefly related the tale of their strange visit to Colonel Fairley's home.

'That's right. It's the Colonel's handwriting – so although it looks like the letter was never posted, he obviously intended to write to Grandfather Lim. Do you know anything about the Colonel – do you remember your father ever receiving letters from him?'

Mr Lim shook his head slowly. 'No – I don't recall the name. But Father did receive a lot of letters – sometimes with foreign stamps on them. He was secretive about them. I'm afraid that my brother Huan and I used to tease him and say they must be love letters from ladies,' he said with a grin. 'But really we always supposed they were something to do with what had happened in China – the destruction of the monastery and the theft of the Moonbeam Diamond. I know that he kept in touch with others who had left the village, but talking about that time always made him very sad. We tried not to ask him too many questions.'

'Do you still have any of the letters?' Sophie asked eagerly.

'He usually burned them,' said Mr Lim. 'But there may be one or two left in his box.'

Song ran to fetch it. They'd opened Grandfather Lim's box once before, when they'd found the notebooks in which he had been carefully tracking Lord Beaucastle. Of course, then they had assumed that was because he had discovered that Beaucastle was the Baron – the same man who had stolen the Moonbeam Diamond, and who cast a shadow over most of the East End. But now Sophie began to wonder whether there could be more to Grandfather Lim's preoccupation with the Baron than they knew.

Song set the box down carefully in the centre of the table: a small wooden trunk, bound in brass. Mr Lim lifted the lid, and then with careful fingers, began to take things out. Last time she had only had eyes for the notebook about Lord Beaucastle, but now Sophie found herself looking keenly at two or three exercise books with densely written pages. One seemed to have been a kind of address book. Sophie took it and began leafing through in search of a mention of Colonel Fairley, whilst Mei and Song examined a bundle of old picture postcards. They were mostly inscribed with short, innocuous messages like '*All well*' or '*Weather fine – writing*'. There was nothing very unusual about them, but they were signed with initials rather than with names – *JB* and *NS*.

Rummaging in the box, Mr Lim pulled out a little tobacco tin, buried amongst the papers. It contained a small stick of red sealing wax – and to their great surprise, a gold signet ring, stamped with the symbol of the lion.

Mei stared at it in amazement. 'Look – it's the same seal that's on Colonel Fairley's envelope!' she exclaimed. 'The lion – like the lion on Grandfather's old cane. But what can it possibly mean?'

It was while the others were staring at the ring that Sophie caught a glimpse of something that made her heart stop. There was a letter nestling between the pages of an exercise book – a letter written in handwriting that she would recognise anywhere. It had been so long since she had seen it that a lump rose in her throat. Her voice faltered as she said: 'Look – everyone. Look at this.'

My Dear Friend,

I write to bid you farewell - I leave tomorrow for the voyage. I will write when I can, but do not expect to hear from me for at least two months. The journey will be a long one and will take me to some wild country, for all Fairley's intelligence points to our man being at present in a remote region of South Africa. I cannot help but think it would be fitting if it were there that I could run him to ground at last - on the same continent that he and I - and Alice - first met. My plans are carefully laid, but all the same. I know that I may fail. You of all people know what manner of an adversary I am facing. If the worst happens, all I ask is that you and Fairley will take care of my girl. There are so few of us left now and it breaks my heart to think of her all alone - or worse, stumbling into the path of the Fraternitas Draconum, without the protection of the Order.

I have asked Fairley to take charge of my financial affairs and have provided him with a copy of my will - as I fear my man of business is no longer to be trusted. I will also leave a letter with Fairley, bidding

Sophie farewell and explaining everything. Happily my greatest treasure is already in her hands she has no idea of its true worth, though it pleases me to see how close she keeps it.

I want you to keep the enclosed to give to her in the event I do not return. You know that I have wondered many times whether I ought to tell her the truth about my work, about the Order - and about Alice's death. But Alice always wanted her to have an ordinary girlhood - the opposite of what her own had been. I am thankful that at least I have been able to honor her in that.

This package will give Sophie all the information she needs when she discovers the truth. I know that you will help her understand it. Please keep it safe for me somewhere hidden - and I pray that I will return before the year is out and reclaim it myself, my task for the Order complete.

—

If I do not return, I know that I may rely upon you and Fairley to help my daughter. You have always been the best of friends to me. I know that you will be at her side, just as you have always, so faithfully been at mine.

My time is almost up - I sail at dawn Thank you, my good friend for everything.
In the name of the Loyal Order of Lions, we shall rebalance the scales.

Ad usque fidelis

R.T.C

CHAPTER TWENTY

On rainy Piccadilly, Sinclair's was a hive of activity. There were only a few days left until the Midnight Peacock Ball, and so whilst shoppers came hurrying up the steps out of the rain, shaking off their umbrellas, in search of fashionable hats and delicious confectionery, tea and cakes in the Ladies' Lounge, or luncheon in the Marble Court Restaurant, the Sinclair's staff were very busy indeed with all the final preparations.

As he hustled through the store with a stack of messages in the Captain's special yellow envelopes, which Miss Atwood had given him to deliver, Billy could see Claudine hard at work behind the plate-glass windows, screened from the street by silk curtains. She was removing the last of the Christmas displays, replacing them instead with *Maison Chevalier* fashions – and of course, displays of *Midnight Peacock* perfume. The scent came in a little glass bottle with a gilt stopper, presented in a purple box covered in a pattern of peacocks and crescent moons: now Claudine was carefully building a pyramid of these boxes against a drapery of brightly coloured silks, accompanied by a large painted peacock, and strings of gold and silver stars.

Out in the stable-yard, old George and a couple of the porters were hefting potted palms out of the back of a van, whilst a group of students from the Spencer rushed by carrying an assortment of paint tins and rolls of fabric. Billy spotted Leo's friend Connie amongst them and gave her a quick wave – but this was definitely not the sort of day when anyone had time to stop for a chat.

After handing his message to the Gaffer in the stables, Billy hurried back inside, along the passage, and out into the Entrance Hall which as usual was thronged with customers. As he passed by the door that led through to the great Exhibition Hall, he could hear a noise of sawing and hammering within, contrasting oddly with the thumping of piano keys and someone shouting 'one-two-one-two-one-two!' and then 'again, from the top, if you please!' indicating that Mr Lloyd and Mr Mountville were rehearsing the dancers. Up the stairs, through the Stationery Department, and past the door to the Library, he almost collided with Madame Lucille, who was hustling out of the mannequins' dressing room, a swathe of *Maison Chevalier* evening frocks draped over her arm.

There seemed to be a very large number of messages that day: one for Mrs Milton in Millinery; one for Jim in Sporting Goods; one for Miss Jenkins in the Toy Department; one for

215

Mr White in the Book Department. After delivering this last message, Billy hurried across the first-floor landing, but then hesitated for a moment by the door to the Taylor & Rose office, before pressing on.

He had to admit he was still feeling sore about what Lil had said. It was true that she had apologised very handsomely for losing her temper, and yet he couldn't help feeling that sometimes she did think of him as a silly little boy. But just because he didn't agree with her – just because he quite reasonably called into question this wild theory about Mr Sinclair teaming up with the Baron – that didn't make him a *mutton head*, he thought crossly.

As a matter of fact, he was just as smart as she was – and quite as good as a detective, even if he didn't get his name up in gold writing on the office door. He was even working on a mystery of his own, not that the girls had shown the slightest bit of interest in *that*. For a moment, he simmered with resentment, but then he reminded himself that all thoughts of the peculiar Lindwurm Enterprises had slipped immediately from his own mind when he had heard that they had once again stumbled across the path of the Baron. But whilst it was true that a mysterious factory that might, or might not, have some connection to the *Fraternitas Draconum* was not quite as exciting as discovering the Baron hidden in a secret room plotting an assassination, he felt certain that it was important just the same.

Now, he began mulling over it again. From what he and Joe had seen in Silvertown, the crates with the dragon symbol might well be full of the powerful new chemical the girl had told them about. What he couldn't understand is why on earth anyone would want to keep a whole lot of explosives in an office building. Surely that would be dangerous, wouldn't it? He remembered the girl's words: it *sets things on fire and makes 'em burn.*

As he strode through the door that led from the shop floor out on to the back stairs that the Sinclair's staff used, it came to him in a sudden flash. Of course! Explosives. Weapons. *Incendiary* weapons! When they had been investigating the disappearance of Veronica Whiteley's jewelled moth, they had discovered that the Baron had been working with a scientist, a fellow named Henry Snow. The Baron had plotted to marry Veronica, so that he could get his control of a rare mineral Snow had discovered in her father's mines, which they planned to use to create a *new incendiary weapon.*

Snow had been arrested of course and the plan had been foiled, but now Billy began to wonder whether the Baron – perhaps with the help of the *Fraternitas Draconum* – could have continued trying to make those new weapons? He might not have had access to the mines, but perhaps they had found another way to make the explosives – and that was what was happening at that factory! It would certainly explain why the crates had the dragon symbol stamped upon them. But what it still did not explain was *why* all those crates of explosives had been moved to that office opposite Sinclair's. Was it just a storeroom – a halfway house of some kind? Or was there some purpose for bringing incendiary weapons to Piccadilly?

Even as he asked himself the question, it all clicked together in his mind – like the final piece of a jigsaw. He spun around suddenly to return to the Taylor & Rose office, his feeling of being offended quite forgotten now, as he leapt down the stairs two at a time.

As he slammed open the office door, he saw that Joe, Lil and Sophie were already there, gathered around Sophie's desk. They all seemed to be staring at a piece of paper Sophie was holding in her hand.

'Billy – come quick – you have to see this!' Lil exclaimed, but he stood his ground and shook his head.

'Whatever it is, it will have to wait,' he said breathlessly. 'I think I've worked out how he's going to do it. I think I know what the Baron is planning on New Year's Eve.'

The cold air rushed against Tilly's cheeks, and her scarf streamed out into the wind, as Mr Pendleton accelerated along the empty road.

'Dashed fine machine, isn't she?' he shrieked, turning for a moment to beam at them both.

'Do keep your eyes on the road, Mr Pendleton!' Miss Leo shrieked back. She looked rather as though she might be sick, but Tilly had never felt half so thrilled in her life. Her insides fizzed with excitement like a sherbet fountain, and she found herself grinning back at Mr Pendleton. Mrs Dawes would have been horrified – ladies' maids were not supposed to grin at anyone, especially young gentlemen – but for once she was much too excited to care. It was hard to believe she was really here, riding in the passenger seat of Mr Pendleton's fine new automobile, on the road towards London, staring in fascination at the various intriguing buttons and levers and dials on the dashboard.

It had only been a few days since Miss Leo had first suggested that Tilly could accompany her back to town, but they had passed at what felt like break-neck speed. There were a great deal of people who had to agree to the idea: Miss Leo had talked to Mrs Dawes; Mrs Dawes had talked to Ma; Ma had talked to Tilly; and then Miss Leo and Mrs Dawes had spoken to Lady Fitzgerald. She was the only one who seemed dissatisfied.

'When I suggested you take a maid with you, Leonora, I really meant someone *older*,' Lady Fitzgerald had said, eyeing Tilly with disfavour. 'Someone who could act as a chaperone – and who could be trusted to be *responsible*.'

'But Tilly is the one that I want,' said Miss Leo in a small but definite voice, lifting her chin in the air.

'If you please, ma'am, I can vouch for the fact that Tilly is a very trustworthy girl,' Mrs Dawes ventured to add. 'She's been properly trained and I know that we can count on her to make sure that Miss Leonora is well looked after in London.'

After what seemed like hours, Lady Fitzgerald had shrugged and sighed and said she supposed she would give her permission *if she must* and Tilly and Miss Leo had exchanged delighted glances. Tilly had been plunged at once into a mad whirl of packing Miss Leo's things as well as her own, and making ready for the journey. Of course, they also had to find time to creep away and examine the secret passage and the secret room for clues. They had boldly ventured all the way along the passageway, and had looked carefully all around the hidden room – but there was not a single sign to suggest that anyone had been living there. It had been Tilly's idea to examine Mr Sinclair's room too – she'd checked the wastepaper basket and even explored the ashes in the grate, looking for the remnants of any papers he might have burned – but to her disappointment, she had found nothing unusual at all.

That hardly seemed to matter now that she was here, squashed into Mr Pendleton's motor with Miss Leo beside her. At first, they had planned to take the train back to London, but then Mr Pendleton had announced his intention to return to town the same day. Originally he had invited Miss Whiteley to drive with him; Tilly had overheard the invitation as she had carefully checked Miss Leo's things were all ready in the hall.

'I say, Miss Whiteley – why don't you drive back to Town with me in the motor?'

Mr Pendleton's voice was hopeful, but Miss Whiteley replied rather stiffly: 'Thank you, Mr Pendleton, but I don't think Isabel would allow that – not without a chaperone. Besides, I don't think we're leaving until tomorrow. Father says he has some important business to discuss with Lord Fitzgerald.'

'I see.' Mr Pendleton's voice was low and anxious. Then he blurted out: 'You – you aren't really going to marry Vincent, are you?'

There was an awkward pause and then Miss Whiteley said haughtily: 'I don't really see why that should be any of your business.'

'But the fellow's a frightful cad! And he's dreadfully rude to you! You can't let them make you do this,' Mr Pendleton said.

'I don't let anyone *make* me do anything,' said Veronica, and she turned and walked away from him along the hall.

Tilly thought Mr Pendleton seemed downcast after that, but he seemed quite his cheerful self again when Miss Leo said that she and Tilly would gladly accept his kind invitation to drive back to London. Tilly had hardly been able to wait to set off. She had packed her bag as quickly as she could with a mixture of frocks and petticoats and aprons, mixed up together with some books and the set of

221

tools that had been Alf's Christmas present – some small screwdrivers and spanners, some pliers and a wire-cutter. 'Never know when you might need a good screwdriver to hand,' Alf had said, with a grave nod.

It had felt very odd to say goodbye to Alf – and Mrs Dawes and Emma, and Lizzie and Charlie, and Mr Stokes, and all the rest. Sarah had looked as though she might cry as Tilly had hugged her and promised to write.

Last of all she'd said goodbye to Ma, breathing in her familiar smell of starch and soap and newly baked bread, and that had been strangest of all.

'Now, you be good, Tilly my girl. And be careful in that London. You get all sorts there. You'll take care of her now won't you, miss?' Ma said anxiously, turning to Miss Leo.

Miss Leo laughed. She looked very happy now that they were leaving Winter Hall. 'Don't worry, Cook – we'll take care of each other,' she said.

Then they were getting in the car, and Mr Pendleton was putting on his motoring goggles. Miss Whiteley came out to wave them off.

'I suppose I'll see you at Mr Sinclair's ball then,' she said vaguely, and Mr Pendleton nodded eagerly. 'Oh yes – jolly good!'

Then: 'Farewell, all!' he called out in a cheerful voice – and a moment later they were off, through the gates, and Winter Hall was growing smaller and smaller behind them.

CHAPTER TWENTY-ONE

'Wait,' Sophie begged. 'So – what you're saying is that you think the Baron is behind the manufacture of these explosives? And that he's planning to use them on the night of the New Year's Eve Ball?'

She felt overwhelmed. She was still reeling from the discovery of the extraordinary letter in Grandfather Lim's box – even now, her eyes kept straying towards it. But now there were new revelations to contend with.

'That's right!' Billy was explaining, all in a rush. 'That's why all those crates are over there in that office! Lindwurm Enterprises is just a front. Really it's the Baron who has taken the office – and he's keeping the boxes there all ready for New Year's Eve. Do you see what this means? *He's planning to blow up the store.* We know he's tried to do that before and we stopped him. This time he's going to use these explosives to assassinate the King.'

'But how can you be so sure that this factory place is connected to the Baron?' asked Lil.

'Because of the *dragon symbol*, of course. But that wasn't all. The factory itself – well there was something sinister about it, wasn't there?' Billy asked, turning to Joe to back him up.

'It wasn't a place you'd want to work, not if you had any choice,' Joe agreed. 'I've seen places like that before – run by the sort of folks that are so busy trying to make a profit that they don't think twice about the people who work for them.'

'Well, if this place does have something to do with the Baron then that doesn't surprise me in the slightest,' said Lil bluntly. 'After all, we know he doesn't care a fig for anyone just as long as he's making pots of money, and getting exactly what he wants.'

'Well that's exactly what he will get, if he succeeds in starting a war,' said Joe soberly. 'He'll be able to make a mint I s'pose, selling a lot of powerful new weapons to the government – or to any other country in Europe, come to that.'

Sophie frowned, trying to fix her attention on what Billy had said. She could see that his explanation made sense – and yet there was something about it that didn't seem quite right.

While she was trying to think it through, Lil spoke up: 'But if Mr Sinclair really is working with the Baron on this – why would he agree to a plan like that? He might want the store to be on the front pages of the newspapers – but surely he couldn't possibly want it to be blown up – and destroyed altogether! That would defeat the point!'

'Exactly!' said Billy, puffing out his chest. 'Isn't that what I've been saying all along? But now we know about the explosives, we *know* that Mr Sinclair can't possibly be part of the Baron's plan. Whoever the Baron is working with, it must be someone else – maybe even that lady that we saw at the factory.'

'You saw a lady?' repeated Sophie in surprise. 'Er – I don't suppose it was a small old lady with white hair, and a velvet hat?'

Billy and Joe looked rather confused. 'No – she wasn't old. Probably about forty,' said Billy, screwing up his face as he tried to remember. 'Very smart with a fur coat and a big hat.'

Lil shook her head at Sophie. 'You ought to forget about the train lady – I'm sure she was just a harmless nosy old woman! But I do think it is rather curious that it was a woman you saw at the factory,' she said to Billy in a more serious tone. 'After all, we've never known the Baron to team up with a woman before. There weren't any women at that meeting of the *Fraternitas Draconum* you saw, were there, Sophie? And women aren't even *allowed* through the doors of Wyvern House,' she finished, sounding quite disgusted.

'The girl we spoke to said she thought the lady might be the boss's wife,' said Joe. 'P'raps it's her husband who is the member of the society?'

Sophie frowned. Her thoughts were all in a muddle. One thing was sure though – they must let Sergeant Thomas know about the factory and the explosives. She got up and went swiftly over to the telephone, hoping he would understand that they hadn't disobeyed his orders. They hadn't *meant* to investigate further – it had just happened.

She asked the operator for Scotland Yard and waited impatiently for the call to connect.

'Detective Sergeant Thomas, please,' she asked the clerk who answered.

'I am afraid Sergeant Thomas is out at present, madam,' replied the clerk politely.

'Do you know when he is expected to return?'

'I'm afraid not, madam. Would you like me to give him a message?'

'Could you tell him that Miss Taylor called – from Taylor & Rose – and ask him to telephone or call upon me as soon as is convenient. It's rather urgent.'

'Of course, madam.'

'Wait – I don't suppose Detective Inspector Worth has returned as yet?'

'I'm afraid he is still away, madam. Is there anything else I can help you with?'

'No – no, I don't think so.'

'Thank you, madam. Goodbye.'

Sophie stayed in the office later than usual that night. After their conference about Lindwurm Enterprises, Joe and Billy had gone back to work, and Lil had gone out on an errand to the theatre. Sophie had remained behind, hoping that Sergeant Thomas would telephone – but there had been no calls.

The truth was she did not really want to go back to her lonely lodging-house room. In spite of their growing suspicions of Mr Sinclair, she still felt better here in the cosy office, knowing that all the usual busy activity of the store was going on around her. Somehow it was easier to contemplate her father's letter here, lying on her desk as though it were just another piece of evidence in a case she had to solve.

Thinking of it like that made her feel a little better. She picked it up once more, trying to look coolly at it as though it was a quite ordinary document and not one of the final letters that her father had ever written – a letter that suggested he had been well aware of what he was facing, and the possibility that he would never return.

She leaned back in her chair, trying to think logically. The letter certainly revealed a great deal. She made a mental list, ticking each piece of information off on her fingers as she went. One: Colonel Fairley and Grandfather Lim had both known her papa. They had been friends – and that was remarkable enough. Two: they had certainly all been well aware of the existence of the *Fraternitas Draconum* – and it sounded as though they considered the society to be their enemy. Three: her papa had travelled to South Africa following the trail of a man who surely could only have been the Baron. Four: he had been all too aware that his mission was dangerous, and could go wrong. Five: he had made careful preparations to ensure that she, his daughter, would be safe and well looked after.

She found herself staring again at the last paragraphs of the letter: *If I do not return I know that I may rely upon you . . . to help my daughter. You have always been the best of friends to me – I know that you will be at her side, just as you have always, so faithfully, been at mine.*

Logic failed her. Her eyes clouded with tears, and all at once, she pushed the letter away. How could he have done that to her – just bid her farewell, and disappear off to South Africa as though it was merely an ordinary military mission? How could it be that the two men he had charged to take care of her had *both* died, leaving her utterly alone? For a moment, the letters on the page swam as she thought how different the last year might have been, if she had had the likes of Colonel Fairley and Grandfather Lim at her side. The unfairness of it blazed through her. Her mother,

her father, Colonel Fairley – every single person who could have helped her or cared for her had been taken away. It was as though the Baron *wanted* to make her as alone as she could possibly be,

Yet there was more in the letter, and now she pulled it back towards her. What had Papa meant when he had said that her mother had had 'the opposite' of an 'ordinary girlhood'? What was the 'greatest treasure' which was 'already in her hands'? What had he meant by 'the truth about his work and the order'? What work was he talking about? For the hundredth time, she traced the shape of the words 'the Loyal Order of Lions'. The lion was important – the lion on the red wax seal, the lion on the head of Leo's cane – it *meant* something. Images of lions and dragons seemed to dance about in her head, like pictures she had seen of old flags and shields: Benedetto Casselli's dragon paintings tangling themselves up with the tapestries at Winter Hall of lions and unicorns and knights and ancient battles. *In the name of the Loyal Order of Lions, we shall rebalance the scales. Ad usque fidelis.* She knew the last few words were Latin, but she had never learned any. She had no idea what it meant.

Most of all, she wondered what it was that her papa had given Grandfather Lim to look after for her. He had said it would give her 'all the information she would need'. After they had found the letter, they had searched

Grandfather Lim's box again – but there was nothing more that suggested even the slightest connection to Sophie or her father. Now she sighed, and sadly traced the shape of his initials once again: *R T C.*

She did not know how long she sat there, staring at the letter, but after a while she became aware that the fire was almost out and she had grown stiff and cold in her chair. The room was very dark, and she knew it must be late – she ought to go before Sid and Mr Betteredge locked up the store for the night. She got up hastily and put on her hat and coat, tucking the letter into her pocket.

As she closed the office door behind her, she realised that it was even later than she had thought. The store was already closed, and most of the lights had been turned out. Here and there a small pool of lamplight was still visible on the shop floor, indicating where someone was working late.

She hurried quickly down the back stairs, and out along the gallery, putting on her gloves as she did so. Below her, the Entrance Hall was quiet and dark, but for the pale gleam of reflected light from the street lamps outside. There was a faint hum in the air, and for a moment, she felt uneasy. She had never quite got used to the shop after hours, dark and empty of people, and now, she jumped at the sight of some shadowy figures moving across the Entrance Hall – but at once relaxed, seeing the familiar figure of Sid Parker.

He had what appeared to be a roll of red carpet over his shoulder, and Claudine was hurrying after him, her feet tapping over the marble floor, and her arms stuffed full of coloured cloths that Sophie realised were Union Jack flags.

Union Jack flags – and a red carpet? They must be for the King's visit to the ball, Sophie thought, staring after them. Her brow furrowed anxiously. Sergeant Thomas never had returned her telephone call. He had promised that he would take care of everything, he had seemed to understand when they had explained that the King must not appear at the ball, and yet here were the staff of Sinclair's, still going ahead with all their preparations for his attendance.

Preoccupied by this, it took her a moment to notice that two more figures were coming out of the Exhibition Hall. One looked around covertly, whilst the other softly closed the door behind them, and then they began hurrying up the stairs together, talking in low, intense voices. Something about them seemed to suggest that they did not want to be seen, and instinct made Sophie step back into the shadows. As they approached, she realised that one of the figures was Mr Sinclair, whom she had not set eyes on since their return from Winter Hall. She watched as the two men passed by without glimpsing her – and then had to stifle a little gasp of surprise.

The man Mr Sinclair was talking to was the police

detective – Sergeant Thomas himself! Was he talking to Mr Sinclair about the party – could he be telling him about the assassination, and making plans to prevent it? But surely if he suspected there was a chance Mr Sinclair might himself be involved, he wouldn't do that? A chill rushed over her as something unsettling occurred. Could it be that the two men were working together to take forward the Baron's plan?

She felt cold as ice. It would certainly not have been the first time they had encountered a crooked policeman, under the Baron's influence. Now, she had the sudden, frightening realisation that she had nothing more than Sergeant Thomas's word that he would help. What if he had lied to them? What if he had really been working for the Baron all along?

CHAPTER TWENTY-TWO

New Year's Eve in London dawned clear and cold, with frost shimmering on the rooftops, and glittering on the branches of the trees in the park. At Sinclair's the staff arrived early, hurrying over the icy cobbles of the stable-yard and in through the staff entrance, full of excitement for the Midnight Peacock Ball.

'It doesn't feel like a normal day. It feels like a kind of holiday,' said Violet, as she came into the cloakroom.

'I can't wait to see the fireworks!' exclaimed Minnie, hanging her hat on the peg. 'I do hope Mrs Milton will let us have a look at them.'

'What I really want to see is Mr Lloyd and Mr Mountville's show. *Midnight Extravaganza*, it's called. Miss Kitty Shaw's going to be starring as the Midnight Peacock!'

'Ooh I'd love to see that!' said Minnie longingly. 'Just think – Kitty Shaw! Though I suppose properly she's Kitty Whitman now she's married to that wonderful Mr Whitman. I wonder if he'll be in the show too?'

'Well I shouldn't get too excited about it if I were you,' said Edith, tilting her nose in the air with all the importance of an Assistant Buyer. 'Mrs Milton told me we're going to be very busy all evening. I daresay there won't be time to see any shows.'

'But maybe we'll get to see the King,' said Violet. 'We'd better practise our curtsies, just in case!'

'Ooh – will we really have to curtsey?' asked Minnie, wide-eyed.

'Of course you will, idiot,' said Edith witheringly. 'That's what you do in the presence of royalty.'

'Fancy being in the presence of royalty!' breathed Minnie. 'I think I might faint!'

Still chattering, the Millinery salesgirls hurried on their way, but a moment later the cloakroom door opened again, and in came Song Lim, hustling out of his coat. Behind him was Sophie, looking anxious.

'No – no one's breathed a word about cancelling the Royal visit,' said Song, as he quickly tied on the white apron that all the staff in the Marble Court kitchens wore. 'I think Monsieur Bernard would go off his head if they did. Everyone's working like mad to make sure we've got the King's favourite dishes ready.' He reeled off the names proudly: '*Fillet de Truites à la Russe* and *ortolons* in Armagnac, and *Chartreuse de Pêches à la Royale* . . .'

He'd never even heard of some of those dishes a few days

ago but already, Song felt like he was staring to understand how things worked in the kitchens of the Marble Court Restaurant. All right, so he might be only a kitchen porter – much too lowly to do any real cooking – but even being in the kitchens with Monsieur Bernard and his chefs was an education. Now, he hurried off, not wanting to be so much as a second late, leaving Sophie staring uneasily after him.

Everyone seemed to be in a terrific hurry that morning. All around the store, porters were whizzing to and fro with boxes, whilst salesgirls hurtled between storeroom and counter and back again. In the kitchens, Monsieur Bernard's chefs were stirring sauces and whisking eggs at break-neck speed, even as Song raced around them, clearing away plates and saucepans. Just before eleven o'clock, Monsieur Chevalier's peacocks arrived in their own special van, accompanied by a handler in white gloves. On the way up to the roof gardens, one of them escaped, and somehow found its way into the Millinery Department where Mrs Milton, who was a little short-sighted, momentarily mistook it for a new *Maison Chevalier* hat and had to be sent home for a lie-down after she realised it wasn't.

Meanwhile, up in the offices, Monsieur Chevalier was suffering from a bad fit of last-minute nerves, and could be heard declaiming that everything was going to go wrong, and if they had only let him create his Venetian lagoon with gondolas everything would have been perfectly all right, until Miss Atwood was forced to send Billy running for a restorative glass of cognac for him from the Gentlemen's Club Room.

Below them, in the office of Taylor & Rose, Sophie was becoming increasingly worried. Desperately hoping to reach Detective Inspector Worth, she had telephoned Scotland Yard three times more, and each time had been blandly told: 'No, madam, I am afraid that the Inspector has not yet returned.' At last, she put on her hat and coat, and hurried out to the post office. She had decided the time had come to send a telegram to Mr McDermott.

Even as Sophie hurried down Piccadilly, Billy and Joe were making their way back into the stable-yard, after taking Lucky and Daisy for a quick walk to the park. The stable-yard was even busier than usual: not only were the usual procession of vans heading out with the morning's deliveries, but many more were arriving, laden with supplies for the ball. Porters were struggling with enormous trunks inscribed with the words *Maison Chevalier*, cases of champagne and boxes of sumptuous-looking fruit were being unloaded, and Mr Lloyd and Mr Mountville's band had just arrived with a van full of musical instruments. As the boys stopped to watch, they saw that yet another van was arriving, pulled by a pair of smart black horses. As it clattered past them, Billy gasped in recognition.

'That's the firework feller, that is,' said old George, nodding in the direction of the big van. 'Come to finish setting up all his fireworks for tonight. Quite an arrangement he's got – he showed it to the lads yesterday. Shame you weren't here, young Billy, you'd have liked to see it. A queer little box he has, what runs on a clockwork timer. He connects it up to all the fireworks with electric cables and it sets 'em off at just the right moment one after another – without him so much as lifting a finger! Like a magic trick it is. Clever feller, I reckon.'

Billy was still gaping at the van. 'But – but – that van – it's got a *dragon* painted on it!' he exclaimed, pointing.

'That's right,' said George nodding. 'That's for his company. Top fireworks specialists, he said. Ah, you can always count on the Captain to make sure Sinclair's has nothing but the best.'

'*Lindwurm Enterprises* . . .' murmured Joe.

'That's the one – knew it was some kind of funny-sounding name,' said George. 'Heard of them, have you, lad? Well he seems to know what he's doing all right. He's got his fireworks up on the rooftops of the buildings all round Piccadilly Circus – peacock colours he says they are, blue and green and purple and the like. Once he's got his little box up there and connected, it'll have 'em all shooting off on the dot of midnight. We're in for a rare treat. You lads make sure you get along to Piccadilly Circus later and have a gander – you don't want to miss it.' He winked at them, and then looked up sharply. 'Here, Tom – Alf – what do you think you're doing monkeying about with that box? There could be crystal glasses for His Majesty himself to drink from in there, for all you know!'

As he shuffled off, Joe and Billy stared at each other and then back at the van. The doors were open now, revealing wooden crates stamped with a very familiar twisting dragon. A tall, powerful man with black hair streaked with white, had clambered down from the van, and was opening up the doors. Billy grabbed Joe's arm.

'Joe – that's *him*! The man I saw across the road in that office – the man I thought I recognised!'

Joe looked at the man for a long moment, and then to Billy's enormous astonishment, he grabbed his friend by the scruff of the neck, and dragged him into one of the empty stables, the two dogs scampering after them, convinced that this was some new and particularly exciting game.

'What's up with you?' asked Billy, taken aback.

'D'you really mean to tell me that you can't remember where you've seen him before?' demanded Joe.

Billy shook his head. 'No!' he protested. 'But he can't really be a fireworks expert – can he?'

Before Joe could answer, they heard the sudden tapping of footsteps, and then Lil appeared before them in the doorway. 'What are you two doing hiding in here?' she asked. She stared around the stable fondly. 'I say, it makes you think of the days we had to work on our cases up in the hayloft instead of having our own proper office, doesn't it? Anyway, I've been looking for you all over, Billy. A funny little red-haired fellow turned up just now asking for you. He wanted to speak to you and said it was fearfully important. In the end he left a message but I had to promise to put it into your own hands and no one else's. He was jolly mysterious about it. Look – here it is!'

She held out a folded note, but neither of the boys even looked at it.

'Turn round,' said Joe in a low, urgent voice. 'No – don't say anything. Just look at that man unloading the boxes from the black van. You recognise him, don't you?'

When Lil turned back to them, her face was as white as Joe's. 'I'll say I recognise him,' she said, her voice wobbling with astonishment. 'Good heavens – what on earth is *he* doing here?'

Tilly stared open-mouthed at the grand edifice of Sinclair's, as she followed Miss Leo up the steps. She knew all about Sinclair's, of course – everyone knew about London's famous department store. In the kitchens of Winter Hall they'd pored over the wonderful photographs of it in the illustrated papers. But now she was really here, amongst all the noise of Piccadilly, the honking of motor horns and the roar of omnibuses, and the great building loomed over her like a temple. She had not realised that any shop could be like this.

A tall man in a smart blue-and-gold uniform swept the doors open with a low bow, as if she were as grand as the Countess of Alconborough herself. Inside, she took in a deep breath of air perfumed with chocolate and spice and a dozen more delicious scents she couldn't even name. They were standing in a huge marble hall, with a magnificent fountain in the centre of it. A fountain – *inside* a shop! Ma would never believe it.

Miss Leo was already hurrying onwards, through the crowds of richly dressed people carrying gorgeously wrapped boxes. Outside the elevator doors, the lift operative, asked: 'Which floor, madam?'

'First floor please,' replied Miss Leo, and they stepped inside. Tilly had never travelled by elevator before, and as it swished upwards, she could hardly decide what to look at first: the cables and weights that made it work, the shiny brass fittings, or the glamorous lift operative in her blue-and-gold uniform and her matching blue boots. Tilly lost her heart to those boots almost at once. But there was no time to look around any longer, for the doors were already opening again, and they stepped out of the lift on to the busy shop floor.

'I suppose all these people are here because of the ball tonight?' she managed to ask, as she hurried after Miss Leo.

'Oh no - Sinclair's is always like this,' Miss Leo explained. 'Look - here we are. This is Sophie and Lil's office.'

She tapped on the door with Taylor & Rose printed across it in gold lettering, and then went inside. In the office that lay beyond, Tilly saw that Sophie and Lil were standing around a desk with two boys and - rather to her surprise - two dogs, one a large Alsatian, and the other a small black pug with bulbous eyes, who came running over to snuffle around them at once. Miss Leo bent down to stroke the dog's silky little head. 'Hullo, all,' she announced. 'We're here!'

But not one of them was listening - or even looking in their direction.

'I must say, I've sometimes wondered about all these beastly files and notes you insist on, Billy,' Lil was saying, her hands on her hips. 'But for the first time I see the point. It's *definitely* him - there can be no doubt about it. The man who helped the Baron try to blow up Sinclair's before, when the clockwork sparrow was stolen. The one who locked us up in that summerhouse in the roof garden!'

Sophie was staring at a photograph lying on the desk. '*Mr Raymond Fitzwilliam*,' she said aloud. 'Former actor. Worked for the Baron - and actually posed as the Baron

241

himself on more than one occasion. Not to mention the fact that he almost had us all killed.'

'Er - ought we to come back later?' asked Miss Leo tentatively.

Sophie looked up from the photograph, and then beckoned them in. 'No - no. Come in and shut the door. I believe we may have figured out what's going to happen at the ball tonight - and I rather think we're going to need your help.'

The six of them sat in a serious circle in the Taylor & Rose office. Tilly had never attended a meeting in a detective agency before, and she kept staring around, trying to take it all in.

Billy had his notebook before him and a pencil in his hand, and he was scribbling notes vigorously. The folder marked '*The Baron*' lay in front of Sophie, open to a photograph of Lil, posing in a tea-gown - and behind her, amongst the grandeur of the Marble Court Restaurant, the figure of a tall, powerfully built man, whose dark hair was streaked with white. He was expensively dressed, with a silver-topped cane, heavy rings on his fingers and a scarf at his neck.

'You're quite certain that this is the man you saw?' Sophie asked, tapping the picture.

Billy, Joe and Lil all nodded. 'He's dressed differently

now – but it's the same man all right,' said Lil.

'He says he works for Lindwurm Enterprises – a company that specialises in fireworks,' explained Billy. 'He's here setting up the fireworks for the display tonight. But we know those crates don't really have fireworks in them. They're explosives. He works for the Baron – and they're planning to use the fireworks as cover for the bombs.'

'So when the fireworks go off at midnight there won't be any wonderful spectacle,' said Sophie. 'Instead there'll be fires and explosions all around Piccadilly Circus. That's what the Baron meant when he talked about chaos on the streets – and setting London alight.'

'But hundreds of people will be there to see the fireworks!' exclaimed Leo. 'They could be terribly hurt – or killed!'

Sophie rubbed her face with her hands. 'We have to try and find a way to stop it,' she said desperately. 'We have to –'

But her sentence was left unfinished. Just then the door banged open again and Jack came striding in, his sketchbook clutched in his hand.

'Oh good – everyone's here,' he said, untangling himself from his scarf. 'Look – I need to talk to you all. I've been sitting in the studio puzzling over that drawing that Lil and

I found in that secret room at Winter Hall, and I rather think I've worked something out.'

'Never mind that now!' said Lil impatiently. 'We've got something much more critical to think about than fussing with drawings.'

But Sophie was already looking with interest at the sketchbook Jack was holding. She had forgotten all about the diagram that Jack had copied from the secret room. 'What is it?' she asked, with a sudden feeling of excitement.

Jack set the drawing down on the desk in front of them. 'I couldn't work out what it was supposed to be at first but I've been looking at it, and I rather think it's Piccadilly Circus.' He pointed with a pencil to the central circle.

'Look – that's Piccadilly Circus itself – with the fountain in the middle. And these are the roads – Regent Street, Shaftesbury Avenue and Piccadilly.'

'And that square with the S on it – that must be Sinclair's!' exclaimed Sophie.

Billy was so excited that he could hardly get his words out. 'Look – look – and that's the dragon symbol! It marks the building across the street. That's the office of Lindwurm Enterprises, where they're keeping the explosives that the *Fraternitas Draconum* have been making!'

'*Lindwurm?*' repeated Jack in surprise.

'Yes – that's the name they're using as a cover.'

Jack stared at him. 'Well it's not much of a cover, is it – if it's something to do with the *Fraternitas Draconum?*'

'What do you mean?' asked Lil.

'Well – *Lindwurm* is German for dragon. They're really *Dragon* Enterprises.'

They all gasped and then Lil snapped her fingers. 'Wait – that boy who came up here with the note earlier. Didn't he say something about Lindwurm Enterprises too?'

Billy had almost forgotten the piece of paper that Lil had given him. Now he quickly unfolded it and read it aloud:

245

STRICTLY CONFIDENTIAL
31 DECEMBER 1909

Dear Mr. Parker,
    Further to our discussion of 24 December
I write to inform you of a suspicious
circumstance at the offices of Lindwurm
Enterprises. Whilst all the crates have
now been removed from the premises,
yesterday a large box was
delivered marked LEE ENFIELD.
I thought you would wish to be
aware of this matter.
Yours faithfully

Stanley Briggs Esq
Douglas Webber Publishing

'Lee Enfield?' repeated Leo, confused. 'Who's that?'

But Billy had read too many Montgomery Baxter stories not to know exactly what the words meant. '*Guns*,' he hissed in a low voice. 'Lee-Enfield is a type of *gun*!'

The office was suddenly filled with a clamour of noise, but Sophie silenced everyone quickly. 'Listen!' she said. 'We've got to work this out – and quickly. Maybe the diagram will help us stop the Baron's plot.'

They turned back to Jack's sketchbook, filled with a new energy. 'The thing I can't puzzle out is what all these lines signify,' said Jack, pointing with his pencil. 'Or this box here, marked CONTROLS.'

'Wait,' said Joe, thinking fast. He turned to Billy. 'What did old George say to us about the fireworks? Didn't he say they were connected up somehow with wires to a sort of box – with a clockwork mechanism that would set them off at midnight?'

'So perhaps CONTROLS is the box?' said Billy.

'And those lines – they could be the wires that connect them?' suggested Sophie.

'But how could a box and some wires set off fireworks – or explosives for that matter?' asked Lil, puzzled. 'Wouldn't they need a flame to ignite them?'

Sophie was frowning. 'Could it be something rather like the mechanism that the Baron used for the bomb in the clock at Sinclair's?'

Tilly had been struggling to follow everything that was happening, but this she understood. 'It could work with an electric charge,' she said. The others turned to stare at her, and she found her cheeks getting hot as she explained:

'If the control box has a clock in it, it could switch on an electric current when the clock hits midnight. The current would run down wires connected to the box and heat up a contact at the end of each wire. That would light the fuses on the fireworks, and then they would go off. I've never seen it done, but I suppose setting it up like that would mean you could create a display where each group of fireworks were set to go off at exactly the right moment.'

'Gosh – how awfully clever!' exclaimed Lil.

Joe was frowning. 'So do you mean to say that to stop them going off – all we'd have to do is cut through or disconnect the wires?'

Tilly nodded. 'I think so.'

'But where *are* these wires?' asked Billy. 'We haven't seen any electric cables being laid out in the street.'

'But the fireworks aren't in the street, are they? They're positioned up on the roofs of the buildings. So maybe the cables are strung up high on the roofs too – all connecting back to the central control box,' said Joe.

'What's that building where the controls are marked?' asked Lil, turning the plan upside down and then the right way up again, as she tried to make sense of it. 'Oh, I know – isn't that the Piccadilly Restaurant?'

'And I suppose all these crosses must indicate where the fireworks are to be set,' said Sophie.

'But – they're all around Piccadilly,' said Leo. 'If these

really are explosives – and they go off . . .' Her voice trailed away in horror.

'I say, Billy, I'm beginning to think you were right all along,' said Lil, shaking her head vigorously. 'Surely Mr Sinclair couldn't do a thing like this. Not harming all those people – not to mention destroying his own store. Look – there's an X on the roof of Sinclair's too.'

'But look,' said Jack again. 'The mark on the roof of Sinclair's is different. It's a small black x – only a few buildings have that mark – most of them have a big red one. Then there's this key at the side. The small black crosses mean F and the big red ones stand for E. What do you suppose it means?'

Billy's face was grim. 'E is for explosive. F is for firework? The big red cross means explosives. The small one could be ordinary fireworks.'

'But if the Baron really wants to create all this chaos – why wouldn't all of the buildings have explosives? Why would any of them be just ordinary fireworks?' wondered Lil aloud.

'Perhaps including some real fireworks helps to conceal what they're really up to?' suggested Sophie. 'And of course, it would also mean that those buildings wouldn't be seriously harmed. Including Sinclair's itself . . .'

Silence fell for a moment as they all took this in – then Lil spoke again: 'Well – it doesn't matter. Whoever is behind this, we have to stop it. If those electric cables are strung up on the rooftops above Piccadilly Circus, how are we going to get up there to cut them?'

'Surely the easiest thing would be simply to get to the control box itself,' said Sophie. She turned to Tilly. 'If we could find it, do you think you'd know how to disconnect it?'

Tilly frowned. 'I . . . I don't know. Maybe – I've never done anything like that before . . . but . . .' She thought of the books she had read, and Miss Jones saying she was one of the brightest pupils she'd had the pleasure of teaching, and Alf saying he'd never known anyone get her head round the workings of an engine like Tilly, and how she had been the one to fix Mrs Dawes' broken carriage clock, when no one else could. Her voice was stronger as she answered: 'But I can try! I suppose the best thing would be to stop the timer. If we can stop that, the explosion wouldn't happen.'

'Very well – so the first thing to do is find this control box,' said Lil promptly. 'We'll have to trail Fitzwilliam and find out where he puts it. But we'd better not let ourselves be seen. If we recognise him then he might well recognise us. Then, after dark, we can creep back – and Tilly can disconnect it.'

'Hang on – I've thought of something,' said Joe. 'Look, if the Baron really has got Mr Sinclair and Sergeant Thomas – not to mention Fitzwilliam – in on his plot, then it's not going to be enough just to stop the explosions, is it? What about the King? Even if the Baron's got these explosives rigged up all around Piccadilly Circus, he can't be counting on those for the assassination. They're too hit and miss. Besides, the King isn't going to be out there in the crowd, he's going to be –'

'Here,' finished Lil. 'Here – at Sinclair's.'

'Oh gosh,' said Leo, her eyes widening. 'Do you suppose that's what the guns are for?'

Sophie took in a deep breath. She looked at Joe and Billy. 'Look – you two should help Tilly find and deactivate this control box. Leave the rest of us to worry about protecting the King.'

'But how are you going to do that?' asked Billy anxiously. 'What if the Baron turns up at Sinclair's – with a gun?'

Lil shook her head. 'He won't do that. We know he doesn't like getting his hands dirty. Besides, people know what he looks like now. He'd be certain to be recognised at once. No – I think he'll have someone else to do the job for him undercover – maybe someone like Fitzwilliam.'

'That fits with what I overheard him saying,' exclaimed Sophie. 'Something about getting the King into position so they would have him in their sights. I didn't know what he meant then – but *sights* means a gun, doesn't it?'

'So the Baron is planning to blow up Piccadilly Circus – while a gunman goes after the King at Sinclair's?' Jack said.

He gave a stunned laugh of amazement.

Sophie stared up at the clock on the mantelpiece. 'That's right,' she said. 'And we've got less than twelve hours to stop it.'

Billy looked desperately at her. 'But – but how can we? We've hardly any time, we don't know who we can trust, we don't really know what the Baron's plan is. I know we've done some dangerous things before – but we're talking about *guns* and *bombs*. Surely we ought to just – I don't know – try again to reach Inspector Worth – or send a telegram to Mr McDermott?'

Sophie shook her head. 'It's too late now. I can't reach Worth, and I've sent McDermott a telegram already but I've not heard anything. I know he's moving around a good deal, so it may be days before he gets it. We can't count on him to appear and save the day. We're alone, and we have no choice. We *have* to save those people – we simply *can't* let the Baron win!'

She stared around at them all: Billy's anxious face, Lil's nodding fervently, Leo looking pale and frightened, Tilly wide-eyed, Joe very grave. All at once, she realised that this was what had sent her father to South Africa. This was why he had risked everything – to stop the Baron once and for all. Now she knew that she must do the same.

Her heart began to beat faster. 'We don't have much time, but if we plan carefully, and work together, we can pull this off. And though we may not be able to count on Scotland Yard or Mr McDermott or even Mr Sinclair to help us this time, there are people who we *can* trust, and who we can call on to help.'

Lil sat up very straight in her chair. 'Sophie's right,' she said. 'We have to try.'

'But Billy's right too,' Joe added quietly. 'No point sugaring it. This is going to be tough. Fitzwilliam is a villain, and he'd be enough to contend with by himself – but we may have to face the Baron too. We know he's fallen on hard times, so he's going to be desperate – and desperation makes people dangerous. We've been lucky before but you all know that we can't afford to underestimate him. He'll stop at nothing to get what he wants. We're going to have a real fight on our hands.'

They all looked at each other sombrely, but then Lil spoke up. 'Well luckily we happen to know quite a few people who are rather good at standing up for themselves in a fight,' she said. She paused and looked over the table. 'I say, Sophie – do you think it's about time we told everyone what we've really been doing at Sewing Society?'

PART V
Murder at the Ball

'Inspector!' exclaimed Montgomery Baxter, in a terrible voice. 'If we do not act, then I fear there will surely be a murder done before tonight is through!'

CHAPTER TWENTY-THREE

Sophie sat still in Monsieur Pascal's chair, as the Sinclair's hairdresser curled, twisted and pinned her hair. The face that looked back at her from the looking glass seemed strange to her – skin lightly dusted with powder, lips softly coloured with lip-rouge. She wore a brand-new *Maison Chevalier* outfit she had been given for the occasion: a green velvet frock with a green and gold sash at the waist, accompanied with high-heeled gold pumps. Monsieur Pascal was humming contentedly to himself as he completed her hairstyle with long gold pins decorated with sparkling jewelled peacock feathers. She felt quite unlike her usual self: the only thing she recognised about herself was Mama's string of green beads around her neck. Now, she put up a hand to feel the familiar shape of them, but Monsieur Pascal slapped it away at once. 'No fidgeting!'

Beside her, Lil sneezed, whilst Monsieur Pascal's assistant dusted her face with a fluffy powder puff. She looked even more stunning than usual in a magnificent gown of dark purple satin and lighter purple tulle, with gold embroidery at the neck, and a jewelled bandeau upon her gleaming hair.

All around them, people were flitting to and fro: Madame Lucille hurrying by with shoes or fans; mannequins, still in their petticoats, scrutinising their faces in the looking glass; dancers helping each other to lace up their costumes, or sitting in corners stitching a ballet-shoe ribbon more firmly into place. The air smelled of greasepaint and powder and the hot, burned smell of Monsieur Pascal's curling tongs – and everywhere the distinctive rich scent of *Maison Chevalier's Midnight Peacock*.

Amongst the hubbub, there had been little chance for her to talk to Lil, but Sophie knew that they were both thinking about the same thing – the evening that loomed ahead of them. They had no very clear idea of what the Baron's plan was, and in spite of their preparations, it was difficult to see how they could possibly stop him. Sophie's heart was fluttering, and she kept casting anxious glances over her shoulder, as though she expected the Baron himself to pop out of the shadows at any moment.

'Stop fidgeting!' scolded Monsieur Pascal again, jabbing her with a hairpin, and Sophie tried to sit still. She reminded herself that it was unlikely that the Baron himself would dare to make an appearance at Sinclair's – and even if he did, it was highly improbable that he would turn up in the beauty salon.

Just then, Mr Mountville came striding in and made a beeline for Lil. 'There you are,' he began briskly. 'Look – there's been a change of plan. I'm going to need you for the show tonight.'

Lil looked at him in astonishment, and then sneezed again as the assistant spritzed on yet more *Midnight Peacock*. 'I say – what do you mean?'

'Kitty has cancelled on us. Says she's unwell – but really it seems she's decided she doesn't like her costume. Of course, you can always count on her for some last-minute drama! Anyway, I'm missing a star – so I need you to take her place.'

'Me?' asked Lil, momentarily shocked into silence. Her eyes shone and for a moment, Sophie knew that she was thinking of nothing beyond the fact that Mr Mountville had chosen *her* to star in place of West End darling Miss Kitty Shaw – and the chance she would have to show everyone what she could do. But then realisation dawned, and her eyes darkened. She shook her head. 'I'm sorry, Mr Mountville, I can't.'

But the theatre producer would not let her finish. 'Nonsense. I've cleared it with Mr Betteredge. Miss Taylor here can easily represent Taylor & Rose tonight. The part itself is easy: for most of the show you sit on the big crescent moon showing off your costume, and then you descend for the final number. Miss Sylvia will go over the dance steps with you just as soon as you're dressed.'

Lil opened her mouth to speak but Mountville cut her off again. 'I won't take no for an answer. The costume will fit you and you're a quick study. You can do this as easy as winking – and don't pretend to me you've suddenly become infected with stage fright! Come on – get out of that dress and Maurice will help you into the peacock costume.'

Lil gave Sophie one desperate glance as Mr Mountville hauled her away, the assistant looking after her in confusion, still clutching her powder puff and scent sprayer.

Quite used to this kind of chaos, Monsieur Pascal merely shrugged and went on skewering Sophie's hair with pins. But Sophie's heart was beating even faster now. If Lil was going to be in the show, that meant Sophie would not be able to count on her help. The task they had set themselves had already seemed difficult enough: now a feeling of dread began to rise in her stomach, as she began to wonder if it was downright impossible.

On the streets outside Sinclair's, there was a hum of excitement in the air, as people began to gather on Piccadilly Circus. A barrel organ was playing beside the fountain, and street hawkers were offering roasted chestnuts, and spiced punch, and hot pies for a penny. People were streaming into the Criterion Theatre and the Piccadilly Restaurant and up the grand steps of the London Pavilion music hall – but the biggest crowds of all were at the entrance to Sinclair's. A procession of horse-drawn carriages and motor cars made stately progress towards the store, and there was a sudden buzz of anticipation as two smart uniformed doormen hurried to lay the red carpet along the steps. People in the crowd stood on their tiptoes eagerly, but there was no sign of the Royal carriage yet: His Majesty was certain to be fashionably late.

Yet there were still plenty of famous faces to be seen amongst the guests. Watching from the pavement, a girl with roses in her hat turned excitedly to the young man beside her. 'Look – isn't that Mr Felix Freemantle, the actor? We saw him in that play, *The Inheritance!*' She squeezed the young man's hand. 'Isn't it funny to think that this is exactly where we first met – on the very first day that the store opened? If it wasn't for Sinclair's, we'd never have found each other!'

The young man grinned at her shyly, and then they both turned to watch as the guests began to make their way slowly up the steps.

It was clear that everyone had dressed very carefully for the occasion. Those ladies who were lucky enough to own such a coveted outfit were attired in *Maison Chevalier*'s latest modes, but even those who were not had chosen their ensemble to match the evening's theme. The onlookers gazed in awe at the parade of feathered turbans, glittering ropes of sapphires and emeralds, and enormous fans of peacock plumes. Society beauty Mrs Isabel Whiteley posed for the press photographers attired in a *Maison Chevalier* robe of gold brocade, whilst well-known suffragette Mrs St James ascended the steps in a flowing gown of teal-coloured satin. Just behind her, Miss Henrietta Beauville appeared on the arm of artist Max Kamensky, wearing an opulent cloak of her own design embroidered all over with peacock feathers.

The gentlemen too were in their finest attire, the usual sleek black and white of their evening dress broken by touches of colour. Here was an exotically patterned cravat, there, a jewel-coloured satin waistcoat, there, the glint of an emerald cufflink.

'One can't help but feel rather a *dandy*,' confessed Mr Pendleton, fiddling with the little buttons on his blue glove.

'But that's half the fun of the thing!' exclaimed Hugo Devereaux, who looked dapper in a peacock-printed neck tie. 'Rather like fancy dress, what?'

The Honourable Miss Phyllis Woodhouse, snug in a velvet frock that perfectly matched her sapphire tiara nodded vigorously. 'I think everyone looks simply marvellous!' she exclaimed.

'Anyway,' put in Veronica, who wore a green *Maison Chevalier* gown trimmed with trails of chiffon. 'We've got more important things to think about tonight than our *appearance*, Mr Pendleton.'

'Oh, quite so, of course,' agreed Pendleton hurriedly.

As they swept on up the stairs, he dared to say something in a low voice to Veronica: 'Er . . . Miss Whiteley. I hope you don't mind me mentioning it but I wondered – that is to say – after our conversation at Winter Hall . . .'

'You want to know if I'm engaged to Vincent?' Veronica demanded bluntly.

Mr Pendleton looked embarrassed. 'I know it's none of my business, but Miss Whiteley, I –'

Veronica looked haughty. 'I've already *told* you, Mr Pendleton. I haven't the slightest intention of having anything to do with Vincent – whatever you or anyone else may think. And I've told him that myself! I don't let anyone make my decisions for me – not any more.'

Mr Pendleton's face lit up as Veronica swept ahead of him into the store – but once inside, they both had to stop to catch their breath. The familiar Sinclair's Entrance Hall had been transformed into a scene from a fairy tale. The high ceiling was festooned with swathes of purple, gold and silver silk, flaming torches and candles cast out mysterious shadows, and the sound of the fountain mingled with the hum of music drifting from the Exhibition Hall. Mannequins in *Maison Chevalier* gowns were circulating with scent sprayers of *Midnight Peacock*, whilst a waiter at once offered them a golden tray set with an array of drinks in extraordinary colours. It was like being in an illustration from a book, Veronica thought: a scene of a fantastical bazaar from the *Thousand and One Nights* perhaps.

'Isn't it marvellous?' gasped Phyllis. 'I've never seen anything like it in my life.'

'Let's look around,' said Mr Devereaux. 'I've heard there's going to be a tremendous banquet in the Marble Court Restaurant.'

'All right – but we have to keep our eyes open,' whispered Veronica. 'Remember that Lil and Sophie are counting on us to help them protect the King.'

They exchanged significant glances, as they set out together to explore the Midnight Peacock Ball.

Somewhere high above them, the kitchens of the Marble Court Restaurant were a hectic clatter of pans and dishes. Song hurried to and fro, ferrying bowls and trays from the stove to the sink and back again. He felt very hot and tired – but he knew that his work here was easy compared to what Sophie and the others had to do tonight. For a moment, he wished he was going to be with them to help, but the frantic rhythm of the kitchens made it difficult for him to think about anything else for long.

Just then, Monsieur Bernard himself came storming past, his face scarlet. 'Paul has deserted us!' he spat out furiously. 'He has gone to join those fools at the Ritz! Today – of all the days – when we are cooking for His Majesty the King himself! And he does not even have the guts to come here and tell me – he sends a *note* – a *note* I tell you – to *me* – Monsieur Bernard! Pah!'

There was an audible hiss of surprise around the kitchen, but there was no time to discuss the *patissier*'s betrayal. Monsieur Bernard was already effecting a swift reshuffle. A skilled *confiseur* was promoted to Paul's old position, one of the *commis* was moved over to replace the *confiseur*, an eager apprentice who had had the job of preparing vegetables was moved over to the stove to take his place. Song marvelled at the way they slotted mechanically into place: it was like watching the great cranes down at the docks changing position.

But now Monsieur Bernard needed someone to prepare the vegetables. The great chef looked swiftly around and his eyes fell on Song.

'Here – you, boy! Can you use a knife?'

For a moment, Song almost could not speak. He had been addressed by the great Monsieur Bernard himself! But he nodded quickly. 'Yes, chef!'

'Let me see you do it. Here – dice the onion.'

Song set down the dishes and took the heavy chef's knife that Monsieur Bernard was holding out to him. It was far finer and more expensive than any knife he had ever used in his life, and for a horrible moment he faltered, feeling suddenly as though he had never even *seen* an onion before, never mind chopped one. But then he gripped the handle and all at once he was back in the kitchen in Limehouse, with his familiar knife and wooden chopping board, and he deftly diced the onion.

It was a strong onion and his eyes began to run as Monsieur Bernard picked up a few of the tiny cubes between his finger and thumb, and considered them attentively. Presently he nodded: 'Acceptable. You will be on vegetable preparation duty tonight.'

Song's heart leapt. It might only be chopping vegetables, but he would be doing *real* cooking – here in the Marble Court Restaurant! Why, he might be dicing the very onions that the King himself would eat! But there was no time to be excited, or nervous. He took up his station proudly, surveying the mound of vegetables he was to prepare. 'Yes, chef!' he said again, and set off at once to work.

'Of course, it's really the colour that makes Monsieur Chevalier's designs so extraordinary,' Jack was saying, as he and Leo ventured through the exotic splendour of the Midnight Peacock Ball amongst a group of students from the Spencer. 'Ladies' clothes are usually so wishy-washy and insipid – all that pale rose and morbid mauve. That's what makes all these wonderful royal blues and violets and tremendous orange crêpe de chines stand out.'

'Yes he's a really terrific colourist,' agreed one of the other students. 'I say – look, there's the peacock screen that Connie painted. Doesn't it look marvellous? She'll be tickled pink!'

'Where is Connie tonight?' asked someone else. 'Surely she isn't going to miss the chance to admire our handiwork?'

'Oh – she's around here somewhere,' said Leo rather vaguely. In a lower voice, she murmured to Jack: 'We must see if we can slip off on our own. We're supposed to be tailing Mr Sinclair!'

'I can see him now – he's over there by the fountain,' Jack whispered back.

Just then, Sid Parker's voice boomed out above the music and the buzz of conversation. 'Ladies and gentlemen!' he announced. 'Mr Lloyd and Mr Mountville's *Midnight Extravaganza* is about to start! Please make your way into the Exhibition Hall to see the performance!'

'Oh – we can't miss that!' squealed one of the students excitedly. 'Let's go and get seats!'

Leo nudged Jack. 'We'll see you in there in a minute,' he said hurriedly. 'Come on, Leo, I want to try one of those splendid-looking drinks.'

As the other students disappeared into the Exhibition Hall for the show, Jack and Leo looked at each other, and then set out determinedly in the direction of Mr Sinclair.

But they had scarcely gone six feet towards him when Leo felt a hand gripping her shoulder.

Turning around, she was surprised to see a woman standing before her. She wore a velvet cloak with a hood that covered her head, and her face was concealed by a mask decorated with peacock feathers.

'Er – can I help you?' she asked uncertainly.

'Leo!' exclaimed a familiar voice, and the strange woman removed her mask and pulled off her hood. 'It's me! What are *you* doing here? Are Lucy and Horace here too?'

Leo laughed, pleased to see her godmother, Lady Tremayne. Now she was back in London, her family and Winter Hall felt a million miles away. 'Oh no!' she said gaily. 'They're still in the country. Jack and I are here with a group from the Spencer. We students helped Mr Kamensky with some of the scenery, you see, and Mr Sinclair was kind enough to give us invitations to the ball in return. What a wonderful ensemble you're wearing! Such a beautiful mask – I really would never have known that it was you!' Her voice faltered, she had realised that far from being pleased to see her, her godmother looked annoyed. 'You remember Jack – Mr Rose – don't you? He was with us at Christmas,' she finished, haltingly.

But Lady Tremayne barely acknowledged Jack's presence. She was still holding Leo by the shoulder, now her fingers clamped her hard, as she said in an urgent whisper: 'You shouldn't be here!'

'Why not?' asked Leo, confused. 'I suppose we're not really properly dressed – but Professor Jarvis said it would be all right, and –'

'You must go home – at once,' said Lady Tremayne firmly. 'This isn't a suitable place for you.'

'What do you mean?'

'Don't argue with me, Leo. Just go – quickly. And whatever you do, don't go out on to Piccadilly Circus tonight.'

Leo frowned. 'But *why?*' she demanded again.

Lady Tremayne let go of her shoulder and began fidgeting with her gloves. 'It – it's going to be very rowdy. There are some rough people out there. You might get hurt! And I know that your mother and father would not approve of you being here. I am sure that Mr Rose will see you home. He'd be better off out of the way too.'

Leo stared at her, puzzled. Lady Tremayne had always been the only person in her life who *didn't* fuss about silly things like what was suitable, and whether or not people approved. What could possibly be wrong about attending Mr Sinclair's ball? Whatever had come over her? As her godmother frowned at her, Leo had the uncanny sense that her godmother had read her mind – that she somehow *knew* that there was something strange and dangerous happening at the ball tonight.

Just then there was a sudden frenzy at the door, and on the street outside.

'The Royal carriage is here!' Leo heard someone exclaim. 'His Majesty is arriving!'

All at once, Lady Tremayne seemed to forget all about what she had been saying. She hastily replaced her mask and hood. 'Excuse me,' she muttered to Jack and Leo, and then she rushed away.

'What on earth was the matter with her?' Leo said, staring after her godmother. 'I've never known her to behave like that before!'

Jack looked anxious. 'Leo,' he said slowly. 'I'm not so sure that Mr Sinclair is the only one we should be watching tonight.'

CHAPTER TWENTY-FOUR

Sophie had been upstairs when she'd heard the roar of the crowd, and she knew exactly what that meant: the King and Queen had arrived. Yet as she came swiftly down the stairs and into the Entrance Hall, she could see no sign of the Royal party anywhere.

The hands of the big golden clock pointed to almost ten, and not far from the store entrance, Mr Sinclair was stepping forward to welcome yet another group of important guests: clapping a young gentleman on the shoulder, kissing a lady's silk-gloved hand, nodding as they exclaimed over the wonderful decorations. He looked tremendously suave and relaxed, not in the least like someone who could possibly be involved in an assassination plot. Sophie stared at him for a long moment, and felt a shiver run over her.

Beside the fountain, she could see that Monsieur Chevalier was holding forth to an admiring circle of guests, his last-minute jitters quite forgotten now. Close by, the society columnist for the *Post* and several fashion journalists

271

were busily scribbling down his every word.

Meanwhile, music was spilling from the door of the Exhibition Hall, hung with a sign reading *Messrs Lloyd & Mountville's MIDNIGHT EXTRAVAGANZA*. She caught her breath – of course! The King's love of theatre was well known, so surely he and his party had gone to watch the show? She slipped quickly through the throng, dodging a waiter and a lady with a peacock-feather fan, and went through the door into the Exhibition Hall.

The big, lofty room had been especially designed with Mr Sinclair's exhibitions and spectacles in mind, and Sophie had seen it in many different guises. She'd seen it used as a splendid picture gallery, as a ballroom for dances, and, of course, as the setting for an exhibition of priceless jewels. Tonight it was different again, transformed as if by the wave of a conjuror's wand into a magnificent theatre, lit up with golden lights.

A stage swathed in velvet curtains had been constructed at one end of the room, where ballet dancers were currently performing before a backcloth painted to look like the night sky. Sophie saw that above them, suspended from the ceiling was a large, silver crescent moon, and reclining upon it quite as comfortably as if she were lounging in her chair in the Taylor & Rose office, was Lil. In Monsieur Chevalier's shimmering peacock costume, she looked more like a queen from an ancient legend than a young lady detective. She glittered from head to toe in blue and green sequins, a rich gold necklace was clasped about her neck, and long gold filigree earrings dangled from her ears. On her head was a diadem of gold, with a spray of peacock feathers in her hair.

For a fleeting moment, Sophie wished she could simply stop and enjoy her friend's star performance – but she knew that she must not delay. She had to find the King. Craning her neck to look around the audience, she saw a dozen different important-looking gentlemen – a tall man in a scarlet dress-uniform, a grey-bearded fellow with a string of medals pinned to his chest. But not one of them was His Majesty. The King was not here.

Up on the stage, Lil had caught sight of Sophie moving through the crowd. She stared down at her meaningfully, and then dramatically threw up one arm into a statuesque pose. She kept smiling at the crowd, every inch the glamorous theatre star – and yet her eyes bored into Sophie, as though she was trying to communicate something. Her arm pointed outwards towards the door – but *upwards*. She was showing her the direction that the King and his party had gone!

With a quick nod to show Lil that she had understood, she darted back through the spectators, and out of the Exhibition Hall, and ran up the stairs to the gallery. Here, little groups had gathered to lean on the balustrade and watch the new arrivals, whilst quite a crowd had gathered around a dark-haired beauty in a jewelled turban, who was laying out tarot cards. A gilded sign proclaimed that this was fortune teller Madame Anna Fortuna. Spotting Mr Betteredge standing amongst the spectators, she hurried up to him.

'I'm looking for His Majesty,' she said urgently. 'Did you see which way the Royal party went?'

Mr Betteredge smiled at her indulgently. 'Hoping to catch a glimpse of the King and Queen? You're not the only one, my dear. The Royal party went that way – I believe they were headed upstairs.'

Sophie hurried onwards. There was no sign of them on the first floor. On the second floor, she put her head quickly into the gentlemen's smoking room, where she glimpsed Hugo Devereaux amongst a circle of young gentlemen chortling to each other in a fug of cigar smoke. He caught her eye and gave her a quick shake of the head. Up she went quickly, through the third floor and on to the fourth, where space had been cleared for dancing. Here, she caught sight of Phyllis and Veronica, amongst a group of debutantes, and as Phyllis glimpsed Sophie, she casually twisted her closed fan and pointed it towards the stairs. That was clear enough – she had to go up.

As she hurried on towards the staircase, the dancers twirled and whirled, and in spite of everything, Sophie stopped for a moment and stared in astonishment. Between the shifting figures, she thought that she had caught sight of a little old lady in a velvet hat watching her from across the dance floor – but when the dancers shifted once more, she had gone.

'I'm sorry I'm so late,' whispered Billy, running across the stable-yard. 'I couldn't get away from Miss Atwood! I swear she has eyes in the back of her head. Thank goodness she asked me to take Lucky out,' he finished. The little dog, who was wearing a special emerald-green ribbon for the occasion, was tucked under his arm.

'Come on,' said Joe urgently. 'We haven't got much time.' He handed Billy a coil of rope. 'Take this. The girls are waiting for us.'

Sure enough, Billy saw that two silhouetted figures were standing in the shadows, with Daisy beside them. Tilly's height and mass of curly hair made her quite unmistakable, but Billy had to blink for a moment at what appeared to be the figure of a small, black-haired boy.

'Mei?' he said. 'Is that you? Are you wearing *trousers*?'

Mei smiled in the dark. 'I borrowed them off Song. Much better for tonight than a skirt,' she explained. 'They're too big for me of course, but I put a tuck in the waist.'

'Look – there's no time to chat about *trousers*,' said Joe urgently. 'We're already behind schedule. We've got to get that box.'

Together, they plunged out into the crowds on Piccadilly. The streets were busier than ever, and Billy saw that a group of policemen were cordoning off Piccadilly Circus to traffic. They fought their way through the throng, and after what seemed like hours, at last emerged beside the Piccadilly Restaurant, above which the big illuminated signs reading *BOVRIL* and *SCHWEPPES LEMONADE* and *DRINK PERRIER WATER* gleamed out of the dark.

Billy stared up at this last sign with apprehension. It looked so high up that he felt dizzy – and yet it was exactly where they were headed.

After their gathering in the Taylor & Rose office, he and Joe had slipped away to trail Fitzwilliam. It had been easy enough to find out where he was installing his control box – in fact, old George himself had pointed it out. The two boys had watched from the shadows as a long ladder was placed at the side of the Piccadilly Restaurant, and then Fitzwilliam went up it with his box, clambering on to the scaffolding behind the Perrier sign. Twenty minutes later, he was down again, the box connected and installed, and the ladder removed. Billy had stared after him in despair. How on earth were they supposed to get themselves – not to mention Tilly – all the way up behind that sign, on the front of the Piccadilly Restaurant, without a ladder and without being seen, to deactivate the box?

To Billy it had seemed impossible, but he had forgotten

that Joe had once been a member of the Baron's Boys, and had more than a few tricks up his sleeve.

'It won't be easy, but I think we can do it,' he had said earnestly. 'We'll have to wait until it's properly dark and the crowds gather – that'll give us some cover. I don't fancy that fellow coming up there after us. We know he's a nasty piece of work.'

'But how *are* we going to get up there?' asked Billy, still baffled.

'See that alleyway down the side of the restaurant? There's a fire escape there – and a drainpipe. We can use that to help us.'

'No chance,' Billy said, shaking his head. 'We'll never manage to make it up there – not without a ladder or a rope!'

Joe grinned at him cheekily. 'Well *we* aren't going to get up there without a rope at all, as it happens. We're going to use a little snakesman.'

'A *what?*'

'A snakesman. It's like when you're doing a housebreak, you see? You've got to find yourself a lad, someone small and thin who won't blanch at the thought of climbing up a drainpipe and in through a skylight. They wriggle in like a snake and then let everyone else in – that's why they're called a little snakesman.'

'But – but – we don't have a little snakesman!' said Billy.

'Oh, I reckon we do,' said Joe. 'I reckon I know exactly the right man for the job.'

Now, as they made their way down the alleyway, Billy turned to Mei anxiously:

'Are you sure you can do this?' he asked, for the dozenth time.

Mei smiled at him. 'Squeezing through that crowd was much worse than this is going to be,' she said, surveying the drainpipe.

Tilly was quickly checking over the tools in her pocket – the little set that Alf had given her – whilst Joe went over the plan one last time.

'Righto – so Mei's going to climb up first, and let down the rope. Tilly and I follow her up, we find the box and disconnect it as quickly as we can. We don't have long until midnight – and we don't want that fellow Fitzwilliam spotting what we're up to. Billy will stay down here on watch with Daisy and Lucky. Do the owl call if you see anyone coming. Everyone know what they're doing? Right. Now, Mei – you ready?'

Mei was making a careful check of the rope that she had now wound several times around her waist. She settled it into position, nodded, and then without saying anything else, she turned and slipped lightly up the iron fire escape, not much more than a shadow in the dark.

Billy's heart was in his mouth as he watched the small,

agile figure quickly swing herself from the fire escape and on to the drainpipe. She clung on to it for a moment like a spider, and then began to inch her way upwards.

'My goodness!' exclaimed Tilly. 'She really can climb, can't she?'

'She's a grand little snakesman,' said Joe proudly.

Billy couldn't help gasping as Mei let go of the drainpipe with one arm, reaching out for the edge of the scaffolding. But a moment later, she was sitting quite happily on the edge of it behind the Perrier sign, unravelling the rope around her waist, and knotting it securely to one of the sturdy metal supports.

Joe gave it a tug to test it and then nodded. 'You first,' he said to Tilly. For a moment, she hesitated, and Joe looked worried. 'Here – you can climb a rope, can't you? I mean, you've got to have strong arms and –'

'Strong arms?' repeated Tilly incredulously. 'I'm a housemaid. I've probably carried half a dozen coal scuttles up two flights of stairs of a morning, before you've even woken up!'

Joe grinned sheepishly and held out the rope to her, and Billy stood watching as they both made their way more slowly up the fire escape and the drainpipe. Tilly had barely reached the edge of the scaffolding when he heard the sound of pounding footsteps, and his stomach lurched.

Spinning around, he saw that a tall powerful man was running along the alleyway towards them. It was Raymond Fitzwilliam, his face twisted with fury.

'Here – what do you think you're doing!' he yelled. 'Get down from there at once.'

Sophie hurried through the Marble Court Restaurant, between exotic flower arrangements and magnificent heaps of delicacies, laid out on gold and silver platters. There were cakes topped with nuts and preserved fruits glistening like jewels, exquisite sweetmeats, piles of fragrant oranges, long-necked carafes of honey-sweet drinks, and bowls of figs and dates. For a moment her mouth watered, but this was no time to think of food – she was on the trail of the King.

She had been certain she would find him here, but as she slipped first one way then the other, she saw no sign of him, and presently she found herself outside on the balcony, hung with flags and rigged up with electric lights, all ready for His Majesty's appearance. For a moment, she leaned against the balcony rail, staring down at the people milling about on the street below.

She sucked in some big lungfuls of freezing-cold air, thinking as she did so that somewhere over there, where the big illuminated signs on Piccadilly Circus glowed out of the dark, Billy, Joe, Tilly and Mei would be putting their part of the plan into action. She knew it would be difficult and dangerous – and crucially important if they were to protect the hundreds of people she could see below her.

Across from her, the windows of the building opposite were in darkness. She realised she was positioned directly across from the office of Lindwurm Enterprises. Of course, they would be empty now, for the Baron would no longer need the office to store his explosives. They were already in position, scattered on the rooftops all around her, she thought with a powerful shiver. Just as somewhere down below her, or somewhere in the store itself was a gunman, planning to murder the King. And even as he smiled and laughed and kissed ladies' hands, Mr Sinclair himself was watching and waiting for it all to happen.

She stared again at the dark windows across the way, puzzled by something. She suddenly found herself wondering why the Baron had ever needed that office at all – simply to store the explosives? Why not have them sent directly from the factory in Silvertown? She thought of the large box marked *LEE-ENFIELD*, and she thought of the Baron saying *make sure the King is in position . . . so we have him in our sights*. And then she was back in the Dining Room at Winter Hall, and the old gentleman next to her was saying: *My trusty old Lee-Enfield rifle would have done the job of course . . . but this fellow had only a feeble little Browning. And at those distances, you absolutely* must *have a long-range rifle if you want to achieve any degree of accuracy.*

She gasped. The pieces had come together. All at once, Sophie knew exactly where the gunman would be – and how he was planning to shoot the King.

'Daisy!' Billy cried out. The big dog leapt forward with a low growl – but Fitzwilliam was wielding a heavy stick. He swung it at Daisy, she dodged away, but then he swung the stick at her again.

Billy took a step backwards towards the rope. There was no need to hoot like an owl: the others could all see what was happening. Above him, Tilly's hands scrabbled on the edge of the scaffolding, and Mei hurried to help pull her up, as Joe scrambled up behind.

Fitzwilliam hit out at Daisy and she whined in pain. 'Take that, you brute!' the man yelled. 'There's plenty more for you where that came from. I'll finish you off – and just wait until I get my hands on the rest of you!'

But before he could make another move, there came the sound of more footsteps running down the alley. To his astonishment, Billy saw that Connie was running towards them. Two tall girls, with purple and green ribbons on their hats, were running behind her.

'Sorry we're a bit late!' shrieked Connie. 'This is Dora – and this is Bunty. They're from the Sewing Society too. We're here to help!' She turned on Fitzwilliam. 'What do you think you're doing? How dare you attack a poor, defenceless dog? How dare you threaten this boy?'

Fitzwilliam stared at her, an evil smile on his face, and then gave a short laugh. But the 'defenceless dog' had taken the opportunity to leap at him again, whilst Lucky wriggled out of Billy's arms and darted forward to bite a large section out of the bottom of his trouser leg.

'Get away,' said Fitzwilliam, trying to hit out at the dogs again. But Connie and the other girls were moving forward towards him. 'What do you think you're playing at?' he yelled. 'Get out of here – scram!'

Connie gave him a very pointed look. 'Oh, I don't think we'll be going anywhere,' she said.

Sophie ran helter-skelter through the shop and down the back stairs. She could see it now in her mind's eye: the bright lights would go on, the King would appear on the balcony just before midnight, the crowds would clap, and the King would wave. And across the street, the Baron's sniper would be waiting in the darkened office of Lindwurm Enterprises with a long-range Lee-Enfield rifle. If it could hit elephants and tigers from a distance, Sophie did not doubt it could shoot the King of England from across Piccadilly. Even as the King fell in full view of the crowd, midnight would strike, and the firework machine would be activated, and the explosives would go off all around Piccadilly Circus.

Except that wasn't going to happen. She wouldn't let it. Halfway down the stairs, she came across Song who was hurrying up with a box of supplies for the kitchens.

'Sophie – what's wrong?' he demanded at once.

Sophie paused, gasping for breath. 'You have to tell Lil and Jack that I've worked it out,' she gabbled. 'The sniper is going to shoot the King from that office across the street. I'm going there now – but you have to go back up to the fifth floor. Warn the others – they have to stop His Majesty stepping out on to the balcony!'

She could not wait to see whether Song had understood. She ran on, down the steps and out into the crowd, her gold shoes skittering across the cobbles.

The *Midnight Extravaganza* was over. Lil had struggled out of the peacock costume and back into her purple *Maison Chevalier* gown with Maurice's help, and with great difficulty had extricated herself from a crowd waiting to congratulate her on her performance. She raced out and up the stairs, looking for Sophie and the others. At last she discovered Veronica, Mr Pendleton and Phyllis standing in a little huddle in the Marble Court Restaurant. Song was there too, looking quite out of place in his white apron.

'Where's Sophie?' she demanded breathlessly.

Song looked anxious. 'She ran off in a tremendous hurry. She said she'd worked out that the King was going to be shot on the balcony, and she said something about going across the street to stop it. She says we have to make sure the King doesn't go out there.'

Lil's heart began to thump. 'Where's the King now?' she demanded, staring around at the crowds.

'We aren't sure – but it's almost midnight! He'll be here at any moment!' exclaimed Phyllis.

'Lil – I'm really worried about Sophie,' said Song urgently. 'If she comes face to face with a sniper by herself . . .' His words trailed away, and Lil knew what he was thinking. Taking on Connie or Bunty at Sewing Society was one thing – facing an armed gunman was quite another.

'Do you know what she meant about going across the street?' Song asked.

Lil cast a look out at the empty balcony. Her thoughts leapt wildly. 'I don't know for sure, but I think I can guess,' she said. 'I'm going after her. You stay here and come up with some way to stop the King going out on to that balcony.'

Across the room, unnoticed by any of them, the elegant figure of Mr Edward Sinclair watched her go, a thoughtful expression on his face. After a moment, he made his apologies to the guests he had been talking with, put down his glass of champagne, and slipped quickly out of the room.

Leo pushed her way hurriedly through the crowds towards her godmother and reached out to touch her on the arm. Lady Tremayne jumped and span around at once.

'Leo – I told you to *go!*' she began in an irritated voice that did not sound in the least bit like her usual self.

'Wait – I have to tell you something. There's a gentleman looking for you – he says it's urgent!'

Lady Tremayne frowned. 'What gentleman?' she demanded sharply.

'I don't know. He wouldn't give his name. He was a tall gentleman and well dressed. He was wearing a gold pin shaped like a dragon. I didn't recognise him but he said he recognised me, and that he knew *you* very well indeed. He said I had to tell you that his plans had changed – and that you're to meet him at once.'

'To meet him?' repeated Lady Tremayne, her eyes widening. 'What? But where?'

'I'll show you,' said Leo. 'I know a quick way. Follow me.'

Her heart was racing as she led Lady Tremayne through the crowds, and up the stairs to the third floor. She hadn't been able to believe that her godmother could really be anything to do with the Baron's plot, but now her anxious face made it all clear.

'Why else would she have reacted in that peculiar way?'

Jack had said. 'She was warning you. She wanted you as far away from here as possible – and there's only one explanation for that. She knows exactly what's going to happen on Piccadilly Circus tonight.'

Now, as Leo hurried on through the Ladies' Fashions Department, where a host of society ladies were admiring *Maison Chevalier* ensembles, and then into Millinery, she felt a dreadful sick feeling wash over her. Lady Tremayne had always been the one person she believed she could count on, the one person that she could trust. She had been hoping desperately that Jack was wrong, but the eagerness in her godmother's eyes when she'd described the Baron had been only too obvious. The horrible sick feeling changed to a hot flash of anger. Lady Tremayne had duped her. She was in cahoots with the Baron. She deserved everything she was going to get.

'Here he is,' Leo said sweetly, pointing to the door of the Millinery storeroom. 'The gentleman – he's waiting for you in there. He said it would be best if he wasn't seen by anyone.'

Lady Tremayne hurried forward and stepped through the door – and at once Jack popped out from behind a display of hats, closed it behind her, and swiftly turned the key in the lock.

'Lil and Sophie told me they got locked in here once,' he explained, removing the key and pocketing it carefully.

'Let's see how Lady Tremayne likes it. And if she's shut up in there for the night, she can't possibly do anything to help the Baron with his scheme – now can she?'

Minnie and Violet were peering out from behind the glass-topped counter, rather confused about what was happening.

'Don't worry about that,' said Jack airily, waving his hand to them. 'Little matter of an – er – uninvited guest. Mr Sinclair's orders, you know.'

Behind the door of the Millinery storeroom, a shocked Lady Tremayne contemplated not the Baron, but only a very annoyed-looking Edith holding a stack of hat-boxes.

Sophie had thought the door to the building across the street would be locked, so she was relieved when the handle turned easily. Inside, she hurried up a dark staircase, counting the floors as she went. First Miss Beauville's, all the lights turned out, then the publishing office, the doors closed, and finally, the fifth floor.

The door in front of her was locked fast, and for a moment she panicked. But Sophie was not the girl that she had been a year ago, and a locked door was no longer the barrier it had once been. Remembering the hairpins Monsieur Pascal had used, she quickly pulled two of them out, and pushed the thin ends into the keyhole. Joe had taught her how to pick locks: after learning how to crack a safe, it had been surprisingly straightforward. Now it only took her a minute's work before the lock clicked, and she was able to push the door open.

She stepped through into a large, empty office. There was almost no furniture, and the crates that Billy had seen were gone. For a moment, she wondered if she had been mistaken and this was just an unused office, but then she caught her breath, as she saw something gleaming on a table under the window. Hurrying over to it, she realised it was a long, narrow rifle.

Breathlessly, she picked it up. The barrel glinted in the dim light. It felt large and cold and mysterious in her hands. She didn't have the first idea about how guns worked – Papa had never allowed her near his. For a moment, she thought resentfully of what he had said in the letter about giving her an 'ordinary girlhood'. 'I'd swap that for a lesson on firearms right now,' she murmured, examining the barrel of the gun. How did it open? Could she damage it – or remove the ammunition? Or ought she just to run for it now, taking the gun with her?

She was so intent that she barely even heard the softest creak as the office door opened behind her. There was only just time to spin around, still clutching the rifle, as a familiar voice spoke:

'Good evening, Miss Taylor.'

CHAPTER TWENTY-FIVE

D own on Piccadilly Circus, the atmosphere had become wilder. A group of children were setting off firecrackers, people had gathered round the barrel organ and were loudly chanting popular music-hall songs, and two lads were climbing up the Eros fountain whilst two angry policemen shook their fists at them. Meanwhile, a tall man with black hair streaked with white, and a blood-drenched handkerchief held to his nose, could be seen trying to escape into the crowd, hotly pursued by some very angry-looking suffragettes.

A young lady found a policeman in the crowd and pulled on his sleeve. 'Excuse me, constable,' she said, rather out of breath. 'I wish to report that man over there.'

'That gentleman, miss?' said Police Constable Potts in surprise. 'Been bothering you, has he?'

'That's right,' said Connie briskly. 'I should say he's been bothering us, all right.'

On the scaffolding above Piccadilly Circus, Tilly had prised away the cover of the control box and was gazing at its intricate workings.

'Quickly!' came Joe's voice beside her. 'We're running out of time! There's only fifteen minutes left until midnight!'

Far below them in the alleyway, Billy's anxious face stared up at them. A wave of panic swept over Tilly. 'I don't know how to do it,' she gasped, staring at the complex mechanism of cogs and wires and dials. 'I can't stop the timer. It's too complicated!' A chill wind blew over the rooftops, rattling the scaffolding, and Tilly felt tears coming into her eyes. She blinked them back frantically. Everyone was relying on her – but she didn't know what to do.

'All right – don't worry,' came Joe's voice. 'Forget about the timer. What about the cables – do we disconnect them?'

Tilly stared desperately at the tangle of thick red and black cables erupting from the machine. 'I don't know!' she said. 'There are so many! We'll never have time to cut through them all! And if we cut the wrong one, we might trip the mechanism somehow – and set the machine off!'

Her heart pounded. It was so easy to understand how things worked when you were reading a book, or looking at a motor-car engine with Alf in the garage, but it was quite another thing when you were high above Piccadilly Circus in the cold and the dark. For a moment she cursed herself, and her wild dream of coming to London. What was she doing here? She could have been safe in the kitchens with Ma.

'You can do this,' said Joe gently. He sounded amazingly calm, Tilly thought, as though they were doing something quite ordinary, not perched up here, knowing that bombs might be about to go off all around them. 'Just take it one step at a time. Red cables and black ones. There must be some difference between them.'

Tilly took a deep breath and tried to collect herself. She had to be rational, she told herself. It was just like the ghost in the passage at Winter Hall. She could not scream and run away; she had to look calmly at what lay before her, however frightening it might be. 'I suppose they could be like the marks on the plan,' she said slowly. 'Red for explosives – and black for the ordinary fireworks.'

Joe nodded. 'That's right!' he said. 'So do the red cables first – that way we've got the best chance of disconnecting the explosives. Where's that wire-cutter? We'll have to hurry.'

The buzz of noise in the Marble Court Restaurant fell silent. The Royal party were here, and in their midst, the familiar figures of the King and Queen Alexandra. Veronica and Phyllis swept into curtseys as they saw the King approach them: large and slow and stately in his black coat, the Star

292

of the Order of the Garter gleaming on his chest. Here and there he paused to nod to an acquaintance, to ask the polite young retainer at his side to make an introduction, or to cough into an enormous silk handkerchief – for as everyone knew, the King suffered from bronchial troubles. Presently, he stopped before the two young ladies and Mr Pendleton.

'The Honourable Miss Phyllis Woodhouse, Your Majesty, Miss Veronica Whiteley, and Mr Reginald Pendleton,' announced the retainer.

'Good evening, young ladies,' said His Majesty, smiling upon them graciously. 'Good evening, Mr Pendleton.'

'Say something!' squeaked Phyllis – and rather to her astonishment, Veronica did.

'Good evening, Your Highness,' she began. 'Er – we have to tell you something. We fear that it would be dangerous for you to go out on the balcony to greet your public. We believe that someone is – well – that someone is trying to assassinate you tonight,' she managed to finish. She grimaced, uncertain what the King's response would be.

For a moment, the King looked at her in astonishment. Then he looked around at his retinue, and began to laugh good-naturedly.

'It's true, Your Highness,' blustered Mr Pendleton. 'You must listen to Miss Whiteley!'

The King smiled at them both. 'My dear young people.

I appreciate your concern, but I have been the King of England for nearly ten years – and I was the Prince of Wales for a very great deal longer than that! I daresay there are plenty of people who would love to see me in the grave – but I wouldn't get on at all well if I spent my time looking over my shoulder for assassins.' He bowed to Miss Whiteley, patted Mr Pendleton on the shoulder and then turned to his retainer and smiled jovially. 'Come on – let us go out and greet the public. And then I believe it will be time for a little more of Monsieur Bernard's delicious dinner.'

Veronica and Mr Pendleton stared helplessly after him as the King made his slow progress over towards the balcony door.

Across the street, Sophie turned to face the Baron.

There he was – tall, distinguished-looking, with the same greying hair, the same unremarkable face. But whilst before he had always been elegantly dressed, now he was no longer so polished – his collar askew and his face unshaven. Yet Sophie barely noticed any of that. She was staring in horror at the struggling figure he had dragged into the room with him. It was Lil, white and shaking, and Sophie saw in horror that the Baron had his silver knife pressed close up against her neck.

'Let go of her!' she cried out at once, but the Baron only laughed.

'No, I really don't think I'm going to do that,' he said. 'You have my rifle – and you're in my way. Unless you're planning to hand it over and let me get on with my business, which somehow I very much doubt, I think I'll keep hold of your companion for now. I rather think she was running over here in such a hurry to try and help you – or perhaps even to try and *save* you? Rather a shame that she ran into *me* instead.'

'*You're* the gunman!' Sophie whispered. 'You're doing it yourself this time. You're here to kill the King.'

'Quite right. Unfortunately, thanks to your meddling, there are very few people left that I can really trust – well, apart from Fitz, of course. I believe you made his acquaintance once before? And Viola too, although I could hardly trust her with a rifle. She'd probably be about as capable of using it as *you* are. But women are of use for some things – and thankfully blood *is* thicker than water. Not that you'd know very much about that, since all your family are dead.' He gave a short laugh, and dragged Lil forwards. 'Do you know, it really was remarkably easy for me to get rid of your parents, when they got in my way. Just like I'm going to get rid of your friend here, unless you do exactly as I say.'

The Baron pressed the knife harder against Lil's neck and for a moment, she whimpered. But then she gathered herself. 'Don't listen to him, Sophie! You can't let him win!'

The Baron gave a delighted laugh. 'Let me win? My dear, I've *already* won. The rooftops of the buildings all around Piccadilly Circus are laced with a new and powerful explosive. In ten minutes time they'll be ignited, and London will be in chaos.'

'You're despicable,' muttered Lil. 'There are hundreds of people down there. Don't you even care that they'll be hurt – or killed?'

The Baron laughed dismissively. 'That rabble? They're of no importance. We are talking about making history.' His eyes gleamed. 'And in history, my people always win the war.' He paused, looking at Sophie thoughtfully for a moment. 'I'll admit, you may have won a battle or two along the way, Miss Taylor – and I must say, that impressed me. Perhaps there's more of your mother in you than I ever gave you credit for. But ultimately, of course, *we* will win. We always do.'

Sophie's heart was pounding in her chest and her grip tightened on the rifle. If only she knew how to use it! But even if she did she wasn't sure she would dare, when the Baron was holding Lil before him in such a fierce grip – she could not risk hurting her friend. Just the same, she knew she could not give up. She had not given up when the Baron had kidnapped her and locked her in his study, nor when he had chased them to the docks of the East End, nor when he'd cornered her in that Chelsea alleyway.

She would certainly not give up now. And so she did the only thing she could think of – she opened her mouth and spoke:

'*We*? Do you mean you and the rest of the *Fraternitas Draconum*?'

The Baron chuckled, and smiled at her as if she were a puppy that had just learned to sit. 'Well well! So you've worked that out, have you? Clever girl. The Brotherhood of Dragons is one of Europe's most ancient, mighty – and secret – institutions.'

'But they're unhappy with you, aren't they?' Sophie hardly knew what she was saying. 'They were angry – after we exposed you, and your plan to get back those paintings went wrong.'

A shadow passed across the Baron's face. 'I'll admit that losing the paintings was an inconvenience. But I'll get them back in time. My mistake was relying on that fool Lyle. That's why I'm taking care of business myself this time. Well, that and the fact that I just so happen to be a crack shot. That was one of the things I was known for in my Army days. Your poor papa on the other hand was never much of a marksman. But he was a fine scout – perhaps one of the best. We made a formidable team – rather like you and dear Miss Rose here. Of course, I killed him just the same.'

'You killed him – and you killed my mother – and you

297

killed Colonel Fairley – and for all we know, you killed Grandfather Lim too,' Sophie went on. Her heart was thumping, but she knew that for every second that ticked away, the less time the Baron would have to carry out his plan. 'You made the Colonel's death look like an accident. You stole his dragon painting – and I suppose you also stole my father's will and the letter he left for me too.'

'Yes, that amused me,' said the Baron. 'I rather liked the idea of leaving Robert's child a penniless orphan. It seemed to me like *justice*. Though I must say I forgot about you after that – it took me quite by surprise when you popped up in the box in the theatre that day. I couldn't possibly mistake *you* for anyone but Robert's daughter.'

He lowered his voice and took another step towards her. 'I still have it, you know. The letter for you that your father left with the Colonel. Oh, he set it out for you all so carefully – such heroic explanations, such fond farewells, such tender plans for your future! It's really quite touching. I can still give it to you, if you like. Put that rifle down – and you and your friend can walk away. I'll tell you exactly where you can find the letter and everything else he left for you. It's not too late.'

The room was very silent. Sophie could hear Lil's ragged breaths and see the rise and fall of her chest. Then: 'I don't believe you,' she said through gritted teeth.

The Baron shifted from one foot to the other. 'I give you

my word,' he said. He looked straight into her eyes. 'I am a man of my word, Sophie, whatever else you might think of me.' For a moment, he gave her a strange smile. 'I do rather admire you, you know. I sometimes think that if things had been different, you could have been *my* daughter. But Alice chose *him*.' He shook his head. 'I forgave them, in spite of that. I forgave him – and treated him like a friend and a gentleman. I told him my secrets. He could still have joined me. He could have been rich. He would have sat at my right hand at the table of the *Fraternitas Draconum*. Together I daresay we could have reached the top. But he threw all that away. He was a *coward*.'

Sophie looked at him steadily. 'He didn't want to have anything to do with the *Fraternitas Draconum*. He joined the Loyal Order of Lions instead – and so did my mother.'

'The Loyal Order of Lions, indeed! That feeble endeavour! I should have known that was exactly the kind of weedy sentimental stuff that would appeal to Robert – all that tiresome nonsense about loyalty and honour and friendship and *doing the right thing*. But I must say I thought Alice was made of sterner stuff. They thought they could stop us but they were hopelessly deluded. Of course, I dealt with that tedious little problem and now the Loyal Order of Lions is no more. Every member of it has been crossed out. Well – except, I suppose, for *you*.'

Sophie stared at him. The idea startled her, but at once

she saw what he meant. If the Loyal Order of Lions had been working to stop the Baron and the *Fraternitas Draconum*, then she and Lil and the others had been following in their footsteps all along. Without even knowing it, they had continued the work of her parents, and Colonel Fairley, and Grandfather Lim.

She had not been alone at all, she saw in a sudden clear, bright flash. She had been part of something since the beginning. Not a family perhaps, but something bigger. They were all part of it: Lil and Billy and Joe; and Mei and Song; and Leo and Jack; and Tilly – and goodness, even Veronica and Mr Pendleton. The thought made warmth swell up inside her and burst out into words.

'I don't care about the letter,' she said. 'Whatever's in it, it won't bring him back.'

The Baron grinned at her, cold as a snake. 'But I know what you *do* care about,' he said. 'The Lions always counted friendship as more important than anything. You care about your friend – so what will you sacrifice to save her?'

Sophie and Lil's eyes met, and for a moment, Sophie was back on the roof garden of Sinclair's, when Lil had been captured and held at gunpoint by Mr Cooper and the Baron's Boys. It seemed like a very long time ago. There had been only one thing she could do then – but things were different now.

Behind them, on the balcony of Sinclair's, Sophie was

aware that the lights had come on in a blaze of gold: she could see them reflected in Lil's eyes. Any moment now, the King would appear.

'You're out of time,' hissed the Baron.

'No,' said Sophie, with a sudden smile. 'You are.'

Even as she spoke, Lil elbowed the Baron sharply in the stomach. In the split second that he flinched and gasped, she twisted with a deft move that Mr Lim had taught them. She hit his arm with all her strength – and the knife fell to the floor.

As she did so, Sophie leapt forward. Behind her, flanked by retainers, the stately figure of His Majesty had appeared on the balcony. The crowd in the street below roared in delight. The Baron gave a yell of frustration and pushed Lil roughly to the side: she fell hard to the ground. He grabbed his knife again and made a rush towards Sophie.

Sophie might not know how to shoot, but she suddenly realised that was not the only use for a heavy rifle. She braced herself and swung the gun as hard as she could at the Baron. For a moment he staggered, but then he was steady on his feet, coming at her again with the knife. She swung out with the rifle once more and knocked the knife from his hands, where it went skidding across the floor in the direction of the office door. But the Baron was too strong, and almost before she knew it he had ripped the rifle from her hands, and was pointing it straight at her chest.

All of a sudden, he began to laugh. 'No!' cried Lil, making a desperate dash for the knife, but as she lunged across the floor to reach it, she saw it come to rest beside a black shiny shoe.

There was someone else standing in the office doorway.

Below them, on Piccadilly Circus, the people were counting down to midnight.

'Ten!'

'Hurry! Hurry!' screamed Mei up on the rooftop, as Tilly feverishly clipped one red wire, then another.

'Nine! Eight!'

Jack and Leo pushed their way frantically through the crowds in the fifth-floor restaurant, towards the balcony where the King now stood.

'Seven! Six!'

Connie came racing back towards Billy down the darkened alley: 'Have they done it?' she demanded urgently, looking up at the small figures working busily above.

'Five! Four!'

Lil gaped upwards from the floor of the office building. Standing above her in the doorway was Mr Sinclair – and he was holding a revolver.

'Three! Two!'

Mr Sinclair looked at Sophie and the Baron, the revolver steady in his hand.

'One!'

It was midnight. Across London, church bells clanged out triumphantly, and on Piccadilly Circus there was a tremendous booming sound. Sophie was vaguely aware of explosions going on all around them, even as she stared at Mr Sinclair – and then a single shot rang out.

Down in the streets below, the crowds went 'Ooh!' and 'Aah!' The sky above Piccadilly Circus was filled with a blaze of light. Fireworks bloomed above them: emerald-green and sapphire, indigo and violet, gold and silver starbursts, illuminating the dark night with rich sparkling colour.

'It's 1910!' whispered the girl with roses in her hat excitedly to her young man. 'I wonder what this year will bring?'

Everyone turned their faces upwards, children swayed high on their parents' shoulders, and up in the windows of Sinclair's, the shop girls and the porters, the salesman and the waiters, the doormen and the kitchen staff had all crowded around the windows to watch too.

'What a wonderful way to ring in the New Year!' exclaimed Mrs Milton, dabbing her eyes with a lacy hanky.

'Now *that* is what I call a spectacle,' agreed Claudine. '*Magnifique!*'

'The Captain's done us proud,' said Mr Betteredge. 'But then, he always does.'

'Where's Edith?' whispered Violet to Minnie. 'She's missing it all!'

But Minnie just shrugged. 'Ooh – isn't it lovely?' was all she said.

Somewhere behind them, they heard Sid Parker call out 'Happy New Year!' and a moment later they were all saying it to each other, kissing cheeks and shaking hands. 'Happy New Year! Happy New Year!'

Up on the balcony, the King himself was admiring the display, and the guests of the Midnight Peacock Ball had come out to join him. Not far away from where His Majesty stood were Jack and Leo, both looking rather tired but immensely relieved – and beside them, Veronica, Mr Pendleton, Phyllis and Hugo Devereaux.

'A very Happy New Year, everyone!' announced Mr Devereaux, before promptly kissing Phyllis.

Mr Pendleton stared at them for a moment, but then, to his great astonishment, he realised that Veronica was standing up on tiptoes to kiss him too.

He broke away, his cheeks scarlet. 'Oh – I say!' he blustered in surprise.

But Veronica just smiled at him radiantly – and then he blushed even more and kissed her back.

Somewhere far below them, in the alleyway beside the Piccadilly Restaurant, Billy and Connie found that they were shaking each others' hands quite vigorously, whilst

Lucky gave a little whine and tried to hide behind Daisy – she had decided that she didn't much care for fireworks. Above them, on the scaffolding behind the *DRINK PERRIER WATER* sign, Joe and Mei seemed to be enacting a kind of victory dance, whilst Tilly grinned out over the magic rooftops of London that she had so long wanted to see.

In the empty fifth-floor office of the building across Piccadilly, the Baron fell to the floor, and London's most famous department store owner calmly pocketed his revolver, and dusted off his hands on an immaculate silk handkerchief.

'Well, then – I guess that's that,' he said.

PART VI
Montgomery Baxter's Casebook

'And so I shall reveal the truth – at last!'
exclaimed the brave boy detective.

CHAPTER TWENTY-SIX

One week after the Midnight Peacock Ball, a much smaller and more intimate gathering was held in the office of Taylor & Rose, London's first (and only) young ladies' detective agency.

Two waiters had been sent along with trays of refreshments from the Marble Court Restaurant. They looked at each other in surprise, eyeing the spread of dainty sandwiches, mouthwatering buns and crumpets dripping with butter.

'What do you suppose they want with all this lot?' asked one, confused.

'Giving a party, I expect,' said the other.

'I didn't think detectives gave parties.'

'Well, they are *young lady* detectives, aren't they?' said the other waiter, as though this explained a great deal.

In the office, Lil accepted the trays, and added the refreshments to what was already an impressive spread. Its centrepiece was the large cake that Song had brought, iced with an intricate design of peacock feathers. 'It seemed like the right thing,' he said with a grin.

It had been difficult to fit everyone in, but now they had managed at last. Sophie and Lil perched on one desk, and Billy and Joe on the other, with Daisy as usual leaning her head against Joe's knee. Mei, Song and Tilly were on the hearthrug with Lucky between them, Phyllis and Hugo Devereaux shared one big armchair whilst Leo took another, with Jack and Connie leaning against the arms. Across from them, Mr Pendleton and Veronica were on the sofa, sitting slightly apart and being overtly polite to each other, although Sophie's sharp eyes had noticed at once that Veronica was now wearing a large and very shiny diamond ring on the fourth finger of her left hand.

They'd even managed to squeeze in Mr and Mrs Lim, who were chatting to Detective Inspector Worth, and of course Mr McDermott who had returned to London just in time to join them for the party. But the guest of honour was Mr Sinclair himself, who sat in their very best chair.

When everyone was supplied with tea and cake, Mr Sinclair cleared his throat and held his teacup aloft. 'It doesn't seem quite right to propose a toast without a glass of champagne – but just the same, I think we should all drink the health of Miss Sophie Taylor and Miss Lilian Rose, the smartest and bravest young detectives in London. And all the rest of you who played your part in helping them to stop the Baron on New Year's Eve.'

'Hear hear!' called out Detective Worth.

'Oh, don't bother drinking our health!' Lil burst out excitedly. 'What we *really* want is for you to tell us *everything*. We want you to go back to the beginning.'

Sinclair smiled at her. 'Right back to the beginning? Well, I'm afraid the beginning goes back pretty far. But we'll do our best.'

It was Detective Worth who began: 'All this really begins with an ancient secret society – the Brotherhood of Dragons, sometimes called the *Fraternitas Draconum*. We still know very little about them: but what we do know is that they are a group of rich, powerful men, who work together to further their own interests. They are active across Europe, and their influence now stretches as far as America. We don't know who leads them, nor where their central headquarters is located – but over the centuries, they have played a key part in bringing about terrible events, such as wars and disasters, to suit their own ends.'

Mr McDermott took up the tale: 'Most recently, we learned that they were conspiring to start a war in Europe, building on tensions between England and Germany. This was at the heart of the Baron's plan. He hoped that the assassination of the King and the attack on Piccadilly Circus would be blamed on German terrorists – and would act as a spark to ignite war. This war would benefit him and the other members of the society, who would be well placed to sell secret information and trade weapons like their new explosives – and ultimately, to profit.'

Mr Sinclair continued: 'Of course, as you know, this plot was a last-ditch effort for the Baron. He had lost most of his valuable assets, and whilst he had once been a senior figure in the society, his fellows had lost confidence in him when his plan to steal the dragon paintings went so badly wrong, and risked exposing them. Now, he hoped to redeem himself – and, we believe, to prove himself to whoever is in charge of the organisation. Luckily he still had access to the factory in Silvertown – and the loyal support of Raymond Fitzwilliam.'

McDermott added: 'You'll remember that Fitzwilliam had once been an actor. That made him exactly the right person to pose as a firework specialist – and lay the explosives in place around Piccadilly. I suspect the Baron enjoyed the idea that all this would happen right under Mr Sinclair's nose, as part of his New Year's celebrations. He might even have hoped that Mr Sinclair would be blamed – or suspected of colluding with the Germans.'

Everyone was listening intently, but Jack spoke up with a question: 'I say – what happened to Fitzwilliam on New Year's Eve?' he asked. 'Is he still at large?'

Connie grinned as she answered: 'Oh no! After Bunty and Dora dealt with him, we found a nice young policeman and I reported him for bothering young ladies – and he got arrested! He was awfully cross. I rather think Dora might have broken his nose,' she added reflectively.

'But of course, Fitzwilliam wasn't the Baron's only ally in this,' said Detective Worth.

Leo nodded soberly. She knew exactly what he was getting at. 'Lady Tremayne was his accomplice. She was the one he met secretly at Winter Hall.'

'That's right. A clever and dangerous woman. Our men had a close eye on her on the night of the ball, but she gave them the slip, disguising herself so she would not be recognised. Happily in the event you and Mr Rose were on hand to identify her – and I must say, you dealt with her most effectively.'

Jack grinned. In the chaos of New Year's Eve, it had been a while before they had had chance to return to the Millinery storeroom, where they had left Lady Tremayne. There, they had found the door had been opened, and Lady Tremayne was long gone, instead there was only a very annoyed Edith, smarting over having missed the fireworks and all the fun.

They had later learned that Lady Tremayne had left the country altogether. Leo's mother had received a hastily scribbled letter, announcing that Lady Tremayne was sailing to New York on personal business, and did not expect to return to England for some time.

'I suppose she must have been duping us all along,' said

Leo now, in rather a small voice. 'I suppose she didn't really care about me at all.'

But Jack looked at her thoughtfully. 'No, Leo – you're wrong. If she *didn't* care about you, she wouldn't have risked taking off her mask, and showing us who she was. But she took the risk of revealing herself and telling you to go home. That was how important it was to her to keep you safe – and stop you getting hurt.'

Leo looked back at him in surprise and gratitude, as Lil said: 'It's just so strange that *she* was the one in league with the Baron all along. We could never have expected that!'

'Well – perhaps not in league with him exactly,' amended Detective Worth. 'It was something more than that. In Mr Sinclair and Mr McDermott's investigations over the past few months, they discovered that Lady Tremayne was not simply working with the Baron – she was his sister.'

'His *sister?*' repeated Billy incredulously.

McDermott nodded. 'Likely she was the one you saw at the Silvertown factory. She acted as the Baron's go-between while he was in hiding. It appears that she was linked closely to the *Fraternitas Draconum* – for although women themselves are not permitted to be members, we believe her deceased husband Lord Tremayne was a senior figure in the society, as well as her brother.'

'I – I didn't even know that Lady Tremayne *had* a brother!' exclaimed Leo.

But Sophie's mind was working in a different direction. 'If you know that Lady Tremayne was his sister, then does that mean you've learned who the Baron really was?' she asked.

Mr Sinclair grinned around at them all, looking rather proud of himself. 'We have indeed – after quite considerable investigation.' He removed a photograph from his pocket, and handed it to Sophie with a flourish. 'John Hardcastle, the youngest son of the Duke of Cleveland, born 1860. Viola Hardcastle, his sister, was born seven years later – and grew up to marry Lord Tremayne.'

'He was an aristocrat?' asked Lil, leaning over Sophie's shoulder so they could look together at the vaguely familiar face of the smartly dressed young man, staring insolently back at them from the old photograph.

'He was. But he was also a rogue, and by the time he was twenty he had been disinherited by his father, and had run away to join the Army. At first he was posted to India, but he soon fell foul of his regiment, and ended up attached to a different battalion in Egypt.'

Sophie looked up excitedly at the mention of Egypt, as Sinclair went on: 'We've confirmed that the Baron – or I suppose I ought to call him Hardcastle – served with Miss Taylor's father in Egypt in the late 1880s. We have also discovered that a young Englishwoman, Miss Alice Grayson, was a resident of Cairo at around the same time.'

'Then my mother actually *lived* in Egypt?' asked Sophie in astonishment.

'That's right – it would appear she was resident there for a number of years, after first travelling there as quite a young girl with her father, an archaeologist studying the ancient tombs. Her father died several years later, leaving her alone in Cairo. Not long afterwards she met Captain Taylor-Cavendish and married him – and they returned to England together.'

'So that was where it all began,' Sophie murmured. She turned to Mr Sinclair: 'From everything the Baron said, I think that perhaps he and my father really were friends once. But then they quarrelled – perhaps when my father married my mother.'

Sinclair nodded. 'You may be right. Of course, the Baron's history is a complicated puzzle. He has always used different names, and has travelled widely. That's partly why it has taken us so long to uncover the truth. There are still many questions to be answered but we do know that he soon became involved in the *Fraternitas Draconum* – and a few years afterwards, John Hardcastle was reported to have deserted from the British Army.'

'After that his movements are uncertain,' continued Mr McDermott. 'We know he travelled in Asia and the United States and was involved in various schemes. Then, in 1897, he returned to London in the guise of the lost Lord

Beaucastle, heir to the great Beaucastle fortune. Of course, by then everyone had long forgotten about the disgraced youngest son of the Duke of Cleveland. The Baron began to establish a foothold in the East End, and he soon became one of the top men at the London headquarters of the *Fraternitas Draconum*. He gained money and power – but he also sought respectability, through his pose as Lord Beaucastle. It seems he hoped to work his way back into the aristocratic circles that had once rejected him.'

'But then that started to unravel,' realised Sophie. 'He lost the East End, he lost his Beaucastle identity, he lost his footing with the Brotherhood, and now . . .' Her words fell away and she found herself staring at the photograph again. It was so hard to believe that the Baron was really *gone*. She thought again of that extraordinary moment in the empty office, when Mr Sinclair had pulled the trigger.

'We're continuing to look into his history, of course,' said Mr Sinclair. 'There's a great deal that we still don't know.'

Billy spoke up. 'Well, what I'd like to know is who "*we*" are,' he said rather shyly. 'Because we all know that you aren't *really* a department store owner.'

Mr Sinclair gave a shout of laughter. 'Of course I'm really a department store owner. My word – Sinclair's would be a very elaborate cover indeed!' But he spoke more seriously as he went on: 'However, I suppose it is true to say that I am not *only* a department store owner.'

He paused for a moment, and eyed Detective Worth. The other man gave him a short nod. 'You should tell them the truth, Sinclair. They've earned that.'

'You're right,' agreed Mr Sinclair. 'Very well. The truth is that I have worked over a number of years as a secret agent for both the American Intelligence Service and with Pickering's, America's famous detective agency. When I decided to come to London to open up the store, I was charged with a job to do.

'I had already had a rather interesting encounter with the Baron in New York, and the US government were becoming curious about him – and also anxious about the *Fraternitas Draconum*. There was evidence of a power base in London – and I was sent here to find it, and to discover the truth about the Baron. As merely an affable American businessman, I had the opportunity to mix with all kinds of people – and to make connections in all kinds of places. I employed Mr McDermott as my private investigator and took him into my confidence – though I must admit that at first we concealed our intentions from our friends here at Scotland Yard.'

Worth grinned amiably. 'And who could blame you?' he said handsomely. 'There has been a little tension between Scotland Yard and our American counterparts in the past. We haven't a history of working well together. Although I rather think all that is going to change now.'

Sinclair gave him a bow of acknowledgement, and continued his story. 'Of course, the Baron knew exactly who I was – and he wasn't at all happy to see me in London. To draw him out, I tempted him with the exhibition of the clockwork sparrow, which I knew he would find irresistible. But I must say I didn't expect that he'd make such a bold move as attempting to blow up my store! Of course, I have you to thank for preventing that.

'After that affair was concluded, I continued my investigations with McDermott's help. Whilst he travelled to Paris on the trail of one of the Baron's associates, I remained in London, making efforts to insinuate myself into Lord Beaucastle's circles. I even attended a ball at his mansion, hoping to use the opportunity to find out more about him. But once again, you were one step ahead of me – and before I even returned home from the ball, I discovered that you had confronted the Baron and his carefully constructed Lord Beaucastle identity was now in tatters.' He laughed. 'I have to admit I was pretty darned impressed with that!

'Now the Baron had lost those assets – and his grip on the East End. His accomplices had been arrested and he was wanted by the police – but he had escaped. Try as we might, we couldn't track him down. So McDermott and I turned our investigations to focus on the *Fraternitas Draconum* itself. Some intelligence work led us to discover that the society had once owned a sequence of valuable paintings by the Italian artist Benedetto Casselli. There was a strange rumour that the paintings concealed a kind of secret code that pointed to the location of a great treasure, hidden by previous generations, to benefit future members of the society. When one of the only known paintings was stolen from a Bond Street gallery, we deduced that the society was trying to regain them. In an effort to lay our hands on the Baron at last, I proposed the idea of an exhibition of paintings at Sinclair's, including the only other known painting. What was more, I also pretended to leave London in order to leave the field clear, and tempt the Baron to strike.'

Detective Worth continued the story: 'Of course, as you know, the Baron used Raymond Lyle to do his dirty work. Lyle retrieved the painting, but also forced McDermott out of the investigation – and did his very best to pull the wool over Scotland Yard's eyes,' he concluded, a note of bitterness sounding in his voice.

'Yet once again, you young detectives went straight to the heart of the problem – and did something that neither I nor Scotland Yard could have done,' said Mr Sinclair. 'You broke into Lyle's apartment – and you rescued both paintings. Well after that, I decided I ought to set you up with your own agency. It was really the least that I could do!'

'After the affair of the paintings, Mr Sinclair and Mr

McDermott took us into their confidence,' explained Detective Worth. 'We've been working closely with them – and the New York team – ever since to continue the investigation together.'

Sophie looked from one to the other in surprise. She remembered how Mr McDermott had warned her against spending any more time thinking about the Baron. 'But – why didn't you tell us that?' she burst out. 'You knew you could trust us – we'd helped you!'

Mr Sinclair looked back at her seriously. 'I suppose we ought to have done,' he said. 'Partly it was habit – I was used to keeping my identity as an agent a strict secret. But partly I must acknowledge that my motive was a selfish one. You had showed me very clearly, Miss Taylor, that you and Miss Rose and your friends could see things and do things that I or Detective Worth here could not. You had made many valuable discoveries already – and I could not help observing that whilst the Baron was intensely cautious and secretive, around you he displayed an unusual carelessness. I admit that I wanted to retain that advantage. I kept you in the dark and at arm's length precisely because I did not want to put the Baron too much on his guard.'

Sophie looked thoughtful, puzzling this out, but Lil bounded ahead as usual: 'What about the assassination plot?' she asked excitedly.

'After the affair of the paintings went wrong, we knew

that the Baron had gone to earth,' explained Detective Worth. 'He knew we would be on his trail, and he left false information for us. One trail appeared to lead to Vienna, where Mr McDermott headed. Another led to the wilds of Scotland, which I determined to follow. Meanwhile, we also discovered the Baron's connection to Lady Tremayne – and Mr Sinclair decided to attend the Winter Hall house party in order to find out more about her.'

'Like yourselves, it did not take me very long to discover that the Baron was actually hidden in the house itself,' said Mr Sinclair. 'Hiding in the East Wing, I managed to overhear some of his conversation with Lady Tremayne – including the assassination plot. I returned immediately to London to inform Scotland Yard of the Baron's plan. Worth and McDermott were recalled to London – but whilst they travelled back, Detective Sergeant Thomas and his men went into action to help me.'

'Golly – Sergeant Thomas must have been astonished when we came in straight after you and reported exactly the same thing!' said Lil to Mr Sinclair with a laugh. 'Especially given that we suspected *you* of being the Baron's accomplice.'

Detective Worth grinned. 'Oh, I imagine that was the least of his worries. This was a matter of international security – and after considerable discussion with the government, the decision was taken to proceed with the ball, in the hope of finally being able to lay hands on the Baron himself. His

Majesty insisted that his appearance should also go ahead as planned, although of course the Commissioner sent many men to the ball undercover to ensure he would remain safe.'

'Our mistake was to assume that the assassin – potentially the Baron himself – would be amongst the guests,' said Mr Sinclair, with a sigh. 'It was not until the very last moment that I glimpsed you, Miss Rose, dashing out into the street in the direction of the building opposite. At that moment it became clear. I followed you at once to the scene – where I found you putting up rather an impressive fight.'

'I *told* you that the Sewing Society was a good idea,' murmured Mrs Lim to Mr Lim, across the room.

'I think he was surprised to discover we weren't quite as feeble and helpless as he thought,' said Lil with pride. 'All the same, it was jolly good timing when you turned up. I really thought he was about to shoot Sophie with that awful rifle.'

'But instead he met his end,' said Mr Sinclair softly. 'It had been agreed by both the British and American governments that we should do whatever it took to stop the Baron. And that is what I did.'

Billy had been writing copious notes in his notebook. Now he glanced up from the pages to look owlishly at Mr Sinclair. 'I *knew* you couldn't have been working with the Baron,' he said. 'I *told* Lil that you weren't.'

Sinclair laughed. 'Well I don't in the least blame Miss

Rose – nor any of the rest of you – for suspecting me,' he said cheerfully. 'After all, you'd found all kinds of unexpected people mixed up with the Baron before. Which reminds me – I hope you don't mind but I've invited an extra guest. I think she should be here by now.'

To everyone's surprise, he got up, opened the office door, and beckoned someone inside. They all turned to look and then, to her enormous astonishment, Sophie saw the little old lady wearing the velvet hat trimmed with violets coming through the door.

'Good afternoon, everyone,' she said, smiling around at them all. She sounded quite different, her voice now a warm American drawl.

'May I introduce Miss Ada Pickering, of Pickering's Detective Agency,' explained Mr Sinclair, offering the old lady his seat.

'Pickering's – detective!' exclaimed Billy, his eyes as round as saucers.

'But . . . but I thought you were just a harmless little old lady!' gasped Lil.

'Well you of all people, dear, should know that people are not always what they seem,' said the old lady contentedly. 'Just because I might not *look* like a representative of Pickering's, it doesn't mean I'm not Pickering through and through.'

'Ada here is one of Pickering's best!' said Mr Sinclair.

'She's been a great inspiration to me over the years – and a dear friend. She's been here working with me for the past month. She also travelled out to Alwick on the trail of Lady Tremayne and the Baron – and I asked her to keep a particular look out for you, Miss Taylor. I knew the Baron had a certain interest in you, and I wanted to be sure you'd be safe.'

'No one ever suspects an old lady,' said Miss Pickering, with a knowing smile.

'No one except Sophie!' said Lil, with an astonished laugh.

But Sophie herself was staring at Miss Pickering, a delighted smile on her face. She was thinking how wonderful it would be to know a real lady detective.

Mr Sinclair was still talking. 'Of course, what neither Ada nor I, nor Detective Worth and his men, had discovered was the Baron's plan to blow up Piccadilly Circus,' he was saying, as Lil poured Miss Pinkerton a cup of tea, and Joe found her a chair. 'That is why we have a great deal to thank all of you young people for. But perhaps especially Joe and Billy here – two young gentlemen that I could not be more pleased to have on my staff – as well as the intrepid Miss Lim and Miss Black.'

It was very peculiar having everyone turning to look at her all at once, but Tilly managed to speak. 'It was Mei who did the hard part,' she owned. 'I've never seen anyone climb like that before!'

'No – your part was much more difficult!' exclaimed Mei at once. 'Tilly stopped the bombs from going off – and she saved everyone!'

Mr Sinclair looked at Tilly speculatively. 'You're certainly a very smart young lady, Miss Black. Very smart indeed. Tell me – have you any interest in studying mechanics – or engineering perhaps? I do wonder if . . .'

'Now, now, Sinclair,' Detective Worth interrupted him. 'I know there's no one like you for spotting talent – but you can discuss Miss Black's future with her later. We've got a story to finish.'

Joe spoke up now, a little shy at talking in front of so many people, but keen to ask his question just the same. 'Excuse me, gents – but what I'd like to know about is this Loyal Order of Lions we've heard about. How exactly do they fit in to all this?'

It was Sophie who answered first. 'Actually the Baron told me a little about that himself before – before – well, before Mr Sinclair turned up. He said they were a group that opposed the *Fraternitas Draconum*. My parents were members – and Grandfather Lim too.'

'I'm rather interested in this Loyal Order of Lions,' said Mr Sinclair. 'I know they don't exist any more as such, but I'd very much like to know a little more about them.'

Song spoke up next. 'Well – we may be able to help you

there. Mei and I – we've been doing some hunting through Granddad's old papers – and we found something . . .'

He took a document out of his pocket, and made space between the cake and tea on the table so he could spread it before everyone:

1 January 1890

THE LOYAL ORDER OF LIONS

We the undersigned hereby commit ourselves to the ancient Loyal Order of Lions. We pledge to uphold the principles of fairness, tolerance, loyalty, truth and justice – and to stand in opposition to the secret society known as the Brotherhood of Dragons, sometimes called Fraternitas Draconum. We shall rebalance the scales.

Ad usque fidelis

Signed:

Colonel Marcus Fairley

Major James Dalrymple

Captain Robert Taylor-Cavendish

Lieutenant Ignatius Davidson

Dr Jasper Bell

Mrs Alice Taylor-Cavendish

K L Lim

Mrs Kitty Kirkpatrick

Count Felix Matveyev

T Riley

the Honourable Miss Noor Singh

'Well bless my soul,' said Mr Sinclair.

'*Ad usque fidelis*,' murmured Jack. 'Faithful until the end.'

'And they were,' said Sophie. She felt tears rising in her eyes at the sight of her parents' names amongst all those others – Grandfather Lim and Colonel Fairley, and those that they would never know.

But Lil was saying: 'I say, Sophie. Don't you think we should tell everyone what else the Baron said about this Loyal Order of Lions? It was rather peculiar – he said that *we* were the final members. But I don't know what he meant by that because I'd never even *heard* of this Order until we saw Sophie's father's letter.'

Sophie looked around at them all. 'I think what he meant is that we were continuing their work – almost without knowing it,' she said slowly. 'Following the same principles, just like they did.'

There was quiet for a moment, and then Mr Sinclair looked around at them all. 'Well perhaps that's no bad thing. The Baron – John Hardcastle – he may be gone, but the *Fraternitas Draconum* are still out there. We know the Baron wasn't the top man – and we have no idea what other schemes they may be plotting. Maybe we need a new Loyal Order of Lions.'

There was a little murmur of approval around the room. Joe found himself catching Jack's eye. On the hearthrug,

Tilly and Mei exchanged quick smiles, and Billy looked up from his casenotes to nod at Lil, even as she said: 'There's still so much to find out, isn't there? I mean, what about the rest of those dragon paintings – and the secret code they contain? I wonder where it leads – and what the treasure is that the Baron wanted so badly.'

'Then there's the *Fraternitas Draconum*,' said Billy. 'It's obvious we need to find out more about them.'

Detective Worth nodded. 'There will be an official investigation. It's being led by some colleagues of mine – a new team, all rather hush-hush for now – but I am sure the Bureau will be very keen to talk to you about what you know.'

'I'd like to find out more about all these people who belonged to the Loyal Order of Lions,' said Song, tracing the list of names. 'Perhaps we could find them – I know the Baron said they were all gone, but we don't know that for sure.'

'And we could try to track down your father's will,' suggested Jack, turning to Sophie. 'Perhaps he left you some money – it might not be too late to get it back?'

But Sophie shook her head. 'I'm sure that would be long gone by now,' she said. 'But what I would love to know is what Papa meant in his letter to Grandfather Lim about the *treasure I've had all along*. I barely have anything that belonged to my parents – only a photograph or two, and this necklace, that used to be my mother's,' she said, touching the green beads.

Mr Sinclair looked at her with interest. 'May I see those, Miss Taylor?' he asked.

She took them off and handed them to him. He turned them over in his fingers, examining them closely, and then passed them to Ada, who did the same.

'Well . . . this is no ordinary necklace, young lady,' spoke up the Pickering's detective. 'I know a little about gemstones, and if I'm not mistaken these beads are a combination of jade, malachite and emerald – and they appear to be very old indeed.'

Sophie stared at her in amazement. 'But surely they can't be!' she exclaimed. 'I always thought they were just any commonplace beads. They were only so precious to me because they had once belonged to my mama!'

'Well it's a good job you've taken such good care of them, my dear. All those stones are very valuable.' Ada coiled the beads in her palm, and then passed them to Lil to hand back to Sophie.

'The treasure you had all along!' exclaimed Lil, her eyes shining with excitement, as she dropped them back into Sophie's open hands.

'But that's not the only treasure,' announced Mei suddenly. 'We've got something else for you too. A present!'

'I'm not sure if it's quite as good as the present you gave

me,' said Song, with a grin. In spite of having disappeared from the kitchens for an hour at a very crucial point on New Year's Eve, with Mr Sinclair's backing, he had been given a permanent job in the Marble Court Restaurant as an apprentice working under Monsieur Bernard – and he now felt that 1910 held all kinds of exciting possibilities. 'But it's pretty good, just the same. That document wasn't the only thing Mei and I found when we searched Grandfather Lim's room.'

He held out a tin box. It looked battered and old.

'It was Mei who found it,' explained Mr Lim, smiling. 'She was the one who worked out where it was hidden.'

Mei blushed. 'I have a hiding place in the bedroom under a loose floorboard,' she explained. 'I remembered that it was Granddad who first showed it to me. I thought maybe he had a secret hiding place like that too – and he did! This was under the floorboards in his bedroom.'

'Open it,' said Mrs Lim, smiling in anticipation.

Breathlessly, Sophie prised open the lid of the box. She didn't really know what she had expected to find inside but it certainly was not a small stack of notebooks, the covers faded and stained from much use. She picked up the top one. On the cover was handwritten in black ink: *Alice Grayson – Diary 1881.*

She stared up at Mei and Song in delight. 'This belonged to my mother!' she exclaimed. She flicked open the pages, which were dense with writing.

Mei beamed. 'They're diaries. *That's* what your father wanted Granddad to keep safe for you.'

They could have stayed there talking everything over in the cosy office all afternoon. Yet at last, one by one, their guests began to drift away. Veronica, Phyllis, Mr Pendleton and Mr Devereaux left to dress for the Countess of Alconborough's supper party that evening, and Inspector Worth was needed back at Scotland Yard. The Lims set out on their way back to Limehouse, Mr Lim looping his arm over Mei's shoulder, and Song flashing a smile over his shoulder as they went.

Leo and Tilly were next to go, and went off chattering happily. They had had a long and interesting conversation with Mr Sinclair, and were going to investigate classes in mechanics and science that Tilly might be able to take: Connie had suggested that Mrs St James might be able to help make arrangements. Of course, they'd already decided that they wouldn't be mentioning anything about that to Lady Fitzgerald, Cook or Mrs Dawes.

Jack followed them. '1910 is looking rather exciting already, isn't it?' he said as he departed. Then he grinned cheekily at Sophie. 'Perhaps this year I'll finally be able to get you to come with me for that coffee at the Café Royal – what do you think?'

'Oh – perhaps!' said Sophie, with a smile.

Mr McDermott nodded at them all before he left. 'I'll drop in and see you tomorrow,' he said to Sophie, patting her gently on the shoulder.

And then at last it was just the four of them – Sophie and Lil and Billy and Joe – and the two dogs, Daisy and Lucky, of course – all sitting together in the office.

'Well,' said Joe.

'*Well*,' said Lil.

Billy closed his notebook with a contented sigh. 'That was a million times better than any Montgomery Baxter mystery. Do you know, I think I might start writing mystery stories myself. I bet I've got enough material for at least a dozen.'

'And I reckon we'll have enough for a dozen more for you too, before very long,' said Joe. 'The Baron might be gone – but I don't think we've seen the back of mysteries just yet.'

'Of course we haven't!' exclaimed Lil indignantly. 'We're a detective agency! Mysteries are our *business*.'

Joe grinned and got to his feet. 'Well, on that note, it's back to business for me. I reckon we'd better take these dogs out – coming, Bill?'

Billy nodded and scrambled up too. 'I think I'll call the first one *The Mystery of the Stolen Jewels* . . .' Sophie could hear him saying as they went out of the door. 'Or no – wait

– maybe that's not exciting enough. How about *The Curious Case of the Missing Musical Box . . .'*

Lil got up too. 'I'm awfully sorry, but I've got to go as well. I'm supposed to go over to the theatre and talk to Mr Mountville. He's talking about giving me a much better part in the play than silly old Daphne De Vere, after my turn in the *Midnight Extravaganza*. Maybe I'll even be allowed to survive all the way through to the third act!' She beamed at Sophie as she put on her hat and then said in a careless voice: 'So I s'pose I'll see you back here tomorrow.'

'Yes, you will,' Sophie replied decidedly. 'And make sure you're not late. We've got lots of work to do. Mr McDermott is coming to see us – and remember, we're going to the Lims' later on.'

Lil grinned. 'As if I could forget the very first meeting of the new Loyal Order of Lions!' she said. 'I say, I'm jolly excited about it all.' She paused for a moment, and they looked at each other and smiled. Then: 'Goodnight, Sophie!'

'Goodnight, Lil!'

Alone now, Sophie went over to the window, and settled down at her desk again. It had begun to snow once more, and for a few minutes she paused and stared out at the falling flakes as they spiralled down on to Piccadilly. Even in the January twilight, she could see that people were still surging up the steps and through the great doors of Sinclair's, or pausing to admire the golden windows, spilling out colour and brightness.

She smiled contentedly, and turned back to look down at the diaries, spread out across her desk in the warm pool of lamplight. She gently touched the blue cover of the first one, and her heart swelled. Then, with very careful fingers, she opened it to the first page, and began to read:

8 May 1880
Paris

I can scarcley believe that I am really writing this from Paris! We arrived last night, after a long journey and a turbulent crossing. On the train, Papa gave me this little book, so I may keep a diary of all our travels and everything that happens to me. I can scarcely wait to document all of the adventures that will surely come about as we continue to journey- through France and Spain, and from there across the Mediterranean to the African coast, and from there onwards - to Egypt...

AUTHOR'S NOTE

Readers of the *Sinclair's Mysteries* will know that whilst the places and people that appear in the series are fictional, some of them are inspired by real-life history. In particular, Sinclair's itself owes much to London's real Edwardian department stores – most of all, Selfridges, which also opened its doors for the first time in 1909.

In this story, César Chevalier is partly inspired by a real French designer, Paul Poiret, whose incredible designs made him one of the most important and influential fashion designers of the 1910s and 1920s. His famous *Mille et Deuxième Nuit* (Thousand and Second Night) party in Paris in 1911, to celebrate the launch of his scent *Parfums de Rosine*, helped to inspire the Midnight Peacock Ball.

ACKNOWLEDGEMENTS

It has been a joy to work with Egmont on the *Sinclair's Mysteries*. Huge thanks to everyone in the Egmont team – but most especially to brilliant Ali Dougal, who understood Sinclair's from the very beginning, right down to the bluebell-scented perfume.

Special thanks to Laura Bird and the design team for creating such a beautiful book and many, many thanks to super-talented magician Karl James Mountford for the stunning artwork – it's been a privilege working with you.

Enormous thanks to my agent and dear friend Louise Lamont – source of endless wise advice, pillar of support in the face of emergency root canals, and all-round Jolly Good Sort.

Thank you to all my brilliant and supportive colleagues and friends – most especially Claire Shanahan, Nina Douglas, Katherine Webber and Melissa Cox – as well as my amazing fellow children's and YA authors. I feel very lucky to be part of such an incredible community.

Thank you to my wonderful friends and family, in particular my husband, Duncan, who outdid himself by inventing a character for this book (Miss Pickering!) and to the whole Hay clan for all their support. Thanks most of all – and very much love – to my mum and dad, who are always my biggest fans.

Huge thanks to all the booksellers, librarians, teachers and bloggers who have so enthusiastically championed the *Sinclair's Mysteries* – it is enormously appreciated.

Special thanks to all the young readers who have read and enjoyed the series. I hope you've had as much fun reading about Sophie, Lil and the gang as I have had writing about them. Most of all, I hope their adventures will act as a reminder that there are many ways – large and small – in which young people can make a difference in the world.

Look out for more adventures
from Sophie and Lil

Taylor & Rose

PRIVATE   DETECTIVE   AGENCY
4th Floor, Sinclair's Department Store,
Piccadilly W1

Discretion guaranteed

COMING SOON!